Night-night, Sleep Tight

Night-night, Sleep Tight

Paul Burman

windeye

www.windeyepublishing.com

Windeye Publishing
Port Fairy, Victoria, Australia

Set in Garamond and Century Gothic
Cover and text design by Windeye Publishing
Printed by Ingram

National Library of Australia Cataloguing-in-Publication entry: (paperback)
Burman, Paul R., author.
Night-night, sleep tight / Paul Burman.
ISBN: 9780648045908 (paperback)
Psychological fiction, Australian.
Australian fiction.

When, our darkest ghosts we go a-courting,
We walk alone, bereft, t'wards our haunting.

Oliver Nailsworth
A Collection of Commonplace Books, 1707-1742

Life is an alphabet without any rules,
The world shows no mercy to wise men and fools.

Anon.
from *A Child's Primer for Alphabet and Numbers*

ONE

I CALL MY MOTHER 'Mother', I call my father Victor. She hated that. He liked it. She hated that he liked it.

It started four years ago, when I was seventeen, but it's almost over now. My mother is dead and Victor is missing and the police want to ask him a question or two.

It's me that's become a ghost, though.

A night of frost. The kitchen is icy. Outside it'll be frozen needles. For an hour or two. Then winter sun.

Filling the kettle and setting it to boil, a bleached whiteness bleeds in at the edges of the kitchen blinds, between the slats. I peel them open and the light is crystallised – intense. The brightness bounces off Angie's garden and is too white, too sharp, like splinters sticking in my eyes. Each blade of grass is ice-crusted, each shrub has become a clumsy caricature of itself. The darker fringe of forest bordering Angie's place offers a softer focus, and I'm imagining myself wandering out there, among the trees, when Stella appears at my side.

I didn't hear her moving about upstairs and when she

stands next to me she doesn't say a word. She has her school uniform on already and looks pale, drawn, so I guess she's had another sleepless night too, although why she can't come down and make the coffee or put the porridge on if she's been awake for a while I don't know.

We're both leaning forward against the kitchen bench staring out, but I know she sees a different forest to mine. She's scared of everything at the moment, is Stella – the trees, the slightest noise – but then she's been ground to shreds of late. We both have. Ground into the ground.

Eventually she says, 'Remember when we were kids and it was winter, how Mum would toast muffins for us over the fire? Hot milk and muffins, with a sprinkle of grated nutmeg on the milk.' Her voice still has a husky rasp to it, from the night of the fire, but even that suits her.

I squint back at the snap-frozen stillness of the day and wish time could be frozen this way too. I'm on the verge of saying something, but she carries on.

'Home-made jam on the muffins. The best plum jam. From the old plum tree down at the back of the garden. Near the bottom fence. Back home. Remember?'

It's easy to romanticise the past, but dangerous.

'That was once,' I remind her. 'She did it once.'

The forest is hypnotic, whatever time of day, whatever time of year. It might sound a strange thing to say, but it's true: staring at a forest is like gazing into the flames of a fire. Except you could walk into this forest and literally lose yourself in it. People do. It's one of the largest forests in the country. Vast and timeless, it stretches beyond all imagination of how immense a forest can be. It's an hypnotic place and its mood is always changing. I love it.

Whenever someone goes missing for more than a day or so, the police send patrols to well-known picnic spots and along the more accessible logging tracks, looking for an abandoned vehicle and a greenish-blue body or two. It attracts all sorts: suicides and murder-suicides, the helpless and the hapless. There are two memorial plaques next to an information board at the Three Creeks campsite, one for a lost hiker and one for two over-playful children who wandered off and never found their way back to home-sweet-home again.

'We'd have hot milk and muffins for breakfast,' Stella continues, 'and then she'd walk us down to the bus stop to catch the school bus.'

I remember the occasion better than she does.

'It was in the afternoon, not the morning,' I tell her, 'after the school bus dropped us off. Just once. My feet were wet and you were in your first year at school.'

'But she used to walk us down to the bus stop in the morning, didn't she? Every morning. And she'd wait there until the bus came?'

Her eyes are welling up and she takes hold of my hand. Her fingers are cold and I fold them inside my own.

'Of course she did. You were only five. I was only eight. She had to.'

'I don't remember seeing other kids' mothers doing that.'

'Why would you? How could you? But they would have. They'd have done it too.'

She comes around a little then and turns to look at me, away from the window.

'Whenever it's frosty and cold like this, I think of hot milk and muffins. I think of us sitting in front of the fire, back home, and toasting muffins, and everything warm and cosy. Don't you?'

I don't. Not anymore. I don't know that I ever did.

'I've got muffins in the freezer,' I say. 'You can have

them for breakfast if you like. Muffins and hot milk. There's no nutmeg though.'

'How would we toast them?'

'In the toaster, of course.'

'It wouldn't be the same.'

'It was only once she did them on the fire. Once or twice at most. There was probably a power outage or something. You make it sound like it happened every day.'

'Maybe there were other days,' Stella says, 'when you were at school, but before I'd started, when I was still at home. Mum used to tell stories and she used to play games with me.'

Her voice has a sharper edge to it now, as if she doesn't care whether she sounds spiteful or not, so I turn to the steaming kettle. Stella can be so self-centred at times.

Momentarily, her talk of muffins and childhood drags me from the safety of Angie's house, which has become my new home these last few months, and takes me back to that other place – Duparc House – to the charred and broken-boned corpse of the place, and a wedge of sick rises from the pit of my stomach, dredging bile into my throat.

'You want coffee?' I ask.

She just nods.

There'll come a time in the future, I tell myself, when the forest will again stretch across and straddle the river at Three Creeks, like it did before the farmers cleared it. Step by step, tree by tree, it'll reclaim the paddocks and swallow up the half-dozen houses – gobble, gobble, gobble – especially the burnt-out ruins of Duparc House, until the place is all wilderness and the houses aren't even a broken memory. After all, there's not much holding it back. Three Creeks is nothing more than a fly-ridden hamlet. It's just a few scattered buildings along the Rudely Road, separated by broad paddocks of coarse grass, and the tragedy of a general store: two prehistoric petrol pumps standing idle out front and too many bone-empty shelves inside. That's all.

Down across the river, nestling alongside it and a little back from the Wallan River Road, there's the campsite and picnic area, and there's the three creeks themselves, cutting across the paddocks in three straight lines. There's two similar campsites further upriver, about twenty kilometres apart, but they're in the middle of nowhere and probably not as popular as ours.

We were always proud of our campsite when we were kids, as if it was something special, but that's because there was little else to make people stop and linger in Three Creeks back then. It was the town's one and only claim to fame... before the fire and Victor's disappearing act, that is.

The ghouls have all been driving out and staring at the house during the last couple of weeks. I know they have. I've seen them. They make a family outing of it, to stare at the house and then head down to the campsite barbecues for a picnic.

It was at the campsite, I tell the police, that I'd seen a white van and a bluey-grey car parked next to one another shortly before the fire, and they asked me to go to the station to identify both vehicles from photographs because I can't tell one make or model from another. While the colour of the car I described was identical to the one Pete Lailer drives these days, I didn't mention his name — not directly — and decided to say nothing about a missing hubcap. I'd have been a fool to do that.

The camping ground isn't much. It's a patch of cleared dirt, four fire pits and a dank toilet shed, but it's marked on the more detailed maps and, almost every summer, little nests of campers seem to hatch there for a night or two. They turn into rowdy mobs in canoes, splashing about in the river, or earnest-looking couples with tidy panniers strapped to their bicycles, or yuppie families with gleaming four wheel drives (and a rack of mountain bikes), swarming in and out.

Every summer, from the vantage point of Mum and Dad's attic window, or standing on the swing, Stella and I would look for the motley assembly of orange, blue, yellow or green tents to sprout down by the river, and we'd shout out that the campers had arrived.

'Come see! Quick! They're here!'

It was a highlight of the year and sometimes we'd set up our own tent in the garden and clamour for a barbecue, or persuade Dad to go for a walk so we could observe them up-close as they fished from the reeds or swam in the black water among the slimy eels and the ugly flecklebacks, or as they drifted along in their inflatable dinghies, drank beer and snoozed. On a still night, dislocated phrases of music and laughter would drift across the paddock, through the garden and up towards the house and, from upstairs, Stella and I might watch the glow-worm flicker of gaslights down by the river.

One year, we made friends with two brothers who were camping with their parents, and they came and played in the garden with us until Mum got all disapproving and sent them on their way. The eldest one wrote me a letter several weeks later, with his photo attached, and asked if I'd be his pen-pal, and I wrote back saying I would, except that was the last I heard of him. I never received another letter from him. I can't remember what his name was.

There was one year when twenty or more cyclists arrived together and stayed for three noisy nights, and in the day they'd pass our house as they flittered to and from the shop. We became extra proud of where we lived for those few days – how important it seemed – but then, of course, like some rare breed of exotic butterfly, they disappeared as suddenly as they arrived and it never happened like that again. We'd reminisce about that year sometimes as if it was part of a Golden Age that had come and gone without us fully appreciating all its nuances at the time, but it was nothing special really. We just made it seem that way.

For the most part, the locals use the campsite as a picnic area. Farmers with their families, sawmill workers, retired couples, teenagers with weed to smoke. Friends will chip in for a slab of beer and a few sausages, to spend a raucous evening around one of the barbecues, car speakers blasting.

We've been going there for years, Stella and me, ever since we started snipping ourselves free of the apron strings, but only if we couldn't get a lift to Lapishot. Except nothing will ever be the same again. Not now. It can't be.

It's all Victor's fault. Victor and her.

Victor used to say, 'Everything happens for a reason, Meg.'

But if he was here now I'd tell him that's clap-trap. I'd say, 'You really think there's some grand puppet master up there pulling our strings, making us walk a certain way for a script that's already written, and that everything's already decided?'

'Well, not as such, but life often works out for the best, you'll see. That's all I'm saying.' And he'd try coaxing me along with that slippery smile he'd begun to adopt, as if to suggest we should all be crazy enough to suspend logic for the right occasion. I can see it now.

Except I'd snap back: 'What's the point in believing there's some righteous reason for the misery in life simply because it's too scary to accept there's no reason at all — absolutely none? That's a coward's faith, Victor. You should know that. Isn't it braver to accept there's no purpose to anything, beyond whatever purpose we create for ourselves, and that all too often things don't work out for the best, but for the worst, regardless of what we deserve?'

I often have imaginary conversations like this nowadays. Usually they're in response to some silly memory or other, but through them I rework my lines until I'm happy with what I've said (or should have said) and have properly worked out what I believe. I suppose other people do this too.

'That's a little bleak, Meg, don't you think?' he'd probably reply, and maybe he'd start worrying I was teetering along the brink of suicidal depression again and he'd start analysing my every look, my every utterance, which would make me really mad.

'Not at all,' I'd tell him. 'We are the only god there is. Each of us is the only god there is. We create the sense as well as the nonsense of the world for ourselves. I'd have thought that was obvious.'

'Oh, Meg,' he'd say, and maybe he'd pull at the cuffs of his shirt, straightening them, and he wouldn't relax until I'd laughed at one of his crappy jokes or gone out my way to lighten the mood myself.

Even so, sweet, foolish Daddy was nothing if not scientific and logical, so I guess his 'Everything happens for a reason, Meg' might've been something he'd lazily trot out simply to give order to a crazy world and make me feel better, safer, saner, about the way things were when they weren't the way I wanted them to be. He probably said it to Stella too. Some fathers like to think they're still protecting their daughters even when we're no longer little girls in party frocks and white socks. They never get over their need to tuck us into bed, whether we like it or not... until, that is, we end up tucking them in bed.

Night-night, sleep tight, watch the bugs don't bite.

The police are looking for you everywhere, Victor. They can't decide whether you're an innocent victim or a suspect on the run, run, run. As if life is ever that simple.

We're all victims and yet we're all blameworthy to some extent too, and no one can truly hold us accountable except ourselves. No one.

All the same, I'm sorry you did what you did and I'm sorry I did what I did. But what's done is done. I know you'd be the first to say it: There's no point crying over spilt milk.

There was a time, not long ago, when Victor was still Dad and when he always brought us back little knick-knack souvenirs from his business trips, such as toy aeroplanes and lacquered, Japanese fans, or sometimes duty-free chocolates and perfume. And when I was little, he'd sit on the edge of my bed and say things like: 'You can be whoever and whatever you want in life,' and 'It doesn't matter what you do or what you don't do, you're my little girl, Megsy, and you'll always be my little girl – no matter what.' Typical Victor.

He'd have sat on Stella's bed and said the same things to her. He'd have stroked her hair and brushed it over her ears, then held her face in his two large hands and given her three goodnight kisses: one on each eye and the last in the middle of her forehead.

Kiss, kiss, kiss.

He'd say these things if we were upset or needed reassurance, as good fathers do. It's who he was. He was also a peacemaker and a master in the art of compromise, although compromise is nothing more than a piss-weak cop-out at times. And cowardly.

When I was small, he seemed tall, but not so much of late. While Mother dried out and hardened as I grew – more walnut than prune – I realised Victor had never been tall at all.

The last time I saw him – before his disappearance, that is – he was only a fraction taller than me and less substantial. His self-assuredness and his lankiness, those gangly arms and legs and long neck, created a false impression, and I'm still surprised it can take so long for a child to know its parent.

'It's been a hell of an evening,' he said, the night of the fire, 'but it'll be alright. You'll see.' Typical.

Back in Angie's kitchen and all that nonsense about muffins and jam, Stella stands in front of the sink while I make coffee and says, 'Mum used to tell stories and she used to play games with me.'

Even though I don't remember, I say, 'With me too. They both did.'

And then I do remember. The memory arrives without me wanting it, but I tell it to Stella all the same: 'She used to sit on the edge of the bed and read me bedtime stories. *Postman Pat, Little Mary.* She must have stopped when I started school, when I could read for myself.'

'Dad would make up stories, but Mum always read.'

'I used to tell you stories. Especially at night. I used to play games with you,' I remind her. 'I always did.'

We used to share a bedroom, Stell and I. That is, until the attic was converted into Mum and Dad's new bedroom and

I moved into their old room.

There was a dark gap between our two single beds, where our dolls would picnic and sleep at night, and this space marked the shared border between her half of the room and mine, with the light cord dangling at the exact half-way mark. We'd lay in bed swinging the cord from one to the other, playing catch or counting who could make it swing the most times before it came to a stop. Sometimes, when she was being a baby and I didn't mind, she'd reach out and I'd hold her hand as she went to sleep.

Practically every night, after our light was turned off, Stella begged me to tell a story. Usually I would, if she hadn't been a pain that day. I might carry on from our dolls' latest adventure and tell her about Barbie and Ken's wedding, followed by their divorce, or if it was close to Christmas I'd tell her about Santa Claus and his reindeer. Sometimes though, if she'd annoyed me, the story would turn to ghosts and vampires, or how poor Rudolph, the favourite, red-nosed reindeer, had been killed and skinned by hunters, and then she'd whine as loud as she could until Mum or Dad marched in and told us to go to sleep that minute or we wouldn't be allowed to watch *Abigail Court* or *The Secret Detective* again before we went to bed, or whatever TV program we were hooked on at the time.

More often than not, the story I told her turned into a game that used our narrow beds as props, and we'd 'play' the story out each night for a week, until we forgot about it and moved onto something new. I'd tell her how our beds were really caravans, tents, space rockets, fortresses, hide-outs, cars, houses, boats – anything I wanted them to be – and we'd each pull the sheets over our head and drift to sleep as we got soaked up into our story.

*

It's winter and ghosty-ghoul dark outside, with rain battering against the window. The hall light has been left on because Stella's still a scaredy-cat, but the bedroom door has been three-quarters closed because I'm grown up and not half as afraid of darkness and shadows. She'll just have to learn, that's all. It's not fair if she always has everything her own way. For a while, we lean across from our beds to play puppet shadows on the patch of wall between us where the light from the hall has made a stage, but when she gets tired she wants to play our story-game again.

'Let's play explorers, Meggy,' she says.

'I don't want to. Not tonight.'

'Oh, go onnnn, Meggy. Just for a short while. You said you would.'

Silence.

'Meggy? Perleeeease.'

'Oh, if I have to. Just for a short while then,' I say. 'We're famous explorers,' I tell her, 'and we're crossing the Sahara with a caravan of camels, which are called ships of the desert.' I've been reading about this, so it's fresh in my head.

After becoming orphans during a fierce sand storm (the rain driving against our bedroom window), we end up camping next to an oasis. Our tents are lined with exotic rugs and blankets, we pick dates and coconuts from palm trees, eat Turkish Delight whenever we want and I have boxes of treasure, which my camels carry, because we're very rich. I'm the richest because I'm the eldest and because it's my story, but Stell is the second richest.

'Can we have something else instead of coconut? I don't like coconut, Meggy.'

'You do in this story. All explorers love coconut.'

'Can't I have more Turkish Delight and more treasure and no coconut?'

'You can have more Turkish Delight, but not more treasure. Besides, it'd be dangerous if you carry too much treasure.'

'Why? Why would it be dangerous, Meggy?'

'Because there are pirates looking for all the treasure they can find. They'll fight you and they'll rob you. They'll outnumber us and I won't be able to help. They'll kidnap you and make you their slave, or they'll kill you.'

I wait for her to say something, to protest or ask another question, but she doesn't. She's gone quiet. So I rattle on with the story for a while, but I'm thinking about pirates at the same time, imagining the next episode.

There are always pirates on the prowl in these stories. Pirates and wild beasts – lions, tigers, bears, wolves – but there's no fighting now because she's fallen asleep and I'm getting tired. Tomorrow night we'll be the pirates and our beds will become galleons, with our dolls as crew; we'll follow secret maps in search of Spanish doubloon, and we'll take prisoners who'll become our slaves, and maybe we'll discover a desert island. I'll be the captain and Stella my loyal second-in-command.

She always gets into trouble and I always save her.

She does. Even now. She always gets into trouble and I always have to save her.

Everything that led up to the night of the fire is getting mixed around and knotted up, but I've got to keep it clear in my head. I must.

What I need to do is unpick and unravel everything back to the very beginning, to stop me from forgetting the *Once upon a time* of what took place and why. It's too easy to get confused and forget the reason for everything otherwise.

Except I can't decide where the very beginning begins. Life is never tangle-free and there's never one place on the crazy skein of things where you can put your finger to pull a thread loose, and say, 'Here it is, this is where it all began.' It always begins someplace else.

TWO

Let's start with the afternoon before the fire.

I'd ended up with the mother of all migraines. Which wasn't surprising.

It started as a dull thud-thud-thud across the top of my eyes, but I knew what was coming and by the time I'd crawled home – to Angie's place, I mean – it felt like a metal bar ramming into my head, pounding it apart with each tiny movement.

How I drove the last couple of kilometres I don't know. Needed to throw up, but couldn't. Had to shut everything down. All I wanted was a heat pack, the nest of my bed and to sleep the night through – to escape my head (and the rest of the world) until it was whole again – so I fed Gustav, slid the bolt on the cat-flap and swallowed a couple of magic tablets.

I dragged shut the curtains, turned off my phone and crept into the warm, treacle dark.

Several hours later, everything changed forever.

According to my clock it was 4:07 when the single car on Nine Mile Road slowed in the dark outside Angie's gate.

There came the crunching of tyres on gravel and then the high beam of headlights sliced a slow arc across the wall. The antique wardrobe was momentarily illuminated by them, followed by Angie's painting of birds flying over the river and then, against the closed bedroom door, the hunched figure of my dressing-gown sprang into the light.

The car stopped and the engine was switched off, but the lights remained on for thirty seconds or so.

I waited. I listened.

Eventually a car door slammed and then another, followed by the rumble of a man's voice.

What was he saying? I couldn't make it out, and strained to hear the second person reply. I strained till I was rigid.

Footsteps scrunched across the gravel, stepped heavily onto the timber boards of the verandah. A knock on the door: a loud, confident knock.

All I wanted was to pull the doona over my head until I was completely wrapped and sealed in a deep, dark cocoon. All I wanted was to hibernate until I was a butterfly or a bear. But I knew they wouldn't go away.

He found the doorbell and rang. Twice.

There was nothing for it. Swinging quietly out of bed, I padded across to unhook my dressing-gown and, without turning any lights on, tiptoed to the top of the stairs and peered through the landing window. I couldn't see their car on the drive. I couldn't see anything other than the corrugated roof of the verandah and the night.

When he rang the bell a third time, I let the sound of it draw me downstairs. I forced myself down, one stair after another, and fought against the instinct to freeze and wait for them to leave. Each step made me tenser, more brittle, but when I reached the bottom I made myself let go of the banister and take two long breaths.

All I could see through the frosted glass of the front door was a darker shadow against the world's darkness outside, so I did what was natural and plucked a golf club from Angie's umbrella stand. Who wouldn't be jittery in the middle of the night? What else could strangers expect, knocking on the door of a remote house at such a time?

'Who is it?' I said, my voice shaking. Didn't sound like me.

'Police,' the dark shadow replied. 'It's Senior Sergeant Mick Droyler. Is that you, Meg? Meg Dapsy? I have Police Officer Wendy Aitkens with me.' He switched on a torch and shone it at himself. I saw something of a distorted face through the crazed glass. It was how I felt.

Still clutching the golf club, I pulled the belt of my dressing-gown tighter and turned on the porch light.

'What do you want? Do you know what time it is?'

'We need to speak with you, Meg. You remember me, don't you?'

Tess Droyler and I went through primary and secondary school together. We hit most every hot-spot of adolescence together too. We were best friends until the day of my abrupt exit from school, after which she wouldn't have anything to do with me. My mother especially liked that I hung around with a cop's daughter when I was fourteen-going-on-eighteen, seeming to think it'd keep me out of trouble, as if her dad's job was a special charm, for pity's sake. What she didn't know was that Tess spent every moment of her teens reacting against every conservative value she thought his uniform stood for and, at that crazy time, I liked her all the more for it. She was unprincipled on principle. She did stuff I never would – took drugs, shoplifted, slept around – which made it harder to swallow when she ended up thinking she was too good for me.

I flicked on the hall light, opened the door.

He said, 'I know it's late, Meg, but this won't wait till morning.'

Removing his officer's cap, he held it by the rim, and the female police officer did the same. He stood in front and she stood to one side, a step or two behind. He was around Victor's age, but she was about my age; maybe a little older. Mick Droyler's always been a big bloke, even without the padded vest of his uniform and all the police hardware on his belt. In his own home, he always looked like a battering ram of a man, although a kind one, I always thought. Solid and reliable.

The cold and dampness of mist swept in with them, but it wasn't this that made me shiver as I shut the front door. We sort of sidestepped one another when I ushered them into Angie's study, where in one long glance he absorbed the crammed bookshelves, the paintings, the photos, the furniture and even the hang of the curtains, as if he was searching for a sign of someone. He did it quickly, but I still noticed, and then he half-smiled and nodded at the golf club. It was a tired smile and more about putting me at ease than anything else.

'You don't need that,' he said.

Angie keeps two golf sticks in her umbrella stand, along with an old-fashioned black-lacquered and brass-ferruled cane and a couple of umbrellas, which she bought from a junk shop. She doesn't play golf, but says they add character to the entrance hall, which they do. One has a bulbous wooden club on the end – a driver – but I'd picked up the iron because it felt less clumsy. I propped it against Angie's desk and pulled the dressing-gown belt tighter. Gustav squeezed through the gap in the door, wound himself against Officer Aitkens' legs, looked up at me and purred.

She reached down and stroked his neck.

'You're bringing bad news,' I said. 'At this time of the night. What's happened? Who is it? Is it Angie?'

He turned his cap between his hands, looked at it, then stopped. 'Can we sit down?'

I felt sorry for him then. I hate it when people feel awkward or distressed on my account, if they're trying to do the right thing by me, which I could see he was.

'Someone's dead, aren't they? Or there's been an accident. That's why you're here. Who is it? What's happened?'

'There's been a fire, Meg.'

'A forest fire?' I made myself glance towards the window for the tell-tale orange glow, even though the blinds were down and the curtains shut. It was the wrong time of year for bushfires, but most people don't think straight if they've just woken up.

'No. A house fire,' he said.

'Oh, where?'

He hesitated. 'Your parents' house. In Three Creeks.'

I blinked, held my breath, stared from him to her and back again. I put a hand out, gripped the top of the settee. 'When? How? What sort of fire? Is she... is my mum okay?'

I gripped the edge of the cushion so tight my hand began to shake and I made myself grip harder. The brittleness of earlier had gone, flushed out by adrenaline or something equally potent; I sensed it coursing through me.

He hesitated again before reaching over and touching my arm. The movements struck me as slow, predictable, and I knew exactly what he'd say before he said it: 'I'm sorry. Your mother didn't get out in time.'

I needed to shout or scream or cry, but couldn't. Instead, like a marionette, I made myself sit down, made myself shake my head, made myself open my mouth, ball my fist against my teeth. And an image of Pinocchio came to mind.

The sound I made was barely audible – more wooden squeak than speak: 'No.'

'I'm sorry.'

I nearly laughed then. Couldn't help it. It was an absurd, nervous response, and only a flash of terror stopped me, turning it into a gulp and a choke. I don't think they noticed, but if they had they'd have assumed it was the onset of hysteria or some sort of emotional tic. They'd see every crazy thing in their job.

Officer Aitkens said, 'Your sister's okay, though. She got out in time. They've taken her to hospital.'

I stopped breathing and all but turned to stone again. I waited for her to correct herself. I waited for the words to reorder themselves. But the moment stretched.

'My sister? Stella?'

'Yes.'

'No, not Stella. She's in Lapishot. She's staying with a friend there.' I was shaking my head.

'We believe it was Stella who raised the alarm. She was definitely in the house.'

That didn't make sense. The room started spinning.

'No.'

He drew a chair up and sat opposite me and she placed herself on the edge of the settee.

I shut my eyes, tried to think straight. Not panic.

'We need to ask you some questions if we can, Meg?'

'Stella? Are you sure?'

He leant forward and placed his hand on my arm again. 'It's okay, Meg. She'll be alright. A bit of smoke inhalation and shock. We'll take you to the hospital after, if you like.'

'But she'd been kicked out,' I said, as much to myself as

them. 'Mum kicked her out. Unless they made up again.' I tried to work out how that could have happened. 'No, she wasn't there. She can't have been.' Why on earth did she go home when she'd said she wouldn't?

I sensed them exchanging glances, the way you can sometimes, and I stopped. I made myself shut up.

Mick said, 'When did this happen? Had there been a problem? Who was she staying with?'

Officer Aitkens unclipped her notebook, all set to write down anything I might say.

I was on dangerous ground, but couldn't straighten my thoughts to find a way forward. I looked across at the golf club. Shouldn't have put it down. Needed something to cling to.

Shallow breaths. Too tight. The air had gone from me. Like a punch in the guts.

'Later,' he said. 'Are you alright? We can go through that another time. Okay?'

I took several deeper breaths, exhaled slowly, made myself look him in the eyes, nodded.

'But can you tell us about your father, Meg? We need to ask about your father.'

Another breath. Focus.

I apologised and he told me not to worry, but to take my time.

Mick Droyler's eyes had a sympathetic warmth to them, the way he looked at you, and it struck me he was unlike any of the other cops I'd come across, not that I'd come across many. He'd always been gentle with Tess too, and it seemed strange now, how determined she'd been to give him and her step-mum such a hard time for those few early years of adolescence, particularly as he was always there for her whenever she needed him; to pick her up, to look out for her, to love her. They both were. At least that's how it seemed. It's not always easy to tell.

He repeated his question and I told myself to get my act together. I couldn't fall apart. I had to think clearly. There was too much happening.

'Dad's on a business trip,' I eventually said. 'In America, I think. Something to do with Demlab.'

He nodded and she took notes. I looked from one to the other. Except now his eyes were waiting for something more from me.

'No he isn't,' he said. 'Your father arrived back tonight; earlier this evening. He was at the house too, although we haven't found him yet.'

I shook my head. I told myself to shake my head, and I did. Pinocchio again.

'Yes,' he said.

'No. Not until Saturday night or Sunday morning. He wasn't sure whether he'd stay over at the airport hotel or not. You're wrong.' I could be emphatic about this.

'He came back early. He was there, Meg. We know that much.'

'No. He would've told me. He'd have called round or phoned.'

He said nothing.

I waited, but still neither of them spoke.

'What's going on?' I asked.

He glanced around the room again, as if he thought Victor might suddenly appear from beneath the desk or leap out from behind the curtains: Peep-oh!

'He definitely hasn't been here? He hasn't contacted you at all? In any way?'

'No. I thought he was still overseas. What makes you think he's not? Why do you think he's been here?'

'You can't think where he might be?'

Again I shook my head, but it was the thought of Stella being back in the house which confused me. Why did she return when she said she wouldn't? Not for a couple of days at least. What made her change her mind?

And every time I thought about this, the air collapsed in me. Too many breaths. Too shallow. Too fast.

I think he realised before I did.

'Slow down,' he said. 'Just take one deep breath.'

'Put your head between your legs,' she said.

Too late. Dressing-gown flying open, I bolted for the downstairs toilet.

Carboxyhemoglobinemia

It's the fumes that kill, not the flames. That's what the research says. I googled it. In house fires, carbon monoxide poisoning is the Number One killer; that and the lack of oxygen. Most people are dead in their beds before the flames are licking at their flesh and bones. They're usually dead before the fire brigade can arrive to rescue them. That's what the research says.

There's consolation in knowing that, I reckon. Wouldn't most people rather drift into unconscious oblivion than suffer the sizzling-skin agony of being burnt crisply alive? They'd rather that for their Dearly Beloved Ones too.

This is how it works: the blood has proteins – haemoglobin – that carry oxygen round the body like little freight train wagons, but the carbon monoxide fumes of a fire hijack those freight trains and stop the oxygen from hitching its ride, which ultimately results in dizziness, unconsciousness, death.

I think I've got that right, but I was never very good at Science.

To treat smoke inhalation, neat oxygen is administered. A concentrated supply helps reduce and replace the carboxyhemoglobins. The ambulance crew would've strapped an oxygen mask onto Stella as they stretchered her off to hospital in Lapishot. She'd have been light-headed, nauseous and tired, but alive.

Not that she should have been there in the first place.

When we walked out to the patrol car and Officer Aitkens opened the back door, I thought she was going to place one hand on my head as I climbed in, like they do in the movies, but of course she didn't, and why should she? They were just giving me a lift to the hospital on their way back to Lapishot because they knew I was in shock and might be a liability on the road. Good community policing is what it was, although I'd have to fork out for the taxi back later.

In the car, Mick Droyler mentioned something and she asked me a question, but my mind was elsewhere. I couldn't focus. I remember the crunching of gravel, the rags of mist, a crackle of static on the police radio. He said something else to her, which I couldn't hear from the back seat, what with the sound of the engine and the air-con fan blasting to clear the windscreen, and then she spoke into the radio and received a reply, but the words didn't register.

Stella would be fine. Stella would be fine. I kept telling myself this. A little smoke inhalation is what they'd said. Taking her to hospital was routine. That's all. She'd be sitting in Outpatients, impatiently waiting. We'd get a taxi back and she'd stay with me a while at Angie's until we sorted things out. I'd make sure Lover-boy was booted out of the picture once and for all and then I'd help her get through her exams. We'd talk once she'd had a decent sleep and I'd look after her, like I always have.

I stared out the window into the night, and Mick and Officer Aitkens were silent. I realised then where we were and that he was taking the long route to Lapishot Road and the hospital, and I couldn't figure why – why not take the Rudely Road through Three Creeks? – until I guessed it was to avoid driving past the house and all the drama there. He was being thoughtful.

Even though the mist petered out as we got deeper into the forest, he reduced his speed. There's always animal corpses littering Nine Mile Road – lumps of twisted, rotting meat – and it wouldn't do to write off a cop car by hitting a deer or a feral goat or something, but all I could see were trees and darkness. The darkness absorbed almost everything and I didn't even think about the poor deer I'd whacked into oblivion a few weeks back, or the way it had snuffled out gobs of phlegmy blood and stared back at me.

Pressing my face against the cold glass of the window, I realised there were different shades of dark in the forest at night and noticed how darkness threw its own shadows. It struck me there might be comfort in this, if only my mind wasn't too numb to find it. All the same, I thought I was doing well and beginning to get everything under control again until, in shifting my gaze up at the sky, the dizziness rushed through me.

The back of the car was too cramped. It was pressing in on me, smothering me. As if the space was shrinking or I was expanding, like Alice in sodding Wonderland. And it stank. One of those synthetic pine air fresheners was clipped to an air vent and, as soon as the heater kicked in and the air warmed up, the shrinking space reeked of deodorised toilet. Piss and vomit.

Had to get out. Had to.

Mick twisted slightly in his seat to glance back at me, and

it was as though my body twisted out-of-control too. 'Are you alright, Meg?'

Hunched at the side of the road, Officer Aitkens placed a hand on my back and handed me a tissue.

'Are you feeling better?'

The nausea was real, but brought up nothing more than the meanest, sourest burp. If only I could have sicked it all up – everything – until not even the bitterness of bile was left. If only I could have sicked up the whole of me until I was inside-out, and then maybe I could've rearranged myself and put back the things I wanted to keep, throw away the things I didn't. If only we could choose.

'Sorry,' I said. 'Thought I was going to heave.'

'No need to apologise. Just take a few deep breaths,' she said. 'The cold air'll do you good.'

I squatted down on my haunches. It was more comfortable like that. For a few precious seconds, I closed my eyes and imagined lying down at the side of the road and sleeping; I imagined what it'd be like to walk off into the thickness of trees and vanish.

'Meg?'

I yawned and tried standing, but stumbled with my back against the car.

'It's shock,' she said.

I took three more deep breaths and, this time, felt the cold thrill of the night air unfurling and shivering through me at last. It brought me round.

Stella wasn't waiting in the fluorescent glow of Outpatients. They'd admitted her to a ward on the third floor. They'd sedated her and only let me look briefly in on her to reassure myself she was okay, but her right hand was bandaged and she was way too still. As for the oxygen mask, the drip, the thingamajig clipped to one of her fingers, the leads and the monitors, none of that paraphernalia convinced me she really was okay. Beyond the mishmash of leads and monitors, I only had their word for it.

The nurse didn't even give me a full minute before ushering me out, despite the fact that the police had brought me there to see her. I could have sat by her and held her hand if they'd let me, I could've made sure she was actually asleep and resting. I could've let the nurses know if she'd begun to wake or call out. I wouldn't have woken her or bothered her, not the little sister I'd always protected.

Besides, she wasn't asleep, not really. She'd been drugged into unconsciousness. Her eyes eclipsed by dark moons.

Without thinking, I touched my own face, stroked the skin beneath my eyes.

Mick Droyler had a quiet word with one of the nurses, then explained to me that the two of them had to go. He told me he'd get in touch later and asked if I'd be alright.

I thanked them both and I meant it. It's a crap job they have to do. I could never do it. And yes, I told them I'd be okay. I *had* to be okay. I meant that too.

But all I wanted was to creep into bed next to Stella and sleep for a few hours of forgetfulness. I'd cuddle up to the wish that when I woke everything would be fixed and dandy and smelling of... roses. What I wanted more than anything else in the world was to wake from the last four years and discover it had been a bad dream.

Instead I was directed to a tacky waiting area furnished with a dozen orange, vinyl chairs and a beige, plastic, coffee table cluttered with old, stained and dog-eared magazines, and a vending machine in the corner. The chair I sat on was ripped so I moved to another, but someone had pressed a glob of chewing gum against the side of that and I accidentally touched it, so moved again. I tried to read, but when that didn't work I flicked through the pictures in a couple of glossies. I stood and paced, wandered down the corridor towards Stella's room, but was shunted out again by one of the nurses who appeared moments later, so returned to the vending-machine and a beaker of lukewarm, coffee-coloured dishwater.

At the window, where the fluorescent light leaked into the night, two moths beat against the glass, trying to get in. On the inside windowsill, among the dust, lay the corpses of several flies and a screwed-up lolly wrapper: *Minties*.

We're either moths or flies. We spend our lives trying to get in or get out. Whenever we catch a glimpse of what will make us happy, something or someone always gets in the way.

I couldn't help thinking about my mother. I knew she was dead, and was possibly even lying in the hospital morgue a few floors below me in the basement, but even so I couldn't remember the happy times. I could only remember the times she went out of her way to make life miserable. That's all she ever did. Ever since I was little. She was the glass wall.

Cousin Gilbert, Aunt Marie and Uncle Drummond visit Three Creeks one weekend. I'm seven or eight, but Gilbert's a year older. Although Aunt Marie is Dad's sister, I only remember one other visit from them, several years later, and that's because they live overseas, working for some oil company, but Gilbert doesn't come on that occasion. He has school exams and can't afford time from his studies if he's going to prove to the world what a genius he is and all that, and so I only ever meet him once.

Once is more than enough.

Until then, I think his name sounds exotic because I've never met anyone called Gilbert before and I boast to friends at school about how my cousin Gilbert is coming from overseas to visit us at the weekend. Afterwards, though, I say nothing. Ever since, whenever I hear the name Gilbert, I imagine that person must be a spoilt sissy and a royal pain in the arse.

It's the main reason I refuse to sign up for my school's Gilbert & Sullivan production when I'm fifteen. I knew I'd hate it.

The adults sit down with coffee, aperitifs or whatever, and we're sent to 'play' in another room. Stella and I are told to show Gilbert our toys or books or to play Monopoly with him, but Stella is being whiny and clingy and is allowed to stay with the grown-ups as long as she's quiet.

'Go play Scrabble with Gilbert, Megsy,' Dad says. 'He's good with words. He won't be so easy to beat.'

'Stella's a bit young for Scrabble,' I hear my mother pronounce, in that loud, exaggerated whisper adults adopt when they want to be clearly heard at the same time as wanting to suggest a note of delicacy or diplomacy or some such nonsense. Each syllable is too carefully enunciated and usually there's a bit of nodding or pointing going on too. As if it matters that Stella had a tantrum last time I beat her. Of course I beat her, I know more words than she does; I'm almost three years older.

But Gilbert and I don't play Scrabble. I show him every room in the house, introduce him to Toby, the school hamster I'd volunteered to look after, and decide to give him a tour of the garden. We tell one another a couple of jokes and I begin to think he's alright.

Big mistake.

It's a cool day, but so still that the raucous of kedamores flocking and shrieking on the edge of the forest sounds as if someone's turned up the volume. There's a blue sky, but you wouldn't call it a blue sky because there are too many clouds in it, and they're those big, fluffy white clouds – the sort that sometimes take on the shape of animals or objects as they sail over. The air smells damp, of rotting leaves and over-ripe apples; brown and spongy apples that have been left where they fell. Autumn.

I'm sitting on the swing and he says: 'Have you seen this?'

'What?' I say.

He has one hand wrapped over the other as if he's holding something and I wonder what precious thing he's been cradling in his pocket all this time: a bird's egg or a pet mouse or a polished stone?

'Smell cheese,' he says, holding both hands up towards my face.

I stand up from the swing, take a step forward and crane down to smell whatever it is.

He pulls one hand back to reveal his fist and smacks me on the nose.

'Cheese!' he shouts and jumps around laughing. 'Gotcha. You're the cheese!'

For a second I don't know whether to sock him back or not, but it didn't really hurt even though it made my nose tingle, my eyes water, and I sort of laugh too. It'll be a good trick to play at school. If only he'd stop jumping around crowing about it.

'Let me do it to you,' I say, balling one hand into a fist and covering it with the other. 'Smell cheese, Gilbert.'

He shakes his head. 'It only works if it's a surprise, silly. There's no point otherwise.' He grabs hold of the rope holding the swing's seat and pulls himself up so he's standing on it, the way I've seen older boys use the swings at school. 'Try it out on your sister,' he suggests and begins to swing slowly backwards and forwards. He has a habit of talking down to me, as if he's a grown-up himself, and I'm not sure whether I admire him all the more for being so much older than me or whether I'm beginning to find him a smarmy-parmy know-it-all.

'Do you want to see if there's any cows in the paddock?' I ask, and he jumps down so quickly I wonder whether he's never seen a cow before. Perhaps they don't have them where he comes from.

We run across the garden and he decides to race me to the fence.

'Beat you!' he crows.

'I'm wearing gumboots,' I point out.

'It's your garden,' he says.

'You're older.'

'And a boy. And faster.'

He wants it all ways, this Gilbert. I'm thinking I might just kick him in the shins and walk away, but guess he'd kick me back, and harder.

'Is that them over there?' he says. 'They're a long way away.'

The herd's grazing down by the far fence, close to the river, with the forest behind, and I begin calling them, but they ignore me.

'Moo. Moo,' I boom, as deep as I can.

'They're not very smart, your cows,' he tells me. 'Our cows would come when they're called. Our cows know their own names.'

'They have names?'

'Of course they do.'

I think he's being stupid at first, except it makes me look at the distant cows and where we live in a different light, and I'm feeling like a country dimwit. Gilbert knows things I don't. He knows more about the things I'd always taken for granted. He has an answer for everything and I can't help but wonder about the cows they have where he comes from and why our cows are so inferior.

'They usually come,' I tell him. 'Usually they do.' I peer into the cow-distance and say: 'It's probably good they're over there because they can be a bit fierce, our cows can. They can be a bit scary.'

'Fierce? Scary?'

'Wild.'

'Boring,' he says. 'This whole place is boring. There's too many trees. I bet nothing ever happens here.'

'It does,' I say, but can't think of a single thing to back me up.

'Like what?'

I look at the herd of cows and the river and the forest, and Gilbert is pressing down on the top wire of the fence that separates our property from the farm. Half a metre away is the electric fence that Mum made Mr Agnew and his idiot son put up after the cows kept leaning over to eat her roses and saplings. They were wrecking the fence and before long they'd be in the garden ruining everything, she said.

'Our cows are so wild we need two fences to keep them from breaking free. They'd stampede and kill people otherwise.'

'Piffle. This one's all rickety. Look at it.' He begins pulling and pushing on the top wire so that the nearest three posts sway backwards and forwards like crazy. 'As for that little fence there, why they could easily step over it or break it down. That's a silly fence. Why have a fence like that at all?'

I look at him and realise he's nothing but a pretender. There's a boy in my class exactly like him – Damien Morrell. He doesn't know half as much as he pretends. He's convincing to a certain point, but then he goes too far and it all disappears. He's just trying to make himself look good. Gilbert doesn't know what an electric fence is and he's probably never been near a paddock of cows before.

'Because it's a magic fence, Gilbert.'

He laughs. 'Sure it is. And fairies dance along it at night.'

'It is. If you touch that fence you disappear. That's why there are no cows on this side of the paddock. They've learnt to be afraid of the fence. Besides, any cows that were over here have probably touched the fence and disappeared. It's nothing to do with the fairies. Honest to God.'

He begins to reach forward, leaning down on our fence to reach the single wire of the electric fence.

'You're such a baby,' he tells me. 'Things just don't disappear. Where do you think they go when they disappear? They have to be somewhere. What do they teach you at your school?'

He sounds like an old man. It's something my grandpa would've asked.

I shrug.

I'm about to say: 'You can touch it if you want, but I wouldn't.' Except he doesn't wait, and I'm glad.

I barely see him touch it, more's the pity, but he must do because he yelps like a kicked dog, spins round in a full circle and goes running up the garden to the house, bawling his eyes out. Suddenly he's a little kid again and I'm left standing there by myself.

'Told you you'd disappear,' I yell after him, but there's no way he hears me.

Five minutes later, I'm drifting backwards and forwards

on the swing, waiting for Gilbert to come back out, when Stella skips towards me instead.

'Where's Gilbert?' I ask.

She stands in front of me. 'Mum says you have to come inside and say sorry to him.'

I know what Stella's after. Neither of us will bother with the swing for months on end, but the moment one of us sits on it, the other's impatient to have a go too.

'You're trying to steal the swing from me,' I tell her.

'No, really,' she chirps. 'Mum sent me out here. You have to go and say sorry.'

'Why? I didn't do anything.'

'You made him cry.'

'He's a cry-baby, that's all.'

'Don't you like him?' she asks.

I shrug, but then remember the trick he showed me. 'Do you want to see a trick, Stell?'

'Okay,' she says.

I stand, turn my back to her and make a show of taking something out of my pocket and arranging it in my hands. I do it better than Gilbert did.

'What is it, Megsy? Show me.'

I turn around with one hand wrapped around the fist of the other and I hold them out to her. 'Smell cheese,' I say.

She takes a step forward and leans forward to smell whatever it is I've found. Quick as a flash, I unwrap my fist and punch her on the nose.

There's barely a pause before her mouth opens into a round, loud wail and, holding her hands across her nose, she runs crying back into the house. I didn't mean to do it hard, but she must've moved forward at the same time.

'Stell,' I run after her. 'Don't tell. I didn't mean to.' But it's too late. It's no good.

Afterwards, there are four of us in the kitchen: Gilbert, Stella, me and Mum. Stella's still whimpering and has been told to hold a cold flannel against her nose. There's talk about it bleeding, but I can't see any blood anywhere. There'd be blood on the flannel or down her dress if I'd hit her that hard. My mother is gripping my wrist and I'm tugging away from her because it hurts, but the more I try shaking her off the firmer she grips.

She wants me to apologise to Gilbert in front of my aunt and uncle, but they don't think it's such a big deal. They remain in the lounge chatting with Dad, who'll probably be pouring more drinks and offering peanuts around, while I'm dealt with in the kitchen.

'I've already said sorry to Stella,' I complain. 'Haven't I, Stella?' And I know Stella will back me up, if only she'd be allowed to speak; she never holds a grudge for long, does Stella. We're friends, the two of us.

'Well now you're going to apologise in front of me and this time you're going to mean it.'

I'm about to tell her that I meant it last time and that she'd know it if she'd been there, but with her vice-hold on my wrist she gives me a shake and I say, 'I'm sorry, Stella.'

'You'll say it like you mean it, young lady. I won't tell you again.' With this, she takes a couple of steps towards the kitchen drawer, dragging me with her, and takes out a wooden spoon.

That's unfair. She's used the wooden spoon before and I still remember the crazy sting of each hit.

'No! I didn't mean to do it. That's not fair.'

'Then apologise.'

'I just did!'

She pulls my arm up and twists me round with one hand — makes me pirouette — and smacks me across the back of the legs, using the spoon, with the other.

'I'm sorry again, then! For the third time!' I'm crying too now, but angry and humiliated that this Gilbert boy is allowed to watch. I point at him. 'Why don't you smack him? He did it to me first. You don't care about that.'

And she smacks me again.

'Now you apologise to Gilbert,' she tells me.

'What for? He hit me on the nose first!'

'You know what for. For making him touch the electric fence.'

'No! I won't. I didn't make him. He –'

Before I can say anything else, she twists me back again, and I try to dodge her swing, but she catches me on the side of the knee instead.

'Ow! No!'

'That serves you right. If you try fighting me, Margaret Dapsy, you'll come off worst.'

'I'm not. You're hurting.' My wrist feels raw, like she's grated the skin off it, but I don't care anymore.

'Then apologise to Gilbert.'

'No, I won't.'

'Apologise.'

'No.'

'In that case you'll go to bed now and you won't have any dinner.'

'Good.'

My wrist is red and I slam the door when I run from the kitchen to my bedroom. For over an hour, I lie in bed imagining how she'll come and say sorry and beg forgiveness for not believing me, once Gilbert's been made to admit he punched me first and that I hadn't forced him to touch the electric fence either. She doesn't though. That never happens. And I hate Gilbert and I hate her.

Just like the back of the cop car, the hospital walls and ceiling started pressing in on me and pushing down on me. My heart was pounding as I ran down three flights of stairs, along the deserted corridor of Respiratory and Cardiology rooms, looking for a way out, and when I pushed through the door from Emergency into the empty, cold night, it was like drawing breath again.

The street was abandoned, the houses had their eyes squeezed shut. I stood on the wide pavement in front of the hospital, taking in lungful after lungful of night air, staring up.

Sometimes, when I look up, up, up into a night sky and stare too long and too hard at the vastness of space, it's as if I'm lifted and flipped around by it until I'm no longer looking up, but looking down, down, down into a vast ocean of blackness that stretches beyond all beyondness, and it reminds me that I'm absolutely nothing in it whatsoever. Of no account at all. No one is. It always makes me realise how space stretches backwards from one infinity, before the beginning of time, and forwards to the infinity that marks the never-endingness of time, as well as sideways to the parallel infinities of Now. It's the measure of before-life and after-death and our few minuscule moments in-between; it's the measure of a non-existence so incalculably vast that it'll swallow the relative nothingness of me and everyone else up forever and ever without even noticing. We exist and die as if we'd never been.

And then I had to stop looking up, before I fell over. I had to focus on the concrete pavement instead, and on the solidness of the trees lining the streets: Norfolk pines, mostly, in that part of town – *Araucaria heterophylla*. I noticed how their roots were lifting the pavement and breaking through it, and I stepped closer, sliding one foot and then the other over the uneven surface.

Out of the blue, this simple action reminded me of an antique clockwork soldier that she – my mother – once showed me. I could have only been five or six at the time. The soldier had belonged to Nan, I think, when she was a little girl, and I remember being spellbound as it was gently lifted from its nest of tissue paper in an ancient cardboard box and placed on the ground. She held it there, carefully winding a key in its back, before releasing it.

It jerked into life and slid one foot out and then the other, and walked in this manner half-way across the kitchen floor until it got slower and slower and halted, and then she wound it up again so it might walk the rest of the way. But it was old and the spring was weak and she put it away again almost immediately, and I never saw it again. She probably squirreled it away in her wardrobe or a box in the attic 'for safe-keeping', except now it'll have perished in the fire.

I don't know why I remembered such a thing, nor at such a time, but there was comfort in mimicking the clockwork movement on a wide pavement in the middle of the night when no one was around to see. Mechanically, I slid one foot in front of the other all the way to the corner of the hospital block, fifty-odd metres away, and felt calmer for it. At the street corner, I paused, switched off from being a toy soldier and turned left. I walked past Pathology, Audiology, the Fertility Clinic and the Brain Injury Rehabilitation Unit. The path was rougher and narrower outside the entrance to the staff car park and the residential apartments, and the broken concrete had been replaced in patches by a thick crust of bitumen, but it was then I realised where the path was leading me. I knew all about Ward 8, tucked away at the back of the hospital.

But I wouldn't give in. I wouldn't let it defeat me ever again. I told myself I had the strength to walk past it, particularly on that night of all nights. It was only a building, after all: a man-made arrangement of bricks and mortar, and there'd be no negative force sucking me back in. Its rooms and locked corridors didn't own any part of me. I'd survived it once, I told myself, but I'd never let it hold me again.

By rights, there should've been a streetlight at the junction with Garrard Road, but it must have failed or been vandalised because it was darker than it should've been. Nonetheless, I turned the corner and walked briskly, one quick step after another after another, until I was dizzy with holding my breath and walking.

Ward 8 was a dangerous place. It would be too easy to lose control and wake up trapped inside.

Turning left again, I took my mind off things by counting footsteps; past the rear of the staff car park, a Goods & Services entrance, Occupational Therapy, ENT, Chaplaincy, and a long strip of administrative offices and consultation rooms. Finally, when I'd got back to the floodlit brightness at the front of the hospital, I took off my shoes and stood barefoot for a minute in the middle of a cold, wet, carefully manicured lawn. It made me gasp. I needed this.

But I'd been outside too long. Maybe Stella was awake and calling for me, except the nurses didn't know where I was. I had to be with her, inside. Pulling on my shoes, I hurried up four flights of stairs – until I realised I'd gone too far and had to come down a flight – and along to Stella's room. I arrived breathless, convinced she'd be sitting up, but she wasn't. She was still out of it. Blissfully dead to the world.

Why shouldn't I sit with my sister? Why place chairs in hospital rooms if visitors aren't allowed to sit and wait?

Anyone else would've been allowed.

Perhaps the police had said something about me.

She reeked of smoke – I hadn't noticed earlier – and seemed smaller under the tucked-in sheet and blanket than she had in years, as if she'd shrunk to a little girl again. What's more, although she usually sprawled in her asleep (she's always been a sprawler, whereas I curl up in bed as if it's a womb), they'd placed her flat on her back with her arms at her side and her legs out straight, all neat and tidy, like a corpse. It was horrible and I wanted to untidy her a bit, so she'd look properly alive.

Inside a polythene bag, which sat in a plastic basket on the cabinet next to the bed, were her clothes. She'd been wearing the nightie I bought for her birthday. How about that? One part of her loves me, one part of her stabs me in the back.

Why had she gone home? After everything I'd done for her. What was said? I needed to know what was said.

She stirred and mumbled something into her oxygen mask – nonsense words – and I moved closer.

'Stella,' I said. 'Stell. It's alright. Everything's alright now. It's gonna be alright.'

Nothing.

'How could you?' I said. 'How could you do that to me?'

Ten minutes later, she began coughing and called out. 'Dad!' Her voice was scratched, stuck between sandpaper and cotton wool, and her mask was slipping off. Her eyes were sort of open – puffy, red-raw slits – but I don't think she saw me. She closed them and mumbled something else, which sounded like, 'Sorry.' Then began coughing again. Coughing fit to burst.

Sorry? It could have been 'Sorry'.

I pressed the Call button next to Stella's bed and ran along to the nurses' station.

'My sister,' I said to the nurse who was already on her way. Why weren't they keeping a closer watch on her? If I hadn't been there, they wouldn't have known.

The nurse adjusted the mask, took note of the monitor, checked the plastic contraption clipped to Stella's finger, did something to the drip line that looped down and into the back of my silly little sister's hand, to increase the dose or something.

Another nurse arrived and directed me out the room, back towards the waiting area at the end of the ward. 'We'll tell you when she's comfortable,' she said.

'She's my sister,' I told her.

'We're trying to make sure she's comfortable and doesn't get into a panic again. We thought we might have to intubate her, but she's doing fine. Really she is. The doctor wants her to sleep.'

'She's not sleeping. You're drugging her to the eyeballs.'

I wondered if one of these nurses had worked on Ward 8 and if that's why they were being such bitches to me.

'So she can rest.' She put one arm close to my back and steered me towards the orange, vinyl chairs. 'Would you like a cup of tea and some toast?'

I was famished, but shook my head. 'No thanks.' I didn't want anything from them.

For almost an hour, I stood with my head against the window, looking out.

Why are the night hours so much longer, slower?

Several small hand-prints were smeared across the bottom of the glass, but these grew less obvious as dawn seeped in from the horizon. To begin with, the new day was nothing more than a slow insinuation of grey, but as it grew and the dark gradually thinned out, it revealed an ocean of trees in the distance and, closer to, housing estates, apartments, shops, lamp-posts and power-lines, the mess of hospital buildings, flat roofs, aerials, antennae, air-conditioning vents... the watery fringe of a weak sun. It began to make me feel panicky and sick again, until one of the nurses came.

'Your sister's awake. She's asking to see you. Try not to get her excited though. It'll be better if she rests.'

As soon as I entered her room, Stella said, 'Meg.' Her voice was a raspy whisper.

'You're awake,' I said, and moved closer.

'Ugh. Tired.'

'How're you feeling?'

'Like a bus... run over.' She winced. 'Stinking headache.'

'Stella,' I said.

She winced again. 'Any Panadol? Anything?'

I nodded. 'In a minute. I'll ask the nurses in a minute.'

She closed her eyes and I held her good hand the best I could, what with the drip and the thing clipped onto her finger, and I thought she'd gone back to sleep until she spoke again: 'How long... how long you been here?'

'A while. They wouldn't let me sit with you, but I've been here, out in the waiting room.' I stopped stroking her hand and waited for her to open her eyes. Her eyelids were swollen; she no longer had beautiful, big, brown eyes, but red slits. 'What happened, Stella?' I asked. 'You went home. Why did you go home? Did you see Victor? Did you see Dad?' I had to know whether she'd try hiding anything. When I thought of her and Pete, I wanted to slap her, except she looked so weak, as if she'd had a good slapping already. I wanted to confront her with what I knew, or some of it at least, but not until I knew everything she knew. 'What happened, Stella? Do you know what happened?'

She closed her eyes again, tried to take a breath, but it caught and she started coughing.

I handed her a beaker of water and she sipped it through a straw. I did the same for her once when she was five and had mumps. I could've only been eight at the time.

'Can't talk,' she said. 'Hurts.'

I nodded, but couldn't let her off the hook that easily. I had to know. I had to know before the police started asking their questions. 'How did it start? Do you know how the fire started?'

She shook her head and sank deeper into the pillow. 'No.'

'No? Really? You really don't know?'

'No. How?'

'I don't know. How would I know? That's why I'm asking you. You were there.' I stroked her hair and she sort of smiled, and I smiled. She stank of smoke. 'Is there anything I can get you?'

'... my head.'

Half-an-hour later, I was sitting in a taxi heading back to Three Creeks. They told me they'd be keeping her in for observation and there was nothing I could do except collect fresh clothes for her and get some rest myself. I tried talking with her, but she could barely keep her eyes open. She wasn't going to tell me anything, wasn't going to admit anything.

'I'll come back later this afternoon,' I told her. 'Let you doze.'

But she was already asleep.

THREE

I NEEDED TO SEE the bones of the house. Sooner or later. I had to.

The taxi driver glanced over his shoulder at me and drifted to a stop. He had crooked, yellow teeth and deep-set eyes, but struck me as a kind-looking bloke; he had one of those tanned faces that's all creased leather and smile lines.

The fire tender was visible through a couple of gaps in the cypress hedge, which I'd only cut back a fortnight before – *Cupressocyparis leylandii*. It was parked in the middle of the front lawn. Above it I could see the upper-half of the house, which wasn't so much smouldering as shrouded in smoke and moist air, and I wondered if the smoke would have drifted down to mingle with the mist on the river.

'This ain't your house, darling? Tell me it ain't your house.'

I'd envisaged the place reduced to a charcoal skeleton, with a few charred and broken ribs sticking up from a mound of ashes, but it wasn't like that. On first glance it appeared untouched. Until I looked again.

The upstairs front windows were blind, empty eye

sockets and there were black scorch marks staining the paintwork above each one, like smudged daubs of eye-shadow. This was where the flames had erupted, splintering glass, burning each eye out. Also, there was something odd about the shape of the roof, the way it sagged.

A pile of ashes and rubble might have been easier to cope with than a tortured corpse. It made the bile rise in my stomach. So instead of getting out and confronting it up close, I kept the door shut and the window closed and scraped together quick breaths.

Besides, there were too many people. I'd imagined having a brief look before asking a neighbour to give me a lift back to Angie's, and we'd get the grief-thing underway and we'd skirt around some of the awkward questions, but there was no way I was even half-ready for that.

I nodded to the driver. 'Yep. *Was.*' Past tense.

'You know about this, right?' His eyes had narrowed, his voice was anxious. Although he was probably younger than Dad – Victor – he looked more weathered, as if he'd had a tough life of working outdoors. He hadn't always been a taxi driver, but a farmer, perhaps, or a builder.

The fire crew were drawing up hoses, tidying equipment, calling to one another as they worked. From where I sat, it seemed they must be trudging across Mother's rose bed, between the roses and over the hellebores, which made me want to smile, except I'd throw up if I did. A police car blocked the driveway and there were another couple of cars I didn't recognise parked out front. A dozen neighbours were milling about, and Shirley-from-the-store was collecting cups and mugs from the roof of the police car and stacking them on a tray.

'Yeah,' I muttered towards the reflection of his eyes in the rear-view mirror. 'I know about it.'

He made the connection then between picking me up from the hospital and dropping me off here. I saw it in his face.

'No one badly hurt, I hope?' he said, and turned in his seat again, but I was fumbling in my bag for my wallet; I had to do something, think about something else.

'Sorry,' I said, holding up a fifty. 'I haven't got anything smaller.' I hated not being able to give him the right money. I know it was only because I was tired and wretched, but it made me tearful and anxious. Sometimes it's the stupid, little things which get to us, while we force ourselves to cope with the big, life and death issues.

'The least of your worries,' he said, and reached back for the note.

When the neighbours and one of the police officers started peering in the direction of the taxi, I slid away from the window. I couldn't stomach the idea of them crowding over me with their condolences and kindness, their offers of casseroles and cakes; nor was I ready for more questions. Later. After I'd slept.

Sure enough, Shirley-from-the-store was about to head my way. There's never been any flies on her. She'd guess it'd have to be one of us, Stella or me, arriving by taxi, all the way out here at Three Creeks. I could almost feel her age-puckered lips against my cheek, her mascara-streaked tears, the cloying scent of the old-person perfume she doused herself in. Just the thought of it made me start to gag.

'You alright, darling?' the taxi driver asked.

I shook my head. 'Can you take me somewhere else? Can you just drive on. Please. Just drive. Go straight ahead.' And I directed him to Angie's house.

Sometimes, when I still lived at home and answered the

phone, I'd say 'Hello, this is Mad Meg speaking.'

It was a private joke, a family joke, which my mother could never find funny. She'd purse her lips into a cat's arse of a mouth and get that frosty look in her eyes, while Stella or Victor might say just a bit too quickly, 'You're the sanest one of all of us, Meg.'

But if I was Mad Meg and Stella was a star (ha-ha!), then Angie was my guardian angel. Until recently, at least. No two ways about it.

When I was seven and Stella was four, we began piano lessons. Mum and Dad decided that learning a musical instrument would be good for us, and it's not something I'm sorry about, even though there were plenty of times I hated it.

Every Saturday afternoon – week in, week out – a dry stick of a man called Mr Thomas would drive to our house, perch himself on one side of the piano stool, pat the space next to him for one of us to join him, then take us through one dull exercise after another. Stella would usually have the first lesson, because she was the youngest, and then it'd be my turn. At the end of the lesson, Mr Thomas would tell our parents whether we'd practised enough during the past week and what pieces we had to work on before the next lesson, and one of them would hand him an envelope with his fee enclosed.

He was a good enough teacher and I got quite fond of him, even though he smelt old and clearly hadn't much clue how to talk to children. However, shortly after I started Year 8 at Lapishot High, he had a stroke and couldn't drive any longer, so we had to go to his house one day a week after school, which was pretty freaky.

One side of his face was paralysed, which meant he couldn't speak properly, and he was forever dabbing at the corner of his mouth with a big cotton hanky to mop up his dribble. Also, he got tired real quick and frustrated when he couldn't make himself understood, and it was a relief when the lessons stopped – I can't remember what the excuse was – even though he'd been a part of my life for many years and even though I wasn't too bad on the piano by then.

Several months later, Angie – Ms Morel, to start with – got a position teaching Art and Music at Lapishot High, and she bought the old Brasovich property out on Nine Mile Road, not far from us. I don't know how it eventuated, or who knew who and who asked what, but it was arranged I'd have a couple of trial lessons at her house (Stella switched to flute that year), which happily turned into regular events. Even though I was only fourteen and she was twenty-two, we became great friends.

She always made a point of looking me in the eyes when we talked, which was disconcerting to begin with because it felt as if she could see what I was thinking, but after a while I tried to do the same. She was attractive and intelligent and everything I wanted to be, except my eyes will never be as gorgeously large or lusciously brown as hers (and I don't think I'll ever stop biting my nails down to the skin, however hard I try).

She had a Bechstein boudoir grand in her living room, inherited from her grandmother, and it stood in front of the French windows so you could sit and play and look across the garden at the very edge of the forest. Sometimes, on warm days, we'd play silly duets with the doors thrown open, while at other times the whole house would resonate to Chopin, Beethoven, Satie, or something more modern like Gershwin, Yann Tiersen, Lennon and McCartney. The Bechstein gave such life to the music, marching and dancing, floating and seducing, that it was hard not to think of the notes drifting through the forest, weaving between the trees and through the tangled undergrowth, and how all the forest's creatures (resting or grazing, predators and prey) might pause at the music's passing to sense its mood (the twitch of an ear, the tremble of a whisker, the shiver through a flank), until it disappeared into the darkness or sank into the humus.

Phrases of Bach and Beethoven, Krakowich and Mozart are all composting out there. A few bars from the *Moonlight Sonata* here, a sodden fragment from *Elvira Madigan* there; mixed in with layers of leaf litter, needles, bark, dead insects, bones and the deep, dank, dark.

At first, Mum or Dad would drive me over to Angie's place once a week, picking me up an hour later. But before long, because the lessons became less of a chore and more about spending time with her, I'd cycle over and back if the weather was fine, or Angie would pick me up sometimes, especially if she was driving home from Lapishot. I loved being with her and the way she made me think differently about things: she was determinedly old-fashioned as far as computers were concerned (had a no-frills mobile, wouldn't do social media, preferred handwritten letters to email), but she was the most intelligent and empathetic person I'd ever come across; what's more, she had the broadest taste in music and introduced me to heaps of very cool bands.

Also, it was because of Angie that I started gardening.

After her first year in the house, she'd been ready to abandon the flower beds and have one big, fence-to-fence lawn because it was too much to tend. As much as she wanted to keep the fuchsias, chrysanthemums, dahlias, daises, lavenders – all the cottage garden plants that Ma and Pa Brasovich must've planted – she couldn't cope with seeing everything look unloved and raggedy. She felt bad about the garden, as if she'd failed it.

'I'm busy enough preparing lessons, correcting, and remembering to eat, sleep and clean the house. As for catching up with friends, finding time to paint and play the piano – having a life – well, I don't have a clue how people do it. I really don't.' She paused, picked up the secateurs lying on the verandah, turned them around and put them down again. 'At the moment, I spend every spare minute trying to stop all this becoming a jungle: picking out bloomin' weeds, tying back plants, pruning them... and before I know it the grass is up to my knees again. Having flowers is all well and good, but...' She stopped, waved her arm in a broad gesture at the garden and was actually on the brink of tears. 'You know what really annoys me, Meg?'

'No. What?'

'It's that my dad'll be secretly pleased and he'll hold it over me forever. He won't say *I told you so*, but I know he'll be thinking it.'

I looked at her. It was the first time I'd seen her like this. Before this moment, I hadn't imagined there was anyone who could unsettle her. She'd always seemed so sure of herself. 'Why? What's it to him what your garden's like?'

She shook her head, pulled a face. 'He wanted me to buy a boring little unit in Lapishot. How horrible! Said this house was too large and too old, that there was way too much garden and how I'd never manage.' She was looking at me in dismay and, even though she was tired and anxious, her eyes were warmer, browner, rounder and bigger than I'd ever noticed before. I felt powerless at not being able to help her and for not really knowing what to say, but more than a little flattered she was sharing this with me.

'I probably shouldn't be telling you this,' she continued, 'but seriously, can you imagine the Bechstein being crammed into a pokey little unit? For one thing, half of it would have had to hang out the window and, not only that, but the neighbours would have had screaming blue fits every time I played. And as for all my bric-a-brac...'

She was able to laugh then, and I nodded and laughed too.

'Do you know what my dad's answer was?'

'No. What?'

'To sell "the bloody Bechstein" and buy an electric piano instead! Said I could plug earphones in so I wouldn't annoy anyone.'

I didn't like her father one bit. He sounded a bit like my mother when she was in one of her moods – it was exactly the sort of thing she'd have said – and I was probably as surprised as Angie when I offered to pay for my piano lessons by helping in the garden. The words popped out before I could stop them, but she was delighted.

It might have been an impulsive offer, but I knew how to handle a petrol mower from helping Dad at home, and had as good an idea as she did about what were weeds and what were flowers. What I didn't know I could learn as I went along. She could tell me what to do. Besides, I enjoyed being with her. It was an inspired, impulsive offer.

The cash that Mum and Dad continued to hand over for lessons went into my bank account and, when they asked about it once, I said it was money Angie paid me for helping in the garden, for looking after Gustav when she was away, for watering the plants and that sort of thing. It amounted to the same deal in the end. I'm not sure they knew exactly what I was doing or how much I'd saved, but they didn't seem to mind. They liked Angie too. It was a win-win arrangement.

What with me having a policeman's daughter and a

teacher for friends, my mother thought she had me well and truly sorted. Not only was I throwing myself into the piano lessons, but I was doing well at school and even had a part-time job that didn't involve being a dreaded check-out chick in dead-end Lapishot.

Poor Mother Dear was born in the wrong century. She'd have been a whole lot happier if Stella and I acted like characters from a Jane Austen novel, confined to a life of embroidery and endless afternoons of lady-like small talk ('stitch 'n' bitch,' as Angie called it). Except I think she had barren spinsterhood and not marriage in mind for us, because she did everything possible to stifle our interest in parties and boys, although there wasn't much chance of this with Tess as a friend. Mum's main concession to the twenty-first century was her insistence that we excel academically – study, study, study; achieve, achieve, achieve – although this was more about her control than our empowerment.

Stella always played the game far better than me. She'd go through the motions of appearing compliant and passively 'girly' in a way I never could, but that's probably because she was accustomed to having me look after her and not having to try too hard. As a child, I was always the tomboy, determined to argue back and fight, even when I knew I'd come off worse, whereas she knew how to smile, agree and still do whatever she wanted anyway. I think Mother hated that in me. I know she did. So she'd have been smug as a Queen Bee when I started spending more time with Angie. She probably thought I was finally growing into someone who could be trusted to act in a civilised and genteelly demure fashion... until everything went pear-shaped and I blew a fuse or two.

Pete was my first real boyfriend. Before Pete, there were

other guys I'd played at going out with, but he was the first I wanted to be with. I missed him when he wasn't there; I wanted to touch and be touched all over by him.

He touched me. In every sense.

He's the only person I've ever slept with.

And I hate him. I hate Pete Lailer.

Bastard. Bâtard. Bastaard. Bastardo.

In every language, he's a shallow, vain, lily-livered mongrel. And a bastard.

There is no word to save him.

The first person we choose to be naked with – and I'm talking choice here, so sharing a bath with Stella when she was two and I was five doesn't count – is one of the first, big decisions we make for ourselves in life. It's bigger than choosing to go to university or not, bigger than the school subjects we choose, bigger than the first job we apply for, because all those things can easily be changed, undone, reversed, and because those decisions always get shaped by other people chipping in. But choosing to share our nakedness and have sex with someone for the first time – body and soul – is nothing less than an Adam & Eve moment. It's revelatory, like discovering there should be delight, not shame, in our body. It's a moment that's bigger than the bible, like choosing to taste an unknown fruit from the very first tree. Once you possess the knowledge of that fruit, you can never un-know it again. It's the leap from innocence to experience. And Pete Lailer was the one I chose to share that momentous occasion with and reveal all of myself to. I was sure he was the one.

Bastard!

I want to be honest. To tell it as it was at the time.

Pete and I arrived separately at Angie's empty house in the middle of the afternoon. It was a warm, sunny day, Technicolor-rich and glossy-bright, even though the previous day had been damp and grey. When I'd stopped by the bridge the afternoon before, the river had been a steely, matt black, whispering an acid coldness, whereas it had a polished silkiness to that blackness now. Summer had returned and there was a razzle-dazzle glare to the light where it bounced off Rudely Road and shimmered into a mirage, and there was the buzz of insects, the darting of dragonflies, the confetti of butterflies – a parade of kedamores and ravens hop-scotching across the road to feast on the litter of their corpses. It was like a closing scene from a romantic film where, after the usual mishaps and misunderstandings, everything was about to come good: the two central characters have found each other at last and are on the brink of their Happy Ever After.

The air was warm on my skin and, wafting from the forest, came the delicious earthy smell of composting leaf litter, drying pine needles, resin and sap. Pete was all smiles and seemed more laid-back than usual, and I could tell I was coming across as happy too, even if I couldn't help being a bit hyper and nervous about what was going to happen next. The day was creating one perfect moment after another because everything was falling into place as if it was all meant to be, and I couldn't help but believe the rest of my life would be perfect too. The power of the day, and of one perfect moment after another, would carry me forward forever and I didn't believe anything could go wrong.

Angie had gone away for the weekend, visiting relatives, but she'd already met Pete after I persuaded him to drive out to her place a couple of weeks earlier. I'd especially wanted to introduce him to her, and we all three had a lazy supper on the back lawn before he took me clubbing to The Urban in Lapishot.

Beautiful Angie, she was delighted for me. 'He seems like a really nice bloke,' she'd said the following day, and offered to lend me a skirt, a top and a pair of earrings, which she thought would look great on me the next time I went out with him. 'He used to go to Delacortes High, you say?'

'Yeah, finished last year. He works at Demlab now, as a computer techie.'

'So he works for your dad, does he?'

'Well, yes, sort of; I guess he does. Although a lot of people work there. I don't think they know one another. Not yet.'

She nodded, smiled, held one of her shirts against me and then another, but shook her head both times and dropped them on her bed. 'He's quite a dish, whatever.'

'You don't fancy him, Angie? Hands off, he's mine.'

'Bit young for me and not quite my sort, but I can still approve your taste, can't I?'

I pretended to consider. 'You can. Definitely.'

She hesitated then, looked like she might say something but had second thoughts, and it was a long enough moment for me to notice and say, 'What?'

'I'm not sure how to put this –'

'What?'

She picked up the skirt I'd tried on and folded it for me, and she placed the earrings on top. 'Well, just to remind you that anytime you'd like a little privacy or a sleepover and I'm not around – if I've gone away for a few days or something – I'm quite happy for you to use the spare room. The spare key is always in the shed. Just check with me first and make sure you tidy up after. You know, like change the sheets, lock up, that sort of thing.'

It took a click and a whirr for me to connect the two conversations together. I didn't know what to say. I was embarrassed, until I turned it into a joke. 'What are you suggesting?' I said in mock astonishment. 'I'm only seventeen. I don't know what you mean, I'm sure.' Nonetheless, I sensed that we'd reached a new point in our relationship, Angie and me. She was accepting something in me which I hadn't fully recognised yet. There were times when she knew me better than I knew myself.

'Hmm. Well, I'm not going to spell it out for you, but the offer's there. As a friend. Just be careful, eh?'

I nodded, was probably blushing, and picked up the earrings and the skirt.

'You'll look gorgeous in those,' she said. 'You could wear them with your white top – the one with the little, shell buttons – and those pixie boots will match perfectly. Or sandals.'

I was useless at choosing what to wear. I think she enjoyed dressing me. Not that she treated me like a doll or anything, but because it brought us closer.

At seventeen, I was drawn to Peter Lailer because he was my opposite in many ways. He was different enough to be exciting – why would I want to be with someone who only reminded me of me? – but there was overlap too in some of what we enjoyed and cared about. We fitted together, it seemed, more like yin and yang than kindred spirits.

I knew he was vain, slightly narcissistic, but at the time I enjoyed how he took pride in the way he looked, both for himself and for other people, because it's not who I was and never will be. I thought he looked like an actor or a musician, even if he wasn't. He had a long fringe of straight, black hair, which swept across his eyes, giving him a deliberately moody, dramatic look, as if he was trying to avoid being noticed, which he definitely wasn't, and it was a habit of his to keep flicking this fringe back. It was probably a habit borne of affectation, but I even liked this weakness in him at the time too.

If I have to be honest, I liked the cut of his jib (a phrase I heard one of my old ladies use not so long ago), and I thought his stubborn chin and determined mouth suggested he was someone who'd fight for what he wanted and wouldn't quickly run away. I liked how he had dimples even when he wasn't really smiling; I liked the kink in his nose (where he broke it as a ten-year-old hurtling over the handlebars of his mountain bike); I liked that he was lean and sinewy from playing hockey and cricket and from so much jogging, and that he had a childish enthusiasm about going to parties and dancing and surrounding himself with people.

It wasn't simply that being in love for the first time redefined me, but that, through being with him and learning to know him, I understood myself better and was happier with who I was.

Anyway, I also liked that he was the same height as me — not taller or smaller — and that, despite the job at Demlab, he hadn't a clue what he wanted to do with his life. His life was an open book, a blank canvas, as far as he was concerned, and he was happy with it that way. I liked the fact that I felt comfortable with him and enhanced by him, and that, with him, I'd do things I mightn't otherwise do. The idea of sex with him seemed natural and inevitable.

I'd forgotten all this until recently — how I felt and why. But in remembering it now, I wish I could wipe it out forever and start again from scratch.

*

Our first time is in the spare bed. Everything is sharpened with those Technicolor-rich hues, and even the timber of the antique double bed and wardrobe, which Angie has furnished the room with, appears warmer, deeper, denser – honeyed. I've never seen the colours of her Gran's old patchwork quilt quite so vivid and alive before. Not only is the afternoon light illuminating the room but, from outside, comes an entire Disney Wonderland soundtrack of blackbirds, starlings, kedamores, ravens, pigeons... It makes me want to laugh, but instead I go to the window and gently pull the blinds shut.

When I turn round, I've got my arms wrapped across my chest; each hand gripping the opposite shoulder.

'Are you cold?' he says.

'No. Not really.'

He stands there, one hand in the back pocket of his jeans, the other hand gripping his car keys, and he flicks his hair back. There's barely three metres between us, but of a sudden it's a mighty distance to travel.

'A little nervous,' I admit.

'Me as well,' he says, taking a couple of steps towards me, arms out.

He doesn't look nervous, but I take a couple of steps forward too and bury my face in his neck, and he buries his in mine.

That's all it takes. Big moments grow from small gestures.

We're quieter with one another than we've ever been and, when he begins to draw up my T-shirt, I almost tell him to turn round while I undress and climb into bed, but I don't. I lift my arms and let him undress me, and I do the same to him. It's only then, standing awkwardly naked, that I step away, draw the bed sheets back and lie down.

'Come on,' I say, but only to fill the silence washing around us.

He moves onto the bed and struggles with a condom before positioning himself on top of me and… well, it's over so quickly I think I might have done something wrong or have affected him some way. This can't be all there is to it.

Afterwards, when I'm staring at the paint flaking from one corner of the ceiling, I nearly use the word *anti-climax*, except for once I know not to speak and to let the silence rise instead. I need to think about what's happened and what it means. It's not what I'd hoped for.

However, Pete's lying there with his hands behind his head on the pillow, looking thoughtful too, and I'm wondering what he's thinking; whether he's alright or feeling frustrated. Until he sighs and too earnestly misquotes what's probably the only Latin phrase he half-knows.

'Post coitum omni est triste,' he says.

I shouldn't laugh, but his smugness and the pretentiousness of what he says gives me the giggles, and he rolls onto his side to look at me.

'What?'

'You're an idiot,' I tell him.

'Why?'

'Is that the best you can do?'

He seems hurt then. Really hurt. 'What do you mean?'

I shake my head. '"Post coitum omni" … whatever. What a load of rubbish.' I'm still laughing, but wondering if there's a way of salvaging the occasion, when he leans across and tickles me, and I squeal, twist every which way and manage to tickle him back.

We're full-on messing around, tickling and wrestling, when he grabs my wrists and holds them hard against the pillow, and I see he's excited again. This wrestling excites him.

'Let go,' I say.

I get him to lay down and I sit across him, the way I've seen in movies. I push his hands back against the pillow, the way he was doing to me, and it's me who finds the rhythm and draws out the pace.

Abandonment is the word that best describes it. I resist at first – am constrained and inhibited – as if I'm doing something I shouldn't, or as if I'm enjoying something I shouldn't, except my resistance makes me awkward. Slowly though, I give myself up to it and this new uninhibited freedom is what's delicious. This is the real nakedness.

I let go of his hands and he fondles my breasts and strokes my nipples as I rise and fall, rise and fall. Floating. It's more than I imagined it would be. It's like being filled and emptied at the same time. Senses swelling to the brink of bursting.

Until they burst.

Being possessed in every sense. Filled and emptied. Bringing us together. There aren't the words to properly describe it.

This time – this after-time – when we're lying next to one another, we're a tangle of happy limbs. I'm looking at him and he's looking at me, and I know I chose the right person to share this Adam & Eve moment with. We're contentedly intertwined and no words need be spoken.

I am new and the world is new.

The afternoon breeze creates a scented hush so defined that I might trace, if I wish, the pattern it weaves out of the forest and through the garden's shrubs, creepers, trees; there are whispers of lemon verbena, white potato creeper, wormwood. It brings with it the irregular tapping of the sash window frame in its runners and the slow dragging backwards and forwards of the buddleia stems along the verandah roof. The cloth blind blows in from the window and drops back again; light and shade, light and shade, highlight and shadow. I stroke Pete's hair. His hand cups and strokes my left breast.

'Are you okay?' he says.

Rather than losing something, I've regained something: a sense of play, childish pleasure, the sense of my own innocence. Not a loss, but a gain.

I smile.

Despite what some people might say, I don't feel cheap or diminished by this and he doesn't look faintly conceited or arrogant because of what we've shared. I've given nothing of myself away even while I've given everything of myself away, but I'm more complete than ever.

I love him and he loves me and that's all that matters. There's a wet trickle down my thigh, but even that doesn't matter. Not now. This isn't dirty. There's nothing dirty in any of this at the time. Only later.

Lying there afterwards is a matter of floating with the slow current of a glorious moment. For an hour or more, we lie entwined, cuddling and stroking one another as the afternoon drifts past, moment by moment, until the current washes us ashore again, lapping at the edge of a new place, and we discover we're both hungry.

I pull on my jeans, throw on a T-shirt and go downstairs to make coffee, cheese and biscuits. Then we shower.

He's made arrangements to go to the gym or play cricket or something, but we're going to meet up later in Lapishot, at the nightclub. First though, we decide that tomorrow we might find our way back to Angie's empty house once more.

I sit at the piano while he finishes in the bathroom and I

watch high clouds scud lazily across the sky, a world away, and there's the trail from a large plane cutting the sky in two. Pete and I have been washed ashore in our new world and everything else drifts by at an invisible distance. It's been such a perfect day and I feel so different now that I let my fingers pick out a few random phrases, but quietly and only while I can still hear him moving about upstairs.

It lasted no more than a day, and then began to unravel.

FOUR

I CUT OUT THE ARTICLE. It was on page 3 of *THE LAPISHOT GAZETTE*.

SUSPICIOUS FIRE IN THREE CREEKS

A house fire in Three Creeks on Wednesday night in which one person died is being treated as suspicious by police. Francine Dapsy (45) died from smoke inhalation after being trapped in an attic bedroom at Duparc House. Also in the house was her daughter, Estella Dapsy (18), who was taken to hospital for observation but later released. Mrs Dapsy was the wife of Dr Victor Dapsy, executive manager of Demlab in Lapishot, which has been repeatedly targeted by Animal Rights activists because of its use of animals for research. An officer of the Fire Investigation Unit said the fire started in unusual circumstances and police are appealing for witnesses.

Pete may have worked for Demlab, but his sympathies were with Action for Animal Rights. Definitely. I know this for sure because it was him that told me all about them.

After the taxi from hospital took me to Angie's, I slept until the early afternoon, and only woke because Mick Droyler was banging on the back door, shouting my name. It was an awful sleep, filled with the most vivid, horrible dreams, and dreams within dreams.

I dreamt I was a child again and my parents were standing in different rooms at home, both frantically calling me to come to them. I could see them even though I was in a different room, but it was as if we were all stuck to where we stood. When I looked down at my feet, I realised I was sinking and that the floorboards were like quicksand and I tried screaming for help, but my voice wouldn't work.

But then I dreamt I'd woken from that dream to find myself where I should be, in my bed in Angie's house – house-sitting for her – and I was thinking about that bad dream about my parents and even realised it's meaning was clear enough, which convinced me I really was awake, even if I wasn't. The moment I heard the front door handle being rattled downstairs, though, I knew something evil had found me and was trying to get in. I don't know how I knew this, only that I instinctively did.

Creeping out of bed, I listened to this evil thing stalking around the outside of the house, shaking at each sash window in turn, but I couldn't remember whether I'd slipped the catches closed on them or not. I listened as it stomped off the verandah, probably onto the lawn, and I took a couple of steps out my room. My bladder was full and I wanted to pee, but was too frightened.

Whatever it was, I could hear it worrying at the French windows next, which is when I remembered (in my dream) that the kitchen door was unlocked. I was frozen where I stood on the upstairs landing, looking down over the banisters and listening, knowing I didn't have time to run down to the kitchen to lock the door before the thing worked its way round there. It would only be a matter of seconds. Besides, the thought of having to run towards that sense of menace and doom filled me with immobilising terror. I had to escape. I needed to get out of the house and speed away from it, except I was in my pyjamas and the keys to my truck were in the kitchen too.

The next thing, I'd somehow leapt from the top of the stairs to the front door and was madly fumbling with the latch and handle to get out when I heard the kitchen door slam and heavy footsteps pounding through the house towards me. Quickening footsteps, getting louder.

I got the door open just in time and was outside, bounding across the garden, jumping the fence into the forest, trying to hold my pyjama trousers up. I ran, but daren't look behind me. I daren't see what was chasing me.

I ran blindly. I ran and ran, thumping and crashing through undergrowth, weaving between trees, branches whipping at my face, until I was so out of breath I couldn't run another step. When I looked around to see where I was, I'd arrived at an area that was all too familiar. I'd run further than I realised because, even in my dream, I knew that this small dell was far from any mapped track, in a protected zone of the forest that would never be logged, and I was convinced I'd escaped whatever was trying to get me. For a moment, I relaxed and caught my breath, pleased I'd outsmarted it.

Even though I was dreaming, I experienced a keen relief – gratitude really – at having come across this secluded spot by chance so soon after moving to Angie's, and at having learnt to find my way back to it, even though there were a couple of times I couldn't find it at all. It's a half-kilometre at least from the nearest track, but I always know when I'm getting close because there's a series of undulating dips and rises, banks and dells, bumping across the forest landscape like gigantic corrugations immediately before it, and then the pines and eucalypts suddenly give way to golden beech – *Nothofagus harlestonii*. There's little in the way of undergrowth beneath their wide-spreading limbs, apart from a few sparse patches of bracken and briar; just a luxuriously soft carpet of leaf litter and moss. And to one side, a couple of hundred metres in, there's a single, massive rock, about three metres high and three metres in girth, which I've climbed and sat on in the past. It was in the small clearing next to this that my dream brought me.

I was getting my breath back and beginning to feel safe, relaxed, when from beneath the pile of leaves over which I was standing came a rustling, followed by a rolling, shifting movement. I jumped back and in that same instant recognised what it was I'd been running from: the fear of the very thing I'd run directly to. More than anything, I needed to turn and start running again, but was frozen to the spot.

Like podgy, white mushroom stalks, fingers began growing up through the mound of leaves. Each blanched finger wiggled as if sniffing the air – sensing it, tasting it – and slowly flexed and stretched out into a whole hand that rose awkwardly, followed by a grimy wrist. There was a moment of stillness, but I couldn't move. I waited. The dead leaves began to shake and flutter as if the ground was some giant, sleeping bird rustling its feathers, and then the earth next to me erupted awake and out of its belly appeared Victor's bloodied and distorted face.

I tried to cry out, but couldn't. His face had a greenish-grey pallor. His slightly parted lips were blue and revealed blood-stained teeth and a swollen tongue. His eyelids were half-open, but his eyes had rolled back and all I could see were the yellowing whites.

'Meg,' he groaned, and grabbed my ankle.

I screamed.

I woke in a breathless sweat. Downstairs, someone was banging against the kitchen door. It took a moment to come round, work out what was happening and what day it was. Someone was shouting my name, except it sounded as if they were in the house.

'Meg! Meg, are you home? Hello, is anyone home? It's the police. Sergeant Droyler.'

Mick was standing outside the back door when I got there, but it was unlocked and he must have opened it to call me. I must've forgotten to lock it.

'Hello, Meg, I was passing. Thought I'd drop by, see how you are. Thought you were out the back.' Again, he was turning his cap between his hands, but more nimbly this time.

'What time is it?'

He glanced at his watch. 'Twelve-forty. Did I wake you?'

I straightened my dressing-gown. 'Doesn't matter.' Despite being dull with sleep and weighted with the memory of bad dreams, I knew what the first thing was I had to ask. 'Have you found Dad?'

'No. There's no news yet. Sorry.'

'Oh,' I said and leant against the open door. 'I thought that's why you were here.'

'Can I come in?'

I nodded, closed the door behind him, filled the kettle.

'How are you, Meg?'

'Slept longer than I meant. Need something to wake me

up.' He could've only had a few hours sleep himself. 'You fancy a coffee? I've only got the instant muck.'

'Perfect,' he said. 'Have you spoken to Stella?'

'Briefly, last night – or this morning – whenever it was. I need to phone the ward and see if she's properly awake and ask if I can see her, or when they're going to release her. Have you?'

'I called to see if she was awake, but she wasn't.' He was standing next to the table, leaning on the back of a chair. 'Sleep is the body's way of healing, the mind's way of coping with shock,' he said. 'It's never easy, this sort of thing.'

'I suppose so.' But I knew those nurses. They could be too free and easy with the sedatives.

He moved back from the chair and seemed to choose the moment I was looking at him to ask, 'Has your dad contacted you at all, Meg? In any way whatsoever? Or has anybody contacted you about him? For his sake, it's important we know if you've heard anything. You must tell us.'

The inference that there might be secret communications surprised me, but shouldn't have I suppose. 'No, he hasn't. I wish he had.' The image from my dream popped into my head, but I made myself shut it out again. 'What do you think's happened to him? Are you really sure he was there?'

'We believe so. One of the cars in the garage still had a docket from the airport car park on the windscreen – the black Audi, which is registered in his name – so we know he returned and that he didn't leave in either that vehicle or your mum's car.'

I shook my head, turned away, opened a tin of biscuits, rattled about with mugs and the coffee jar. I washed and dried a teaspoon, even though there were half a dozen clean ones in the cutlery drawer.

'I don't believe it,' I said.

'I'm sorry, Meg. This must be hard for you. Could he have come home and left again – before the fire, perhaps – and be staying with a friend, for instance? Is that the sort of thing he might do?'

The hardest thing was not knowing what other people knew or didn't know.

'Why would he?'

He said nothing. Just waited.

'What, like a mistress?' I said and laughed. 'Is that what you mean?'

'Or just a friend,' he suggested.

I shrugged. 'I don't know. I can't think why he would. I don't think so.'

He placed his hat on the table. 'There are other things I have to ask you, Meg. You understand, don't you?'

I poured water into the cups and stirred the coffee. I carried the cups to the table and put them down. I pulled out a chair for myself and motioned for him to sit.

'It's alright. I know you do. You're doing your job. Ask whatever you have to.'

'I have to ask about the fire.'

Holding my cup so the coffee steam drifted across my face, soothing my eyes, I registered the beginnings of a headache, or left-overs from the previous day's migraine, but didn't want to remember that. Yesterday belonged to a different lifetime, like an old skin I needed to shed and leave behind. 'What about it?'

'If you have any ideas how it might've started?'

'You mean like an electrical fault or something? It could have been. The wiring was ancient. Needed replacing years ago. Mum was always going on at Dad about it.' My hands, my arms, my legs began trembling; I pressed my feet against the floor, gripped my cup in both hands, took a deep breath. 'There'll be an investigation, won't there? That'll find out how it started, won't it?'

Turning his cup in his hand, he said, 'It was deliberate, Meg. It was arson. Someone set that fire.'

I looked from him to my coffee, then sat my cup back on the table. How does a person handle such news? Do we immediately howl and rage or reject and deny?

'I'm sorry, Meg.'

I placed my hands in my lap and shook my head. 'No.'

'Meg, I need to know if there was any more trouble out there, since… well, since that business a few weeks ago.'

This was hard. Harder than I'd imagined. It was making me light-headed, but I needed to focus. I had to shift my gaze and refocus. Outside, the sky was bright blue, as it often will be after a night of mist, and I couldn't see a single cloud from where I sat. There was a smear on the window above the sink, probably from where I swatted a fly the other day. On the floor, next to Gustav's food bowl, lay a scatter of dry biscuits, which he'd shaken out in disgust, and I told myself I had to get more of his favourite tins of meat from the supermarket in Lapishot next time I was there. I made myself focus on trivia. I focussed on the pin-board of Angie's postcards, newspaper clippings, quotes, the three old-fashioned prints of birds: the peregrine falcon (*Falco peregrinus*), the kedamore (*Cracus garrulus*) and the coodylark (*Lullula nocturnes*). These were names I had learnt and could recite.

'Meg?' He'd taken out his notebook and pen and was poised to write.

'Sorry?'

'Did your parents have any more trouble since –'

'Since the Bunny Brigade? Action for Animal Rights?'

He sort of smiled. 'Those animal liberation nuts, yeah.'

I couldn't help but think of that word – *KILLER* – daubed in red paint across the front of the house. Victor had played it down, but it freaked *her* out and she made him phone the police. It came with the territory, Victor told me later that day, and all the Human Resources manager at Demlab could give the police was the name of a bloke who'd lost his job a couple of weeks previously after being caught stealing stationery, conical flasks, lab coats, that sort of thing. Usually, it was the laboratory or admin building that got targeted, Victor told me, although staff vehicles were damaged in the car park once. He made it sound like it had gone on for years.

It was me who discovered the graffiti, when I arrived to pick him up on my way to work, before Stella had left for school. It was Stella who discovered the clothes slashed on the washing line. It was Mick Droyler who followed it up that day. Small world, this place. Too small. Dangerously small as it turns out.

'No,' I said. 'No more trouble. None that I'm aware of. I think it was a one-off. On the house, anyway.' I looked him square in the eyes, made a point of it. 'They wouldn't do that, would they – set fire to the house? They wouldn't have come back a second time?' But before he could answer, I joined the dots for him: 'You think they're connected, the graffiti and the fire, don't you?' Scraping my chair back, I stood, but was a bit wobbly. 'You think the same people did it? You think they've got Dad, don't you?'

He leaned forward as if he was going to stand too, but remained sitting and ignored my questions. He didn't tell me there was more graffiti sprayed across the house that previous night, or anything like that either, but he repeated his question. 'Were there any more problems, Meg?'

I raked my hands through my hair, leaned against the edge of the table and sat down again. 'No. Dad didn't say there'd been anything else. No threats or stuff...'

'But? You sound as if there is something.'

'It might be nothing. I hadn't really thought about it before. There was no reason to.'

'What is it?'

I took a long breath. I had to be careful, not only about what I told him, but how I told him. Besides, it had only occurred to me when I was in the taxi that morning, after leaving Stella at the hospital.

'It might not be important,' I said, and hesitated.

'Go on.'

'Well, there was a car and a van parked down at the campsite not long ago, near Mum and Dad's house. The thing is, they were there again on Tuesday –'

'The Tuesday just gone?'

'Yes, I think it was Tuesday. Around five o'clock. Or possibly Monday. Well, either way, I noticed them because they'd both been parked in exactly the same position about a week or so before.'

'At the campsite?'

'Yes. Near the barbecues.'

'I see.' He scribbled a few notes.

'I know it's probably nothing, but you don't get many visitors stopping there during the week in winter. Not usually. Not parked together like that.'

'No, that's good, Meg. That's good. Can you describe the vehicles? Was there anything about them that stood out or anything else that struck you as unusual? What about drivers and passengers? Did you see anyone?'

'Well, that's one of the things which was odd and why I

noticed. Both times, it looked like they were deliberately parked next to one another, side-by-side; there was maybe a couple of people in the front of the van and a person in the car, but they were just sitting there. Of course, I was only driving past, but it struck me as weird, and reminded me of a film where they were dealing drugs or something. That's what crossed my mind, especially the second time, and why I remembered. Because it looked suspicious. I thought I was being over-imaginative.'

'A car and a van, you say? What colour was the van?'

'White. It was one of those vans that look like a box on wheels. Fairly new. The sort freight companies use.'

'And the car?'

'That was a bluey-grey colour.'

'Do you remember what make it was?'

'No, sorry. I'm no good at recognising cars.'

'Well, do you know anyone who has a car like it?'

Again I hesitated. Probably shouldn't have – not then. 'No. No one. They're quite common, I think. A sedan, not a hatchback.'

He scribbled his notes, leaving a long silence, and it made me afraid I'd been too helpful or not helpful enough, or had remembered details a person wouldn't normally remember when they're in shock. I couldn't be too specific, but it wouldn't be helpful if I was too vague either – nothing more than a trail of breadcrumbs.

'Okay. Do you think you could call into the station and have a look at some pictures then? See if you can identify the makes and models of both vehicles?'

'Sure, if it'll help. I'll call in later.'

'That'd be good. Thanks. Is there anything else you remember? Anything at all?'

I was tossing up whether to mention that the car had a

hubcap missing. 'No. I don't think so,' I said.

He flicked to a different page in his notebook. 'What about problems at home, Meg? Was everything okay between your mum and dad? Any problems with neighbours? Or boyfriend problems for you or Stella? Definitely no threats or nuisance calls that you're aware of?'

Again, I gave myself a few moments to consider. It's not that I was sleepy any longer, but I didn't think it'd hurt to seem that way. Most people would be exhausted.

My parents might raise their voices at one another, but they rarely shouted and never swore. It wasn't their way. Instead, when they were arguing, she'd get all snappish and make terse comments or play the martyr, while he'd ignore her or be polite to a fault, which made her madder still. Well, that's how they were in front of Stella and me. She'd make a point of pegging out her grievances around the house in every gesture, utterance and silence – especially those sharp silences – and he'd respond by going to work early or disappearing for a walk by the river, or he'd go out of his way to amuse Stella and me. There were occasions when the tension between them would stretch across breakfast, lunch and dinner, and all I'd want was for it to snap; I'd long for there to be a shouting and a clearing and an ending. Usually it'd last until Victor decided enough was enough and he'd apologise or offer a compromise or cave-in completely, and he'd justify it by saying life was too short to spend it arguing. If he was feeling particularly adamant about something, he'd ignore the issue, pretend everything was hunky-dory and that he wasn't even aware of her passive-aggressiveness, until she had no choice but to push that particular gripe onto the back-burner.

I got bogged down with remembering this, but when I glanced up I caught a flicker of how Mick Droyler was looking at me. It was only the tail-end of a moment because he looked away when I caught him out, but I'm sure he'd been staring at the gap in the front of my pyjama top, revealed by the bagginess of my dressing gown. Not that he could see anything, not that I've got much to show, but it made me realise he was no different to any other guy, young or old. They're all wired the same. It didn't matter that he was a policeman and roughly the same age as my dad. He covered himself well, though, by darting a look around the room – coffee cup, biscuit tin, table, window, cat bowl, pin-board, ceiling light, my ruffled hair – as if it was his policeman's habit to be looking at everything, everywhere, every second. But I found his clumsiness in this reassuring. It made me feel safer.

'Anything at all?' he said.

'Sorry, what was the question?'

'Problems, nuisance calls –'

'No,' I replied. 'Nothing unusual.'

'Nothing?'

I wondered what Tess was up to and whether I'd ever forgive her enough, for dumping me the way she did, to catch-up with her again one day. I shook my head.

'We need to know everything, Meg. However unimportant it seems. Tell me why Stella had been kicked out. You said she'd been kicked out and shouldn't have been home last night. What was that all about?'

'It's boring, family stuff,' I told him, glancing back at the kitchen window and the smudge I'd left there. 'No big deal.'

'Your mother's dead, Meg, and your father's missing. You need to tell me everything.'

'Oh, yes. I forgot. Sorry.' And for a brief, delicious moment I had.

There wasn't any choice but to give him something. All

the same, there was no way I was going to tell him and his little notebook every dirty, little secret. No way.

The reason Stella was kicked out didn't seem such a big deal at the time, except our mum had to make a drama out of everything. She'd make a drama out of nothing and a crisis out of the drama. Not that I intended telling Mick Droyler that. When I said about Stella getting kicked out of home, what I should have said was that Mum told her not to come back if she stayed at her friend's house overnight – the night before the fire, that is. There's a subtle difference, of course, but our mother was an expert in manipulation and the blame game, and it certainly wasn't the first time she'd used that line. She'd done it to both of us, whenever it suited, except Stella decided to be most unStella-like and push the point. As a rule, she avoids conflict, does Stella, knowing she can sweet-talk her way round almost everyone, but not this time.

Dad was in America, on his business trip, and Stella phoned me on Tuesday morning while she was waiting for the school bus. By the sounds of it, she'd been crying.

'Megsy, I'm so angry. Mum can be such a bitch at times. I've just had a massive row with her.'

I was heading to work, landscaping the garden for a new house on the other side of Lapishot, but I pulled over to talk. She doesn't often get upset, but she was then.

'What's the matter? What about?' I asked. It was a cold, drizzly morning, but the forecast was for it to clear.

'Jasmine's eighteenth. About staying over at her place.'

'You've stayed there heaps of times,' I said.

'Exactly, except Mum won't have a bar of it. She says it's too close to my exams to stay over on a school night.'

'It's not at the weekend?'

'No, Jasmine's mum works shifts and, well, it's just worked out that her party has to be tonight. Almost everyone's turning eighteen this month, so it's hard to fit them all in across the weekends. Anyway, the long and the short of it is that I told her I was going, that I didn't let my friends down – especially my best friends – and she more or less told me not to come back.'

'Oh, Stell, no.'

'Yes, she did. She said: "If you're not back through that door by eleven o'clock, young lady, then don't bother coming back through it at all."'

'Sounds familiar.'

'Except this time she meant it. I know she did. You know what she's like. It's only because she doesn't want to be on her own when Dad's away, even though I said I'm sure you'd stay and keep her company if she wanted. She's also got it into her head there's a boy involved and she said some horrible things. Oh, Megsy...'

I waited for her to stop crying – a snuffly mix of upset and anger – and I made the best soothing noises it's possible to make over a phone. When she was settled again, I said, 'So is there?'

'Is there what?'

'A boy. Is there a boy involved?'

I heard her blowing her nose and could imagine her dabbing her eyes with a tissue, standing in the bus shelter where we'd caught our school buses year-in year-out.

'Well, yes, sort of,' she said. 'Except she doesn't know that for sure and I wasn't going to let on about it after some of the things she said. Can you imagine? But it's complicated, Meg, and I really need to have a chat with you about it.'

'About your boy? Why? You're not going to elope are you?'

She laughed. 'No, it's nothing like that. I can't say now, not over the phone, and the bus'll be here in a minute, but there's something very special I want to ask you. The biggest favour I've ever asked.'

'You want to stay at Angie's with me? You want to bring your boy over to Angie's?' It made me feel good to be able to offer this.

'God, no, we don't need to do that. Look, perhaps I could come over in a couple of days, when all this has blown over, and we'll talk?'

'Sure. No worries.'

'But I'm certainly not going back tonight or tomorrow night either. I'll let her stew.'

'So you're staying with Jasmine?'

There was a moment's pause. 'Well, that's the official story.'

'Stell!'

'Jasmine's all worded up and there's so many people kipping down at her place that her mum won't notice what time I leave –'

'You're staying with this boy? Who is he?'

'He's very special, Megsy. That's what I want to talk to you about. I'll move in with him tomorrow if Mum really kicks me out. He'd love me too.'

'I bet he would. But what about your studies, Stella? You've only got a few months of school left. Don't wreck your chances of getting into uni, will you?'

'Not a chance. He's cool with that.'

'Who is he? Anyone I've met before? He's obviously not at school if he's got his own place. He's not married, is he? He's not messing around –'

'I could hardly stay with him if he was. No, really, that's all part of what I want to ask you. I've got a big favour to ask, to see if you're okay with something and what you think about it.' There was a moment's hesitation. 'Look, I've got to go, the bus is coming. It's not something I can ask over the phone – really – so we'll catch up soon, alright? Perhaps Thursday or Friday?'

'Okay. I guess.'

'Great. Love you.' And she was gone.

Mick kept his notebook open after I'd finished my story, waiting for me to offer more, I suppose. When he looked across at me, it was as if he was glancing over the top of a pair of invisible glasses, and the way he did this reminded me of Tess. She used to look at people the same way sometimes. They have a similar shaped jaw-line and chin too, which I'd never noticed before, although his face is obviously broader, more masculine.

'So who's the fella?' he asked.

'What fella?'

'Stella's fella.'

I shook my head. 'How would I know? We never got to talk, did we?'

It's always best to use a truth to hide a lie, and I noticed he drew a line under whatever it was he'd written. He could ask Stella that himself.

The instant I relaxed, I realised how hungry I was. I was famished. Not for biscuits or snacks, but for a fry-up: steak, eggs, tomatoes, mushrooms – the lot.

'Have you eaten?' I asked. 'Would you like lunch?'

He smiled. 'I'm fine, but you go ahead.'

'I can't remember the last time I ate a proper meal. I had a stinking headache yesterday afternoon; came home and went straight to bed.'

With him sitting there, ready to scribble down every

word I uttered, I wondered whether I should wait until he'd gone so I could concentrate on whatever he was asking, or whether I should start cooking straight away. I didn't know how long he'd be, but I couldn't afford to get light-headed again either.

'I feel bad...'

'Go ahead, Meg. A person can forget to eat when they've got all this going on. It's never easy, but you still have to look after yourself. It's important you do that.'

I started rattling about with taking eggs and tomatoes from the fridge, olive oil from the cupboard, and searching for the piece of porterhouse steak I know I had, but which wasn't in the fridge or freezer any longer. I was sure I hadn't eaten it; nor all the mushrooms for that matter.

'Tell me about the graffiti, Meg.'

That caught me. Totally. My knees buckled and my hands were shaking. I almost dropped the frying pan, except I shoved it down with a clatter, leant against the kitchen bench and told myself to take a deep breath. Push it out, draw it in. Keep breathing.

'Are you alright?' He was standing next to me, pulling a chair out for me. 'Put your head between your knees.'

I focussed on each breath.

'I keep getting the shakes,' I said. 'It comes over me in waves.'

'That's shock,' he said. 'Stay like that for a minute. You're not going to faint on me?'

I shook my head and almost laughed. He had his hand on my back, resting there. I could've stayed like that for ages, but after a minute or two I pulled myself together and sat up. The nausea had returned and I doubted I'd be able to eat without throwing up, but at least I was thinking straight again. I was still shaking, but made myself carry on.

I could have asked him to leave and he would have, but instead I said, 'What about the graffiti?'

'Tell me what you remember.'

'That was… ages ago.'

He said nothing, waited for me to continue.

'And I already have. Dad did too. When you spoke to us at Demlab, remember?' I folded my arms across my stomach and pressed down.

'Yep, I know, but memory's a funny thing, Meg, and you've already remembered something extra that might prove useful, with the business of the van and the car and seeing people hanging around. In the light of that, I really need to hear about it again and anything your Dad might have said afterwards.'

'You do think those Animal Rights nutters set the fire, don't you? You think they did it. Have they claimed responsibility or something?'

'I can't say. I really can't. We have to look at every possibility, that's all. There'll be other people investigating this, Meg. You know that, don't you? It won't just be me. Fire investigators will be arriving soon, if they haven't already, and I have to make sure they've got all the information they need. They'll want to talk to you and Stella, and they'll probably ask the same questions all over again. We have to work this way if we're going to find out what happened and who's responsible.'

'I see. I suppose so.'

He didn't want to know every detail about that morning a few weeks back, when I discovered the graffiti, just the ones that mattered, but this is much the way it happened:

With breakfast in my belly and the first coffee of the day kicking in, I was hurtling along Nine Mile Road from

Angie's. The sun wasn't so high it had shaken the night's autumn chill from the forest, but even though it was only four or five degrees outside, it looked set to remain a clear morning; there was a sharp brightness to the sun and a smoothness to the eggshell blue of the sky. Victor had asked me to pick him up from home and take him to work because his car was in Lapishot for a panel-and-paint job (some moron dented his front wing at the supermarket car park and drove off without even leaving a note on the windscreen). This suited me fine as it was about time I spent a couple of days pruning and weeding at Demlab, where Victor sweet-talked the guy in charge of Buildings & Grounds into giving me my first landscape maintenance contract. I'd probably give Stella a lift to school too, I thought, and save her a trip on the bus, if it wasn't too early for her.

My foot was a bit keen on the pedal, perhaps, skimming along on such a fine morning, and I was humming away to a happy song. In short, I was feeling good about the day and forgetting to be cautious.

Victor always argued that it was quicker on the main road because it's sealed and you can't push your luck on unsealed roads, but that's a boring route, with too many dog-legs, milk tankers and tractors. Besides, unsealed or not, I'd timed them both and the forest route is a minute quicker at the very least. Once, with Stella, I almost shaved a full two minutes off, but you'd be mad to risk driving like that too often.

Nonetheless, it's usually when you're being ultra-sensible and not crazy at all when crap happens. It's when you least deserve it. Before you know it, it's as if you've hit a random moment of chaos drifting through the universe; it sucks you out of your seasoned comfort quicker than you can blink, spins you into limbo for a flash and then gobs you back out again – splat! Inside of an instant, something dramatic happens and everything's ripped apart.

Which is much the way it happened.

There were puddles in the ruts from the previous day's rain and scatterings of fallen branches, but the main thing to always watch for was livestock and wildlife. Already, that morning, three escaped sheep had run in a nervous huddle down the centre of the road outside Angie's place when I pulled out. Even so, while hitting anything that size would do damage at whatever speed you're driving, it's the swerving to avoid them that keeps the undertakers busy. There's a local joke about trees being slower to get out the way than rabbits, and outcrops of rock being a tad slower still, but it's a cautionary tale that's almost impossible to remember, I reckon, when, during the split second that instinct cuts in ahead of reason, you slam on the brakes and swerve to avoid something you'd be happy to see skinned, stewed and on your plate at any other time.

Perhaps it was because of that happy song and the desire to play it again, but the moment I glanced down to select Back Cue on the media player, two young deer bounded through the forest, cutting a line across the road a few metres ahead of me. They were fast. Damn, they were fast and big.

Instinct-bloody-instinct made me brake and swerve to avoid the first, but in doing so I hit the second.

There was a sickening series of thuds as I collected it head-on, and my truck almost rolled as I bumped and dragged over the top of it. I slammed on the brakes, but was immediately fighting the steering wheel, which was pulling for all it was worth in the wrong direction. For a second, I saw I was going to get thrown off the road and...

like I said, there's no shortage of trees. All the same, I remembered to steer into the skid, as I'd been taught, and gradually came out of it again.

When the spray of muck settled and I shook to a halt, I'd done a full ninety-degree turn, but was still on the road. Just. The road was half-blocked about fifty metres back by the fallen deer.

The other deer had vanished and the forest was silent and, more than anything else in the whole world at that moment, I hoped it had been a clean kill. By which I mean an instant kill, so I wouldn't have to put the damned thing out of its misery.

Since getting my licence, and like most everyone else I know, I've hit rabbits, one fox and a sky-full of birds, which is one of the hazards of living in the country. But I'd only heard of two other people hitting deer, which made me feel damned unlucky, although both those cars were written off and the driver was killed in one, so I guess I could be thankful for my bullbar and high axle.

I approached it slowly. It was a juvenile buck and seemed pretty dead at first, but when I got closer I could see the thing was breathing and quivering. There was a dark slash down its side and a thick mass of blood pooling underneath and bubbles of snot and blood bubbling from its nose and mouth. I moved a step closer. No way would it be getting up in a hurry.

It was the closest I'd been to that kind of dying before. We were both frightened, except our fears were different. I was as much afraid of its fear and of what I had to do as anything, and I wished the damned thing would hurry up and die without me.

I waited a minute and the quivering stopped. There was no movement. Its stare became distant and glassy and I was relieved it was over. I was off the hook. But then, when I took a step towards it, a deep tremble tensed its flank and it started breathing urgently.

It had been a powerful beast, solid with sinew, muscle and coarse hair, and its hooves were more pointed and rigid than I'd imagined, but with each gurgled pant of breath the bubbly froth of blood and mucous from its mouth and nose grew less, so that the rhythm of its living and dying was in the ebb and flow of that snotty mix. How I wished the bloody thing would die.

When it blinked and tried raising itself, but couldn't, I knew I had to do the deed. I didn't have a choice. I could never forgive myself otherwise. I needed a large stick or a wheel brace or, better still, the back of my spade. I had to finish it off. Living in the country, it's a lesson everyone's heard: only the lowest coward would let a creature like a cow, a deer or a dog suffer a slow death. I'd become responsible for it the moment I hit it.

'Crap, bloody hell and shit!'

Before I could start over-thinking what I had to do, I ran to the back of my truck and pulled out my heaviest spade. I still hoped it'd die while I was about this, but I had to run to create the momentum to keep me going. I took a deep breath, ran back and, giving it a wide berth, approached it from behind.

I told myself not to think, just to swing high. Which was fine until it began moving. It lifted and arched its head back and seemed to lock onto me with its eyes, but I told myself it was the deer's fear I was seeing, not mine, and there was no way it was going to clamber to its feet and gallop away into the bush, skippety-skip, leapety-leap. Its Bambi days were over.

It carried on staring at me, both eyes swivelled back, and

there was a fresh flush of crimson bubbles. I watched it watching me until it couldn't keep its head up any longer and lay down and was still again.

Deep breath.

I swung the spade as high as I could, barely pausing before bringing it down with all the force I'd got. I smashed the back of the spade against the side of its head.

A loud metallic thud rang out, but also the crack of bone, the squelch of tissue.

Dragging the spade away, I tried not to look, but couldn't help seeing the eyeball out of its socket, the dislocated grin.

I gagged then, but quickly sucked in another deep breath and hit it again. To be sure. In case it was only unconscious. And once more. I had to see it through.

Once I'd wiped the spade clean on damp, roadside grass and rinsed it in a muddy puddle, I made myself turn and look fully at the dead thing and the mess I'd made of it. I wasn't finished, though. I had to get it off the road.

It was a lump of meat, that's all. Nothing more. It couldn't hurt me, I told myself, not unless I let it. The worst was over.

Rubbing my hands together, as if to pull a shrub out the ground, I grabbed close to the hoof of a hind leg – it could be a fallen branch – and dragged with all I'd got, but there was no shifting the thing. It was far heavier than it looked.

I was tempted to leave it then, in the hope someone beefier than me might come along, except it was blocking the road and might kill the next poor bugger if they didn't see it in time. I glanced at my watch, wondered whether I should phone Dad, but then realised what I could do.

Jogging back to my truck, I drove close to the deer and grabbed a bundle of rope from the tool chest. The collision had made a mess of my bullbar, written off a headlight and wrecked the number plate, but hopefully the winch still worked. It was an ancient beast, my truck, but solid. I tied one end of the rope to the two hind legs of the deer and hitched the other end to the winch hook and, reversing onto the verge, dragged the thing off the road.

After I'd washed my hands in another puddle, I sort of took stock of myself and realised I was okay. Actually, I was better than okay. It was as if, in confronting and overcoming the death of this thing, and my part in it, I'd achieved something life-affirming; as though a significant coming-of-age had sneakily tucked itself in with the incident. As if having this brief dance with Death was more a rite of passage than my awful eighteenth birthday had been. I was a survivor and could now survive anything. It had done me good. I was taller than I was ten minutes ago.

Apart from the obvious damage to my truck, everything underneath looked okay as far as I could tell. There was none of the green fluid I once had from a fractured brake-line and no steam from a broken radiator. The bullbar needed straightening and I'd need a new headlight, but that was all. The insurance would cover it.

For the rest of the journey through the forest – along Nine Mile Road, before turning left onto Wallan River Road – I drove at a stately pace. I only increased speed as I crossed the bridge and the house came into sight.

Victor was running late too, it seemed, or I'd left much earlier than I thought, because he wasn't standing in the driveway checking his watch when I pulled up. Maybe he'd cancelled his first meeting. Either way, such considerations didn't carry much weight on the scales of Life & Death. When I glanced in the visor mirror to make sure I didn't look too wrecked, I could even smile at the new, stronger me, before pushing open the door and clambering out.

But there it was, as if some spiteful bastard was looking down from above and was more than ready to point an accusing finger at me. Scrawled in large capitals, in blood-red paint against the white render of the house, each letter streaking down the wall, was the word *KILLER*.

Its starkness froze me, then dizzied me.

Leaning against the bonnet, the world spun a little, but when I re-focussed the word was still there.

It couldn't be.

KILLER.

I walked slowly towards it, across the lawn. This was a harder thing to confront, in a strange way, than the deer itself, because there was no logic to it. It didn't make sense.

I tentatively touched the letter *K* with the tip of my little finger. It was red paint. Not blood. And growing tacky, which meant it had been there a few hours and couldn't be anything to do with the deer. Nothing at all. Unless prophetic.

The front door opened.

'Ah, there you are, Meg,' Victor called. 'Excellent timing. I'll just grab my jacket and briefcase. Oh, and here you go, before I forget, your Mum's got a magazine for you.' He waved something in the air, but then stopped and stepped out. 'Meg? Are you alright? You look like you've seen a ghost.'

'You've had visitors.'

'No,' he said. 'No visitors, thank God. Too busy for visitors at the moment.'

'Yes, you have,' I told him. 'Haven't you seen this?'

'Seen what?' He smiled as if I might be playing a joke on him, like April Fool or something. He glanced quickly at Mother's rose bed and lowered his voice. 'We haven't had Graham's cows through the front again, have we? Your mum'll be ...' The words trailed off.

Each of the scrawled letters was about a metre high, but even though you could tell they'd been sprayed with an aerosol they'd streaked with the moist night air.

'Oh, I see.' He stepped down onto the lawn, as if to better appreciate its message. 'Those Animal Rights nuts,' he said, shaking his head. 'Your mother'll like this even less.'

Typical. He was more concerned by my mother's reaction than by the actual graffiti or that a bunch of fanatics had come all the way out to Three Creeks in the middle of the night to vandalise his house. Didn't he feel threatened or violated by this?

It wasn't something I'd given much thought to before, but it made me wonder how often he must receive poison-pen letters, death threats, that sort of thing, because of Demlab. Quite often it would seem, if his calmness was anything to go by. He'd never talked about it, but with Mother the way she was it wasn't surprising. Better to play it down or say nothing.

He pulled a face when she called from inside the house.

'Who's left the front door wide open? We'll have all the flies in.' And she would have shut the door, I guess, if she hadn't poked her head out and seen Victor and me standing there. 'Oh, you're here, Meg. Are you running late? Your father was frightened you'd forgotten him. What...'

She didn't have a chance to say more because Stella ran out, laughing her head off. She had a pair of Dad's boxers and a pair of Mum's knickers in her hands and was stretching the knickers out for us to see. 'You'll never guess what,' she began, and I noticed they'd been shredded – slash cuts through both pairs – until she spotted what we were looking at. She put a hand to her mouth. 'Or maybe you will.'

'Hello, Stell,' I said.

'Hi, Megsy.'

'You've had visitors.'

Mother looked from that streaky word – *KILLER* – to her knickers, and back at Dad. Her face twisted with horror and bewilderment. 'Give me those,' she managed to say, snatching them into a bundle and fleeing indoors.

Stella shrugged and dabbed at the graffiti with her finger. 'It's still wet.'

'Hmm.'

'I was looking for a clean school shirt on the line. Thought an owl or a squirrel or something must've clawed your underwear to death. Didn't like your taste. Guess it wasn't an owl.'

'Probably not,' I said.

'Hmm, visitors,' Dad mumbled and loosened his tie.

Mum stormed out, tightly wound. 'Have you called the police yet? You need to call the police. Get them out here straightaway. Who'd do such a thing? You'll have to phone Demlab and tell them you won't be in today.'

He looked down at the magazine he was holding and seemed momentarily puzzled by it. 'Why won't I? Why won't I be going in?'

'I'm not staying here –'

Then he gathered himself. 'Of course I'll be going in. You can phone the police, can't you?' You could almost see him measuring his tone, weighing his words. 'You can show them what's happened as well as I can. It's not going to take two of us. I've got a meeting to get to, remember?'

'I'm not staying here alone. Not with lunatics on the loose. It'll be those Animal Freedom terrorists. I don't know why they –'

'Then go visit Claire or someone. Wait until the police

have been out, if they can spare anyone to come all the way here just for graffiti, that is, and go visit Claire afterwards if you want. I thought that's why you needed your car today, so you could catch up with her?'

'It's not why I wanted it at all. I told you that already. I knew this would happen. Sooner or later it was bound to happen.'

He sighed. 'Why was it bound to happen? I've worked at Demlab for twenty-two years. They've never been to the house before. I don't see why it was bound to happen.'

'Those Animal Rights terrorists, they ought to lock them up.' She began walking away, but as quickly turned back. 'You'll just have to be late to work, won't you? They'll cope without you for an extra hour, I'm sure. Besides, there's not much point in me phoning the police because it's you they'll want to talk to. It's only because of your damned job – that's why. You phone the police. You're the one who should phone them.'

He pushed a hand through his hair and looked at his watch. 'I'll phone from the car,' he said, absent-mindedly handing the magazine to me. Then, straightening his tie, he walked towards the front door for his jacket and briefcase.

She stood with her arms folded and her hands gripping her waist. 'So I'm supposed to stay here by myself with these lunatics running wild and... and that scrawled across my house, while you run off to work? Well, thanks a lot, but if –'

'It's a bit of graffiti, not the end of the world. Just mindless vandalism from spineless cowards who'll have fled hours ago. If we lived in town we'd get it all the time; we wouldn't think twice about it.'

'Well, we don't –'

Stella said, 'I'll stay with you, Mum. I can easily take the day off school. Anyway, I've got nothing important on and I'll get heaps more study done at home.'

Victor raised his eyebrows and Mother hesitated, but I gave Stella a kiss and moved towards my truck. It was always good to see her outmanoeuvred.

When I climbed into the cab, Stella was standing back, examining the effect of the graffiti as if it was street art, and Dad was saying something to Mum, who was ignoring him. She slammed the front door and he blew a kiss at it. Glancing at his watch again, he said goodbye to Stell and strode across the lawn to join me.

I waited a moment before turning on the ignition and he winked.

'It's not very nice for your mum, but she'll calm down, my love,' he said. 'She always does.'

FIVE

THE LAPISHOT GAZETTE, page 1:

THREE CREEKS ARSON ATTACK
DEMLAB MANAGER MISSING

Police have revealed that Demlab's Managing Director, Dr Victor Dapsy, 45, whose Three Creeks' home was destroyed in a fatal arson attack on Thursday, has been missing since the night of the fire. A police spokesperson expressed concern for Dr Dapsy, who was targeted recently by animal rights group A.A.R. in its campaign against Demlab International and the use of animals in laboratory tests. Dr Dapsy's wife, Francine Dapsy, died and his daughter was injured in the fire, which Fire Investigation officers believe was started with an accelerant. Police are refusing to rule out that Dr Dapsy, who had recently returned from an overseas conference, may be the victim of foul play and are appealing for anyone who was in the vicinity of Three Creeks last Wednesday night to contact them.

When I saw it on the front page, I couldn't stop shivering. My fingers turned to ice. I thought I was going to shatter into tiny pieces.

But I didn't. I held tight.

Pete told me about Action for Animal Rights. It surprised me, his interest in ethics, politics, direct action – something other than himself – and I liked that he might be a dark horse after all. Made me realise he was more than a pretty boy with a slightly irritating fringe-flicking habit, but that he had a few ideas and values too, even if I didn't always agree with him. He showed me some Animal Rights links on the net and we watched a couple of their videos together.

There was one of a battery farm raid where the A.A.R. used bolt cutters to break into the sheds, and it showed how the chickens had lost their feathers and looked sort of freaky, not like chickens at all, and how the activists released them all. Another video showed the A.A.R. doing this Special Forces-type attack on a beagle-breeder's house, where two guys strung up an effigy of the owner in the garden and sprayed graffiti across the house, while another pair broke into the garage and set fire to a Mercedes and a Land Rover; then they tossed a couple of rape alarms into the gutters and left. All in less than ten minutes.

Pete laughed his head off. 'That's cool,' he said, and I could tell he liked the idea of dressing up in a black ski mask and breaking into buildings in the middle of the night with the justification of a cause behind him. Even if he'd never have the guts to do it himself.

<u>A.A.R. – Action for Animal Rights</u>
The founding members of Action for Animal Rights, Kevin Whitloach and Suki Maurelais, are currently

serving prison sentences for their involvement in the kidnapping of 9 year-old Emilie Villier, grand-daughter of cosmetics tycoon Ralph Villier. Despite the organisation being outlawed, the A.A.R. has increased its activities as a leaderless, cell-based movement, regularly claiming responsibility for attacks that target:
• breeders of animals used for research;
• research laboratories and employees of research laboratories who use animals as test subjects;
• manufacturers and employees of manufacturers who commission research that uses animals as test subjects;
• perpetrators of (and profiteers from) cruelty towards animals.

Despite its illegal status, a number of websites openly promote A.A.R. aims and objectives, and continue to identify it as a 'militant, counter-terrorist movement that ... actively protects the rights of animals and prosecutes any individual or organisation that contravenes such rights.'

No wonder they had Demlab and Victor in their sights. It's a massive relief to read about the kidnapping.

Since he's been gone, I've been remembering all sorts of things about Victor. Stuff from childhood. I try not to, but I can't help it.

I'm standing at the door of their darkened bedroom and watching Victor sleep. I'm eight or nine. It's the end of the afternoon and I've never caught him sleeping like this before. It's unheard of for him to go to bed in the day, but he's been to Japan (I think) for meetings, and arrived home only a short while before, when Stella and I were still at school.

I tiptoe across the carpet, so the floorboards don't creak, and stand over him.

He sleeps on his back. There's the dark shadow of stubble across his face, which makes his chin and cheekbones more pronounced. His lips are drawn back faintly in the grin of a pleasant dream and I want to touch the scribble of laughter lines at the corner of his eyes, to smooth flat the creases, but his brow is slightly furrowed too, as if he's thinking of something even now, and I know he needs his rest.

Stella comes bouncing up the stairs one loud step at a time and I want her to be quiet. I lean down so I might catch the sound of his each, warm breath, but he opens his eyes wide, as if he's been awake the whole time, and reaches out to grab me.

'Hello, monster,' he cries, pulling me down, and I squeal and laugh and he's got me on my back, with one arm clamped round me, and he's tickling me until I'm fit to burst.

'Stop it! Stop it!' I laugh, squirming and wriggling to escape, which is when Stella runs in and jumps on the bed too, half-crushing me.

'Dad!' she shouts. 'Me too, me too!'

All I'd seen from the taxi was the front of the house, but I needed to see it all. I needed to witness the shrivelled guts of the place up close and to poke a stick at them. Before long, the police would be asking me to identify our mother's body, but I wasn't up to that yet. Confronting the house would be a first step. Besides, I needed to get clothes for Stella.

It was the middle of the afternoon and I parked out of

sight against the bank of wattle on Wallan River Road, a good hundred metres from the junction with Rudely Road, so the neighbours wouldn't notice if they looked across or happened to drive past the front. The last thing I wanted was the awkwardness of kind words, soft shoulders, invitations to dinner.

There was a 'secret passage' between the old limbs of rambling wattle – *Acacia perambulare* – which Stell and I made when we were kids. At first, we built a den amongst the smooth-barked branches, using one stout branch as a seat and another as a look-out post, but over time we extended it into a dog-legged tunnel, which became a short-cut out of the garden in recent, teenage years whenever we headed down to meet friends at the barbecue area by the river. The side of the tool shed camouflaged the tunnel's entrance, while the narrow exit was usually draped in the season's tender foliage.

That afternoon, I noticed track marks from a wheelbarrow pressed into the soil and it made me uneasy about sneaking through the hedge, as if instead of entering the secret garden of my childhood, it had become a garden with darker, adult secrets. I'd have liked to turn back, but couldn't. Snapping off a piece of dead branch, I scratched at the soil until I'd obliterated the track, and then kicked leaf litter across the disturbed area. I saw a film once where a cowboy or American Indian did exactly the same.

Stepping out from behind the shed, there was the back of the house. Except it wasn't a house. Not anymore. Not from this angle. It was a carcass, surrounded by a mess of rubble and... and I couldn't understand why there was so much furniture and rubbish strewn across the lawn.

I looked for the garden bench, which was the last place I'd sat with Victor, but it must have been buried under the pile of splintered timbers and remnants of plasterboard. The grass around it was churned up, sodden and muddy. There were oily puddles across the patio, soggy rags, dark shards of glass.

At first, it was impossible to see beyond the blackened walls, the broken windows, the mess across the garden, the smashed panes in the roof of the cactus house, but then the crazy obviousness of what was different struck me: a portion of the upstairs wall had completely burnt out, exposing the back of the bathroom sink, with the bath next to it and the shower against the far side of the room. It was like peeping into a dolls' house, except someone had stood on the roof and broken the spine of this one.

I stood, stared, hardened myself.

Despite the softening sweetness in the air of all the water that had been hosed onto the place to saturate the last embers, it still had a bitter edge of smoke and wet charcoal to it. Flecks of soot and ash covered everything. The new, outermost leaves of wattle had given up their translucent yellow-green to a drab, smutty opaqueness, and there were streaky-black smuts on my jacket and jeans from where I'd pushed through the branches. The entire roof of the shed was coated and the clothes hanging on the washing line were smothered with black smuts too.

The air was still and the clothes rigid. I reached for one of Dad's once-white business shirts, which was bone-dry now, and checked Stella's T-shirts, but they were all wrecked. A light blue pillowcase and a maroon hand towel lay scrunched and filthy on the ground, as if several firemen had wiped their boots on them, and I went to drape them over the line, but they were beyond keeping.

As for the house...

It looked larger for having part of the wall missing, and

yet, beyond that trick of the eye, also managed to appear smaller too. Physically bigger for being opened up and drawn out across the garden – like a disembowelling – but essentially diminished for being laid bare and reduced to scorched timbers, splinters of glass, fragments of plasterboard.

No loss, though. I refused to entertain any sense of loss. *What's done is done.*

After all, it hadn't been a home since I couldn't remember when. I'd happily be the one to drive a bulldozer through it, flattening its carcass into the earth and burying its bones once and for all. I'd have done it right then if I could.

Taking a long, bitter breath, I doubted there'd be any clothes fit for Stella to wear. At best, everything inside would stink. I'd probably have to buy her a whole heap of new stuff in town, just so she could leave hospital. And that's what I was doing, standing in the back garden, trying to work out how much a set of clothes might cost, when that obnoxious detective first appeared, marching round from the side of the house, scribbling something down on a clipboard.

The moment he saw me, he pointed his clipboard and shouted: 'Oi, you! Stay there! What do you think you're doing?'

As soon as he opened his mouth, I could tell he was an arrogant prick.

Picking up his pace, he strode over, squelching across a clear patch of grass, keeping an eye on me all the time, as if he expected me to run and was ready to give chase, which tempted me to do exactly that: to turn and out-run him. With his tacky brown suit and wispy, thinning hair, I thought he was middle-aged at first, but as he got closer I guessed he was probably in his early-thirties.

'You've got no right being here,' he told me. 'This is a crime scene. What's your name? How did you get in?'

What an idiot.

'This is my parents' house,' I told him. 'I have every right to be here. Who the heck are you?'

Reaching into his pocket, he took out his wallet and flicked it open. There was a fancy official badge and a flash of words: *Detective Steven Somebody-or-other.*

'I'm investigating the fire,' he said. 'I'll need some identification from you too. A driver's licence for starters.'

Reaching into my pocket, I pulled out a clean tissue. 'Licence is in the truck, but my name's painted right across the sides and back of it: *Dapsy Landscaping & Gardening.* Will that do?'

'Dapsy, eh?' He was about to write it on his clipboard of papers, but flipped back to his first page before nodding some sort of acknowledgement. 'And where is your vehicle, Ms Dapsy? How did you get in here? I didn't see you arrive.'

I poked my thumb in the direction of the wattle hedge and the road. 'Through the back gate,' I said.

'Back gate?'

'Sort of.'

He glanced at the hedge, but didn't seem convinced. 'This is a crime scene; you can't be wandering around. Besides, it's not safe.'

'I have to get clothes for my sister. She's in hospital. I'm heading in to see her.'

'Where's your car keys?'

'In the truck, with my licence.'

He shrugged in an off-hand way, as if to say I must be mad leaving my truck open like that.

'This is the country,' I pointed out. 'There's not many car

thieves wandering out the forest at this time of day.'

'Let's take a look, shall we?'

'At what?'

'At your identification,' he said, gesturing with his clipboard for me to lead the way. 'So you're the eldest daughter, is that right? Margaret?'

'It's Meg, not Margaret.'

Without giving him the chance to say another word, I slipped between the side of the shed and the wattle hedge, making him trot along to keep up. Didn't want him lingering in my secret spot.

Out on the road, I swept my hand along the side of the truck. 'There you go: *Dapsy Landscaping & Gardening*. Like I said.'

'Why'd you park all the way down here? Why not come in the front, on the drive?'

'Didn't want the neighbours rushing round. Kind words don't always make things easier.'

He flicked a look at the front number plate and then back at his clipboard, and was, I realised, merely confirming information he'd already received, and I wondered what else he knew or thought he knew about me. When he noticed the damage to the bullbar, he made a show of sizing it up. 'Been in an accident?'

Fancied himself as Sherlock Holmes.

'Hit a deer. Are you investigating that too?' I knew I was being a smart-arse, but officious pricks like him always bring it out in me these days.

'Do any other damage?'

'The deer wasn't looking too smart,' I offered, before adding: 'Took out the front light, but had to replace that straightaway.'

'Ouch, that would've hurt,' he said, as if wanting to be all friendly now, which made me trust him even less. 'Might just take a squiz at that licence, Meg.'

When I reached into the glove compartment, he took a step back and I could feel him watching my every move, as if I was the sort to pull a wheel brace on him or have a gun tucked away, for goodness sake.

'Squiz away, Steven,' I said, handing over my licence.

He glanced at it, glanced at me, handed it back and peered into the open tray of my truck.

'You've got a flat,' he said with a nod at the tyre of my upturned wheelbarrow.

'I'd noticed.'

'Mind if I have a look?' He lifted the wheelbarrow a fraction to see under it; cast the briefest of glances at the strimmer and chainsaw, the collection of forks, spades, edging tools; unscrewed the lid from the can of petrol and sniffed it, sloshing it about to see how much was in there.

'Sniffing petrol's a bad habit,' I said, but got no smile.

'It's half-empty,' he pointed out.

'Or half-full.'

'How often do you refill it?'

'Depends how often I empty it.'

He smiled then, but a caustic smile. 'Roughly how often?'

'Depends how many lawns I cut... roughly.'

'When was the last time you filled it up?'

'The day before yesterday. At Greens, on Lapishot Road. About nine in the morning.' I had to curb my mouth, I knew I did, but I was tired and his rudeness brought it out in me.

The prick wrote everything down, which I suppose he had to, and then leant into the cab and looked under the seats, pulling out a broken trowel, a biro, a half-box of tampons, but didn't bother pushing any of it back again.

'Looking for something in particular?'

'Apart from the accelerant?' he said, with a nod in the direction of the petrol can.

'You bastard. My mother died in that fire.'

'And your father disappeared. Yes, I know. Has he contacted you at all? Or have you received any news about him?'

'No. Have you?'

'I can't let you go into the house, I'm afraid, and I'll have to ask you to stay off the property until the investigation is concluded and it's been made safe – if it can be.' He stood back again so I could move round to the driver's door.

'Don't worry, I don't intend to. It stinks. There's a bad smell around.'

He smiled at that too. 'I guess I'll be talking with you later, Meg.'

'I guess you will, Steven,' I replied, climbing in and pulling the door shut.

<u>The forensic science of fire</u>

Fire investigators have been copping bad press in recent years. I checked out the science behind this stuff on the internet, after meeting Stevie of the brown suit and retreating hairline, and discovered that a number of long-standing beliefs about how fires begin and how they burn have been discredited of late.

According to the articles, innocent people have been convicted and imprisoned (at least two were executed in the United States) because the 'science' developed by early fire investigators went unproven and unchallenged for decades. Too many assumptions were based on general observations, flawed logic and anecdotal evidence, which, in the absence of proper, detailed studies, were passed on as 'gospel truths' from one generation of investigators to the next. Thanks to their 'unequivocal' testimony, innocent people have been convicted for manslaughter or murder, and one woman had her children taken from her and placed in foster care when investigators asserted that an accidental fire was deliberate.

Recently, though, heaps of these assumptions have been challenged and dismissed – like how hot certain types of fire will burn and what particular scorch patterns might indicate about the cause of a fire – even if it's too late for those poor unfortunates who've been hung out to dry.

Stella was watching television. She was listening to the sound through earphones and didn't hear me enter, and I couldn't tell what the program was, but I stood at the door to her room and watched her watching.

'Stella,' I said, stepping closer, and she saw me.

Pulling out her earphones, she put her arms out and I walked over and put my arms around her, and she cried.

'Oh, Megsy,' she sobbed.

'It's okay, Stell,' I said, hugging her tight and patting her on the back, comforting her, the way Mum never had – not for years, anyhow. 'You're safe now. I'll look after you. Everything'll be alright again. Really it will. You'll see.'

It was a *Neighbours* repeat on the TV.

'It's awful,' she cried.

'It is. It's awful.' I leaned back to take a better look at her. 'I was here last night, you know, but they wouldn't let me stay. They wouldn't let me sit with you, not for ages.'

'They told me you were.'

She reached towards a packet of tissues and I drew one out for her.

'I was here for hours,' I said. 'I talked with you at one point. We had a conversation.'

'Did you? Did we? I don't remember?'

'You were out of it. You wanted Panadol. The police came by this morning, but you were… still snoring away.'

She smiled, but then gasped and began a new helter-skelter of crying. 'And Mum…'

'I know. I know.'

'I was such a bitch to her the other day,' she sobbed. 'We argued, Meg. If only we hadn't argued.'

'You mustn't blame yourself. It's the way she was.'

'She's dead. She's dead! I can't believe it.'

I passed the packet of tissues. 'That doesn't change the way she was. It doesn't make everything in the past our fault, you know.'

'I suppose not.'

'The past is just the past, that's all.'

She looked at me strangely for a second, but glanced at the TV and said, 'There was a fire on *Neighbours*.'

I remembered the episode. 'Can I turn it off?' I stood to find the switch, but she'd got a remote tucked in the crease of blanket at her side and simply pressed the Power button.

Walking to the window, I looked at the dull expanse of flat roofs below, then sat on the edge of her bed again. It seemed she was waiting for me to say something, as if she knew I had something to say. 'They think it was deliberate, Stell, and they can't find Victor. He's missing.'

She looked as if she was still waiting for me to speak, as if she hadn't heard me, but slowly shook her head, blinked and shifted her focus to the blank TV screen.

'Stella.'

Nothing.

'Stella! They can't find Dad.'

She sort of came back, but not completely, as if she was on the verge of drifting away. I'd only seen her vacant like that once before, when she was a little kid running a fever with mumps, and I automatically put my hand to her forehead.

'No,' she said.

'No what?'

She gradually returned from wherever she'd gone and I noticed again how pale she was and how weird her breathing was. The dark rings under her eyes looked like stains.

'I don't believe it,' she said. 'No.' Each breath was shallow and fast. She was beginning to pant. 'I won't believe it. I won't.'

I put my arms back around her. 'It's alright. It'll be alright.' But I reminded myself too that some of this was her fault. She'd played too big a hand in what had happened.

'They kept saying... last night... kept asking... about Dad.' Tiny breaths.

'It's alright, Stella.'

She pushed me off and struggled to swing her legs free, to clamber out of bed, regardless of the leads. She pulled the plastic clip off her finger, scratched at the tape that held the drip in her arm. 'Didn't imagine it.'

'Imagine what? What are you doing? Where do you think you're going?' She was panicking and the panic was rising in me too. 'Calm down, Stell. It'll be okay. Imagine what? What do you think you saw?'

Her words were quick, faint breaths: 'Why would he? Why would anyone...?'

I tried to hold her back, but she got the tangle of sheets out the way and slid from the bed. She stood for about two seconds before fainting.

I expected the nurses to tell me to leave, but the day shift was friendlier than the night shift.

'She probably got up too quickly,' one of them said, which is all they knew because she wasn't saying a lot when they helped her back to bed. 'Did you want the toilet?' she asked, but Stella's shoulders began to lift and she grabbed a tin bowl sitting on the side stand, and Stella threw up.

The other nurse smiled and said, 'Better out than in. Try and get her to drink a little when she's settled again. Just small sips though.'

One took away the sick bowl, while the other checked Stella's drip, placed the clip back on her finger, reset the monitor to read her temperature and held her wrist to take her pulse.

'That's fine,' she said after about a minute. 'How are you feeling?'

Stella shrugged. 'Better, I guess.' Her eyes were red and brimming, and she had me worried. I couldn't tell whether she was hiding something or not.

'She's been through a lot,' I added.

The nurse smiled again. 'A bit less woozy?'

Stella muttered something.

The nurse topped up the plastic beaker from the plastic jug of iced water and offered it to Stella. Even the ice cubes looked plastic. 'Sip this slowly and give us a call when you need the toilet.'

Five minutes later, Police Officer Wendy Aitkens arrived and I wondered where Mick was. She asked how I was and introduced herself to Stella.

'Do you feel well enough to tell us what you remember about last night?'

'She just passed out and vomited everywhere,' I pointed out, but she waited for Stella to reply.

'Can Meg stay?' Stella asked, which was a relief.

'If you'd like her to.'

Stella blew her nose, pulled the sheet up and sighed. 'What do you want to know?'

'Tell us everything you remember.'

'About the fire?'

'About what happened.'

'I'll try.' She coughed and took a sip of water, but it seemed now like she was putting on a bit of an act. 'I went to sleep around eleven, or just after,' she began, and her voice started off even weaker than before: more raw, as if dragged from the bottom of her throat. 'I must've gone straight off and been in a deep sleep because when I got woken – there was a loud crash or a shout or something – not sure what – it was almost two. I thought –'

Officer Aitkens stopped scribbling in her notebook. 'What was the exact time? Can you remember?'

She paused, considered. 'Um, yes, I do. I glanced at my phone. It was 1:47. I remember that.'

Stella's always been good with numbers.

Officer Aitkens made a note and motioned for her to continue.

'Anyway, I thought maybe I'd imagined it and must be dreaming, like how sometimes you dream you hear a noise and it seems real, but as I was drifting off again I smelt smoke.' She swallowed hard and took another sip of water. 'It was strong and I thought it must be a bushfire or a farmer burning off, so I looked out my window, but couldn't see anything.'

Stella stopped and seemed agitated again, so I held her hand.

'What happened next? Tell me everything you remember. Did you hear any more noises?'

'That's when I heard the smoke alarm, I think. It wasn't the one outside my room because the battery was flat and it'd been beeping away the week before so I took it down. But I realised the smoke was coming from inside the house, from under my door, and not from outside.' She appeared to drift into the memory and then shuddered. 'I know you're not supposed to open doors if you think there's a fire, but it was automatic; I couldn't help it. Anyway I didn't think it was a real fire. It never crossed my mind. My first thought was that Dad was having a midnight snack and had burnt the toast and that maybe it was him I'd heard banging about in the kitchen, except the smell was wrong. It was a different sort of smoke.'

She coughed some more and reached for the beaker of water again, but her actions were too considered. She hadn't been coughing like that before. All the same, the dark rings under her eyes were real enough.

'So you saw your father during the evening?'

'Dad? Yes.' And she almost smiled, but then winced.

Officer Aitkens wrote something else down, then said, 'Did he often get up in the night, your father, for midnight snacks or that sort of thing?'

'Not all the time, not often, not that I know of, but he used to complain about being a bad sleeper, didn't he, Meg?'

I nodded and stroked the back of her hand. 'He did.'

'It always took him a while to get his hours back to normal after he'd been on an overseas trip – jet lag – which is why he tried to keep those trips as short as possible.' Again she turned to me: 'Wasn't it?'

'It was.'

'How about your mother? Was she a good sleeper?'

Stella shrugged and I chipped in. 'She claimed she wasn't, didn't she, Stell? She said Dad always disturbed her sleep with his tossing and turning, stopped her from having a proper night's sleep herself, so she got a prescription she sometimes took – some sort of sleeping pill. I don't know whether she really needed them or not, or how often she took them.'

'Sometimes she'd sleepwalk,' Stella said.

'Who, Mum?'

'Yes, you both did, although you were the worst. You used to freak me out sometimes because I'd wake up and find you standing over me, but Dad laughed a couple of times about Mum doing it too.'

'I never knew that,' I said.

'Apparently she'd stopped for years, but recently – the last couple of years – she started again.'

Aitkens nodded and scribbled her notes. She glanced at what she'd written and said, 'You opened your bedroom door. Was the handle hot?'

'No, I don't think so. Why?'

'What happened then?'

'The hallway – it was full of smoke – I couldn't see a thing. It was thick. And the smoke alarm... I guess I panicked. I remember shouting out, screaming for Mum and Dad, and trying to get down the hallway, to call upstairs to them, but I couldn't get there because of the smoke. That's when I heard more bangs and crashes, as if things were falling and breaking, so I ran back to my room and climbed out the window.' Her voice was normal again now.

'Your room's on the ground floor?'

Stella and I both nodded.

'And their bedroom was upstairs?'

'They had the attic converted a few years back,' I said.

'And it was you who called Emergency Services, wasn't it?'

Stella nodded again.

'How did you do that?'

'What do you mean?' she asked, but then realised what she was after. 'Oh, I grabbed my phone before climbing out.'

'Smart girl.' Aitkens smiled, but I couldn't tell whether she was being genuine or if there was a hint of doubt there.

Stella's mobile was sitting in the plastic basket, on top of her clothes, and I was about to show her it was there, to prove Stella still had it with her, but she changed the subject.

'Did you see anyone or hear anything when you were outside, like voices or a car engine or anything?'

Stella was shaking now. Genuinely shaking. I could feel her hand trembling and see it in her clenched shoulders, and I wanted to stop the questions, but couldn't. She'd have to give a statement at some point and it'd be better if I was with her when she did.

She closed her eyes as if trying to remember. It took ages for her to reply. I wasn't sure what she was up to, but it worried me.

'No, nothing,' she said eventually, and pulled her knees up to her chin and pulled the sheet further up too. She dropped her head, rested her forehead on her knees for a few seconds before looking up again and shivering.

'Are you cold?' I asked.

The room was warm, but she said yes and so I began straightening her blanket and pulling it up for her. Aitkens had been standing at the end of the bed until then, but now she took my bag off the chair and sat.

'You're doing well,' she said. 'Just a few more questions before we leave it for the moment, okay?'

'Okay,' Stella agreed.

She lowered her notebook and gave Stella another encouraging smile. 'You'd had an argument with your mother, I gather, and you weren't planning on going back to the house for a few days. What made you decide to go back last night?'

Stella froze and spat a look at me, although I'd had no choice but to tell the police about the argument and why I was surprised she'd been home.

Closing her eyes, she took another couple of quick breaths and I wondered whether she was about to be sick again.

'Dad phoned and asked me to come home. He'd got back from his conference early and found out... well, that Mum and me had a falling out. It was just one of those silly things. It wasn't about anything really. Nothing important. We had a chat and a hug – you know, a mother-daughter moment – but she was tired so she went to bed early and... and I had a heap of homework to do, so I went to my room and did that and later I chatted online with friends for a while, and that's about it. It was no big deal. Really.'

I stared at her in disbelief, but then quickly looked away. She was lying and I couldn't think why. For starters, her argument with Mum had been the end of the world when she'd told me about it. I also knew that whatever was said, when she returned home, wouldn't have ended up in hugs all-round. No way. There'd have been a scene, a massive row. I'd have been surprised if Mother was talking to either her or Victor by the end of an evening like that.

As if this wasn't enough, Stella dug herself in deeper. She looked more relaxed now, as she brought her arms from under the bedding and wrapped them around her knees, embracing her legs, locking herself in place. She had a bit more colour.

'So, until your dad phoned, where had you been staying? Not with Meg?'

It was a trap. If Officer Aitkens had been briefed by

Mick Droyler, she'd have already known the answer, and I wondered why she was trying to trip her up?

Stella barely paused. 'With a friend in Lapishot,' she said. 'My best friend had a party the night before last, on Tuesday – Jasmine – it was her eighteenth. Wasn't it, Meg?'

It was easy for me to see her sleight of words because I knew the truth she was masking, and could see how she was trying to avoid telling an outright lie by giving two unrelated answers, but it wasn't right and it wasn't fair that she should try and make me complicit in this of all things.

All the same, the police must be familiar with this type of evasion because straightaway Aitkens said: 'So you were staying with this Jasmine friend? Is that what you're saying? You stayed with her overnight?' She was shrewder than she looked.

I couldn't let Stella get caught out, though. She hadn't a clue how much I'd told Mick Droyler over coffee.

'I thought you were staying with your new boyfriend,' I said as pointedly as I could.

She hesitated, but turned her hesitation into a cough and said, 'Only for a short while.' Although she stared at me a bit too long.

'We'll need names and addresses,' Aitkens told her.

'Why?' She seemed surprised.

'Because the fire was deliberately started and your mother died as a result, and because your father's missing. This is a very serious investigation, Stella. We need to know everything that might be relevant.'

'I don't see why any of that's relevant.'

'That's not for you to decide.'

She bit her lip and stared straight ahead, avoiding both of us.

I put my arm round her, tried to encourage her, but it

was easy to see where this was going. It reminded me of the early stages of a chess game being played out, with one predictable move after another falling into place, but Stella never had the patience for chess – all that looking ahead and mapping of possible moves. 'Stella,' I said. 'Come on.'

She didn't respond. She sat there, chin against her knees, all locked up, biting her lip and staring at nothing.

It was Officer Aitkens who broke the stalemate. She turned to me and said, 'Meg, would you mind leaving us for a few minutes?'

I wanted Stella to protest, but of course she didn't.

'Stella needs me here,' I said, except Stella wouldn't say anything and I could see she was crying.

I wanted to turn and tell her I knew who she'd been staying with and how she'd betrayed me, but I couldn't. If I'd done this, I'd have had to explain exactly how I knew and then too much else might come spilling out, which would've been the end of it: *The End*. No *Happy ever after*.

'I'll call you back when we're ready,' Aitkens said. 'Thank you, Meg.'

It's not as though I was given a choice. I headed towards the waiting area and heard the door to Stella's room being shut.

I stared out the window at the mish-mash of hospital buildings below, at the city skyline, at the forested horizon, but it was hard to focus on anything. Over and over, I told myself I'd survive. Whatever it took. By hook or by crook. Even if I had to nail Peter-bloody-Lailer to a cross in the process. Amongst the scatter of magazines on the table was the *National Geographic* I'd tried skimming through the previous night, and I flicked it open at an article that half-interested me – *Of Venice and Vampires* – except I couldn't stop thinking about what Stella was saying.

Ten minutes passed before I was summoned back. Officer Aitkens had her cap in hand and looked ready to leave. There was nothing in her expression I could read, but she handed us each a card and said, 'I'll leave you two to talk, but if either of you remember anything else here are my contact details.' After she'd squeezed past, I shut the door behind her.

Stella was less agitated for having had her little chit-chat without me. She was sheepish, perhaps, but that was all. This from the little sister I've always looked after.

I waited, but she said nothing.

'What?' I said, and sat down. The seat of the chair was still warm. 'What was all that about?'

'Try not to be cross, Meg.'

'About what? What's going on?'

'I know you're going to hate me. Try not to hate me.'

'What?' I said again. 'What can you tell her that you can't tell me?'

I gave myself a point: word perfect, not a glance out of place. This was the way it had to be. For both our sakes.

She raked her fingers through her hair and drew out a tress in front of her face, as if to examine it for split ends, but then self-consciously brushed it back and placed one hand in the other. She was always playing with her hair or fixing it, was Stella – stroking it back, putting it up, shaking it down, straightening it or curling it – because she knew her hair was blonde and gorgeous, but at that moment it was dull and lank. 'This isn't going to be easy,' she said, 'but it's not as if... Well, you remember how, the other morning, when I phoned you, I said I wanted to discuss something important? That I had a big favour to ask?'

I waited, said nothing, until she began to insist: 'I *did* say that. I was going to talk about it with you.'

'Yeah, I remember.'

'Well, it was to do with my boyfriend. The one I was staying with.'

'I know. You told me that much. I asked whether you wanted to bring him over to Angie's. I was trying to help you, like I always do.'

She looked away.

'For goodness sake, Stell –'

'Meg... it's... He's... the same boy you used to go out with – a few years ago.'

I let several seconds pass. A solid moment.

'Pete? Peter Lailer?'

She nodded. 'Honestly, I didn't realise who he was at first. Really, I didn't. I didn't make the connection, and he didn't realise I was your sister, not to begin with. We've only been going out a couple of weeks or so. But, as soon as I realised, I tried to talk about it with you; I wanted to. I didn't want to hurt you. Wanted to make sure you were okay with it. That's what I meant when – well, over the phone – it was never the right moment. You were always working or I was... It just sort of happened, Meg, and, well, you know...'

I sat there. Silence has its own nuances. Timing is every-thing. 'What? What do I know?' Silence. 'How could you?'

'He's important to me, Meg. Really important. It was too late by the time I realised.'

'He was important to me too!' The words slipped out before I could stop them. I didn't mean to say it and wished it had never been true, but there it was. All that mattered now was that I get her away from him. 'No, Stella. You can't have anything to do with him. You have to keep away from him. He's bad news.' Then, with more bitterness than I could ever have faked: 'I know things about him you don't.'

They were wasted words. She'd stopped listening and was

crying again, staring at the blankets and shaking her head. 'No, that's not fair. I love him, Meg. He loves me too. It's more than three years since you and him...'

I wanted to grab her and shake her. 'No, listen, you can't. Not just because of me. He's bad news. I mean it.'

'What? Why's he bad news? Why shouldn't I see him?'

There was no way to tell her. I didn't know how to say it and I had to be careful. 'Just take it from me, he's a royal bastard. You can't see him. You mustn't. I mean it.' It was the best I could do and I hoped it'd be enough – for that to be an end to it – so I didn't have to think about it anymore. I wished that could have been the end to it all.

She blew her nose and looked at me strangely again, the way she had earlier. 'Sometimes you sound exactly like Mum,' she said. 'You even look like her when you talk like that.'

It was a slap in the face. She knew what she was saying. After everything I'd done and the way I'd always looked after her. For a moment, I wanted to slap her back. I stared at her, but swallowed hard and blew my nose. There were secrets I didn't want Stella to know – anyone to know – unless there was no other choice. At least I could be glad of the graffiti.

I looked down at my fingers. Took a moment. Considered. Dad taught me how to play chess, but more often than not I'd beat him.

'Did you know he's an Animal Libber?' I eventually said.

'Who? Pete?'

'Yes. If you must know, he's right into it – hard core. The A.A.R.'

'Since when?' she began and her confusion was clear, but then she said: 'So what? That doesn't mean anything?'

I shook my head as if she was being stupid. 'Stella, the

police think it was Action for Animal Rights who started the fire. It was them before and they think it was them again.'

'No, you're just saying that.'

'Pete Lailer's part of that.'

'No.'

She slid from crying to wailing again, my little sister, and I hated having to do all this, really I did, but it was for her own good – our own good. Her words were snotty and wet, but there was a thread of doubt there too.

The door opened and one of the nurses from earlier stood looking bewildered for a moment. 'Is everything okay?' she asked.

'He's using you like he used me,' I told Stella. 'And he'd have known you were my sister. Of course he did. That's the sort of creep he is.'

'No, I don't believe it,' she sobbed. 'No, he didn't. I know he didn't.'

'He's A.A.R.'

'What's going on?' the nurse said. 'I think maybe you should go now. Let your sister rest, eh?'

I picked up my bag and was in tears now too. I'm never in tears, not normally, but these had been the shittiest couple of days and I knew I had to leave before I said too much.

'He wouldn't... No... I can't...' she blubbered.

'Think about it, Stella. Where do you think Dad is? They've probably got Dad too.' Which made me cry even more.

We were blubber and flubber, us two.

People say I look like my mother and that Stella looks like Victor, but that's not true. People walk about with their eyes shut or they see what they expect to see. They say I have her eyes and her mouth, but that's nonsense. Besides, it's personality that counts, not looks, and we were chalk and cheese, her and me – always. I used to think I was more like Victor, but I don't think so anymore. I am my own person.

SIX

Pete and I, we shared paradise for a day. And then it unravelled.

It's a second day of butterflies. Cabbage whites. They fill the sky – possessing and possessed by it – and the sky rings like a polished wineglass with the sharp clarity of its blueness. It's so wide and high and clear that, again, there's a cinematic, dream-like quality to the day. I look up, up, up, until I imagine I'm looking down, down, down, into a flittering universe of white wings dancing the vast cerulean blue, and there's nothing to tell up and down apart. I turn round and round, diving into the day, until I'm dazzled and dizzied by the sharpness of the sun, by the knife-edge highlights of this Technicolor-rich world and by the deepest, richest shadows a person could imagine.

I've arranged to meet Pete at Angie's, but my mother interrogates me before I leave and perhaps I'm a little too vivacious in my enthusiasm for the day; as if that should be a sin.

'You were over there most of yesterday. I'd have thought you could just give that cat of hers enough food for a meal or two and be done with it. Don't you have homework to do?' She smiles, but I'll realise later it was part of her act.

'I'll do it there. It's quiet there.'

'It's hardly noisy here. What with your dad away and Stella at her sleep-over, I'd have thought you'd be making the most of it.'

'I like the atmosphere at Angie's. Besides, Gustav's a bit highly strung; he starts going bonkers if he's left cooped up in the laundry all the time. He'd probably claw the washing machine to death or something.'

She raises her eyebrows and returns to her dusting. I can't get over how much time she spends cleaning and tidying, especially when Dad's away for more than a couple of days. It's almost obsessive. I'm learning to bite my tongue about weird parental behaviours, though, because I got into a massive argument for commenting on it not long ago.

She picks up one of her silver-framed photographs of Stella and me in our first years of Primary School and gives it a quick flick before wiping the sideboard on which it sits, between the cut-glass sherry decanter and one of her precious Wedgwood vases. 'Anyone would think you don't have a home of your own.'

She can't quash my happiness. It's heedless to the point of being reckless. 'I'll practice the piano while I'm there. It's such a beautiful day, don't you think?'

Her silence might be taken in any number of ways, but I totally misread it at the time. She polishes the fingerprints off the decanter, then lifts and polishes the stopper before dropping it back in place with a clink. I run upstairs, two at a time and grab my bag.

Pete's sitting in his car, listening to music, waiting for me. He's early.

I haven't had Betsy, my little blue bomb, long – just a few

weeks after getting my P-plates – and I love the quick freedom of her, even if she's a bit small and old-fashioned. I still have to catch the school bus because Year 11 students aren't allowed to drive to school, but no longer do I have to cycle over to Angie's, pushing against the wind; not unless it's a beautiful day and I want a different sort of freedom.

He's parked on the road in the broad shade of a gun oak, near Angie's drive, and he's obviously got the air-con running because all the windows are shut. I pull alongside in Betsy and blow him a kiss and he unwinds his window.

'You park in the garage,' I tell him. 'I'll pull up behind.'

It's not that I'm worried about her neighbours, because the closest farmhouse is well and truly too far away for them to have a clue who's calling or what's going on, but I feel I should be discreet nonetheless. It's more instinct than wisdom.

After he's parked his car, he stands and waits to open my door for me.

'Hi,' he says. He dips his sunglasses, which are dripping with reflections, and grins.

'Hi.'

'It's a warm one,' he says, sliding his sunnies into the breast pocket of his shirt.

'It's a beautiful day,' I say. 'I wish every day was like this.'

'Me too.'

We kiss with me pressed up against one side of Betsy and there's a delicious urgency in our kissing, the fierceness of our embrace. When my bag slips off my shoulder and I drop my keys, I notice the short shadow stretching out from Betsy – the shadow we're standing in – is purple, which is the first time I've noticed how shadows can have colour.

'Look at this,' I say to Pete, picking up my keys. 'She's got a purple shadow.' I move my hand through it to see if my skin will be purple too.

'It's just a shadow,' he says, stroking his fingers through my hair.

Maybe it's a combination of things – our memory of yesterday, the closeness of our embrace, the prospect of making love again shortly – but even though it's only twenty paces or so from my car to the front door, we walk across the lawn tightly holding hands. It feels to me as if we're both frightened of letting go of one another, as if we're too aware we're stepping from one significant moment to another and that both these moments are bigger than we are. By stepping into this new moment, we each believe we'll grow into it – well, I do – but that doesn't make it any less awesome. At the same time, I'm beginning to feel almost as though this part of my life has been somehow cast into a film, and while there's a thrill to this heightened sense of being (through knowing the weight of each breath, being able to unpeel the tones in each colour and shadow), I don't want it to become so much so that it turns plastic and unreal.

At the front door we manage to let go of one another and Pete pushes his hands through his hair while I fumble at fitting my key into the lock. The verandah sits in shade, but the butterfly bush – *Buddleja macroflora* – which overhangs one end, casts a shadow that might be burnt umber or sepia.

With the door shut behind us, we tumble into kissing again. It's a tumbling and falling headlong. Down, down, down. Intoxicating.

His hands steal their way inside my T-shirt; I have one hand in the back pocket of his jeans and one hand fumbling with the buttons of his shirt.

Down, down, down.

I open my eyes and look past him into the hallway.

'Wait,' I say, breathless, pulling myself back.

'What's up?'

It's stuffy in the house and the light is more subdued with the blinds and curtains half-shut, so I need to open them and throw wide a few windows, but I really should see to Gustav too. I want this to be right, as if it's our house and we belong here, not jammed up in a dark corner against the front door, with all these other things that need to be dealt with pressing in on me.

Pete follows me into the kitchen and into Angie's study, but he drifts off into the lounge while I'm stroking Gustav and cleaning out the litter tray. I run upstairs to let the light and air into those rooms as well, and downstairs I can hear Pete tentatively tapping out a few notes on the Bechstein. There's no tune to it.

'I wish I could play the piano,' he says when I join him.

I draw the curtains fully back, raise the blinds and open the French windows. Later, we could sit on the verandah sipping iced tea (if there's any in the fridge), looking out across the garden at the forest. I might play for him too.

'You should learn,' I tell him. 'I could teach you the basics, if you like.'

'If I could play, I'd start my own band. You should do something like that. How long have you been playing? How long would it take to learn, do you reckon?'

'I don't know. I started when I was little. I was seven.'

'Ten years? I wouldn't have the patience for that.' He runs his fingers across several notes in a trill and I'm about to show him where Middle C is, how to play a couple of chords. 'I think I'd rather play the guitar,' he decides. 'A guitar's more sexy, don't you think?'

I shrug and can't help but smile. 'My sister plays the flute,' I say, and have no idea why I'm telling him this. 'She used to play the piano, but now she plays the flute.'

'At least you can carry a flute around with you. I don't think you'd be lugging this thing around from gig to gig, would you?'

'I don't play for other people. I've never wanted to. I play because I like the way music works.'

'Really? What a waste.' He hits one note and then another. 'The white ones are ivory, aren't they? Elephant tusk.'

'Ebony and ivory,' I say, laying my fingers across the keys, for the sake of touching them. Ghosting a song: C Major, F Major, G Major, A Minor, F Major. 'I don't mind playing for friends – special friends.'

'Would you play for me?'

'I might do. Later. We'll see.' And I gently close the fall-board over the keys, knowing full-well I will.

'Later?' he says, putting his arms around me.

'Later,' I say.

With the French windows open to our beautiful morning, the room is flooded with fresh light and the air is a warm current we could happily swim in and drown in together. It'd be the easiest thing in the world today, now we're moving towards that hallelujah moment. We kiss and press against one another and there are things I do, like bite his lip and rake my fingers through his hair, down his back, which I've never known to do before, but which grow naturally out of the moment and being with him, like reflexes never called upon before. Similarly, I know it'd be 'liberating' – I can think of no better word – to undress one another and make love right here, with the outside day flowering in through the French windows and brushing against us, almost as if we were out in the garden itself.

Except I think about Angie's rug and not wanting to

leave a stain and spoil things between her and me, and I know we should stop and move upstairs. He kisses my neck and unhooks my bra, and I want to melt – to melt into him, with him – and I take his belt and loosen the buckle.

If he was to take me into the garden right now, I'd let him. I'd run naked into the forest with him. Away and away.

'I would unhook the moon for you,' I whisper against his ear, and mean it.

It was Angie who taught me this beautiful expression – 'Je décrocherais la lune pour toi' – when she was helping me with my French homework once, but it's being with Pete that's taught me what it means. It'd sound corny if I said it to him in French, though, and he wouldn't understand anyway, so I whisper it in English.

We are both breathless and all we can do is whisper.

He looks at me. 'What?'

I shake my head. 'Come on. Let's go upstairs,' I say.

He holds the waist of his trousers with one hand and lets me lead him awkwardly upstairs by the other.

We have the sheet over us and he's on top of me, his face buried against my neck and shoulder; I can feel his heart pounding against my breast, can feel his warm breath panting next to my ear. He's come (again too quick), but he's still inside me and I have my arms around him. I'm gazing at the bleached, white ceiling and enjoying holding him here like this.

That's what makes me realise: when the light changes. It's only a whisper; not like the sun has been blotted by a cloud or anything, but as if a breeze has moved the bedroom door. When I shift my gaze to look down, past the foot of the bed, she's standing there.

I gasp and stiffen, and Pete winces at my sudden

movement. He begins to turn, but I hold him where he is.

She's standing in the doorway. My mother.

'Well I never,' she says.

Pete tries to lift himself again, to see what's going on, but I can save him this embarrassment and I draw my hand up so it's behind his head.

'What are you doing here?' I ask.

'I thought I'd bring you some sandwiches for lunch and see how your homework was going, but I can see you're... busy.'

I close my eyes and am aware of a cramp growing in my leg. I'm aware of Pete's penis slipping out of me. When I open my eyes, she's still there, steely-eyed, hard-mouthed. There's no way she'd have merely come over to bring me lunch. That's not the sort of thing she'd do. Not ever. I know she's checking up on me.

'I didn't hear you arrive,' I say, but it's hard to get the words out with Pete a dead weight on top of me.

'The French windows were wide open,' she points out. Then she says, 'You can explain yourself later.' And she turns and leaves.

This time I hear her footsteps on the stairs and I hear the front door closing behind her.

'Who was that?' Pete says.

'That was my mother.'

'Shit,' he says. 'Oh fuck.' And laughs.

'Get off me now,' I tell him. 'Move off. You're hurting me.'

He slides off and I pull the sheet up to my neck, and I'm listening for her car door or for the engine to start, but it doesn't. The light in the room has completely changed now. The colours have faded, the brightness wilted.

I sit up and get out of bed, pulling the sheet off to drape

around me, leaving Pete naked and curling on the mattress, while I stand at the window.

'The bitch,' I say. 'She parked down the road, a couple of hundred metres away. She did that on purpose.'

'I don't see why I should feel as though we've done something wrong. We haven't. We're not children. I'm not a child.'

We're downstairs, in the kitchen. There's a blue Tupperware box on one corner of the table, with a few sandwiches and an apple in it, but I know her better than that. She must have been suspicious – I was too enthusiastic – but she'd have needed an excuse to check up on me. She hasn't made sandwiches for me in years.

'I'll come back with you, if you want,' Pete says. 'So it's not just you.'

'Would you? Would you really do that?'

'If you want me to. Maybe they'll realise then.'

'It's just her. Dad's away on business at the moment.'

'Even better. Maybe she won't go off at you if I'm there.'

'She might go off at both of us.' I'm gnawing at the skin of my fingers and I'm angry – so angry – but we'll get over this. We'll get over this because Pete's the best thing that's happened to me. I have to hold onto that.

He puts an arm round me and draws me close. 'Really? Would she? Well, I'll still come with you if you want.'

'Thanks, Pete. That means a lot. Honestly. There's not many blokes who'd do that, I don't think.'

'Your dad won't sack me when he finds out, will he? That could be awkward.'

I shrug.

'You can always say we weren't doing anything, but just fooling about,' he continues. 'You could say we hadn't gone the whole way.'

'I don't think so.'

'Well, you could tell your mum it's not just a casual thing, but that I'm serious about you.'

'You don't know her. You don't know what she's like. She's so old-fashioned. Uptight and old-fashioned. She even gives my dad a hard time. Sometimes I haven't a clue how they ended up together. They're so... unsuited.'

He smiles at that, I smile at that, because we're not like that. It's our last moment of confidence in one another.

After I've stripped the bed, done the laundry, sent Pete on his way, I have to return and face her. There's no point in staying at Angie's. I won't be able to do homework now and I certainly can't play the piano.

It's a horrible drive and, when I pull up and park Betsy in the driveway, I don't want to get out. In the space of an hour or two, one of the best days of my life has become one of the worst. I haven't a clue what's going to happen next.

My mother is on the phone in the sitting room when I walk in, and I hear her saying: 'She's here now. She's just walked in the door. I'll speak to you later.' A few seconds pass and she calls out to me. 'I think you owe me an explanation, don't you? What have you got to say for yourself? That was your father and he's not well pleased with you, as I'm sure you can imagine.'

The sitting room was the darkest room in the house because the windows looked out onto one side of the garage, which blocked most of the natural light, and yet it was always regarded as the 'best room'. It was Mum and Dad's posh room, where they entertained visitors, so we always had to be extra careful not to wear out the carpet, not to place drinks on the side tables without mats (lest they leave a stain), not to scuff the upholstery. When we were kids we didn't play in this room, but even as adults got told not to slouch on the sofa, not to perch on the arms of the chairs, to put the cushions back how we found them. With its heavy curtains, dark-varnished woods and stink of polish, along with the boring prints of one still life after another, it always felt more like a shrine to a previous age than a room to relax in and, but for the piano (an upright Steinway), I didn't often go in there.

'He was quite upset,' she says.

'That's the first thing you do, ring Dad? What's the point of that?' I'm standing in the doorway and all I want is to fast-forward to a better moment and a better place than this.

She gets up from the armchair and smoothes her skirt. 'He phoned here, if you must know. But he certainly has every right to know what you're up to; he's your father.'

She appears calmer than I imagined so maybe she's going to be okay about this. Maybe she somehow understands, woman-to-woman and all that. Nonetheless, I'm embarrassed and I'm not sure what to say. I don't believe her about the phone call, but I let it go.

'Thanks for the sandwiches,' I try.

She blinks. 'What on earth do you think... after everything... How dare you?' She points a finger down at the settee in front of her. 'You come and sit there, young lady. You sit down right there.'

I place my bag on the carpet, the damned lunchbox on the sideboard and I move to the settee, but she doesn't sit down and neither do I. She stands staring at me, she looks me up and down as though I'm something a stray cat's dragged in, and I try to look abashed. I want this to be over and so I look down for a moment, but I can't stay that way for long. It's not who I am.

'What?' I say.

'I hope you're ashamed of yourself.'

I look her square in the face and take a moment to consider, even though I know the answer. I won't betray any part of my relationship with Pete. I won't. I'd definitely reach up and unhook the moon for him if I could. 'No, I'm not. I've done nothing I'm ashamed of. I'm a little embarrassed perhaps, but –'

'Don't start your word-games with me, Margaret Dapsy. Not now. Not after what you've put me through?'

'What have I put you through?'

'You might not be ashamed of yourself, but I am. Can you imagine what it was like for me finding you... like that? My own daughter! To say nothing of the fact you lied to me, have been lying to me for goodness knows how long.'

'When did I lie?'

'In pretending you were going to Angie Morel's to feed that cat of hers and do your schoolwork, when really what you were doing... Do you know what men call girls like you? Girls who do what you were doing?'

I bristle, but I'm more than ready to let her damn herself. 'What?'

'Sluts, tramps, tarts. There's nothing clever about what you were doing. You think you're so clever, but that's not clever. Anyone can do that. Women who can't do anything else get paid to do that. And as for whoever it was you were with, he won't stick by you. He'll take what he wants and then he'll drop you. He'll drop you as soon as look at you.'

'Did you just call me a slut? Are you calling me a whore? My own mother –'

'And you needn't start putting words in my mouth either.'

'You –'

'Oh, Meg, how could you? How could you? How could you cheapen yourself like that?'

'No! I haven't cheapened myself. I love him. He loves me.'

'You were in bed with him. You let him... You're only seventeen.'

'I didn't "let him" do anything – him more than me. It's not like it used to be in your day, you know. We decided together. It's not unusual –'

She snorts in contempt. 'Well, how very grown up.'

'Other people... Lots of my friends –'

'You're not other people. Your father and I didn't bring you up to throw yourself at the first boy who comes along – the first thing in trousers that turns your eye. Do you know how common it makes you look?'

'I –'

I'm about to say something, to protest, but she holds her hand up and points her finger at me. She shakes her head and says, 'Tell me you used something. Tell me you took preautions. You'd better not be... I won't have it. I won't have you throwing everything away. How could you?'

'Contraceptives?' I delight in using the word she can't. 'Of course we did. We're not stupid. There's no way I'm going to get pregnant.'

She sits down, back in the armchair, but I remain standing.

'There are times when I don't know you, when I don't know who you are anymore.'

I can imagine this. I really can. I think it must be hard for parents when their children leave them far behind. 'I know,' I say.

Things are calming down, I reckon, as if we're past the worst. She was worried about me getting pregnant and what people might say about her, and I wish I could reach out and touch her. I wish we could hug and cry and understand one another, and so I sit down too, but she stands then and walks to the window.

'Who was he? Who was the boy?'

My hands are clenched and I must have been biting the inside of my lip because I can taste blood. 'His name's Pete. We met a few weeks ago.' I'm not going to tell her how this weekend was our first time together, nor that it was my first time with anyone, because those words don't belong to her; it's not the sort of thing I should have to say, especially to her and especially not as a defence. 'He's not just anyone, like you said; he's special. He wanted to come back with me and meet you.'

'I don't want to know.' She's got her arms crossed and I wonder what she could be looking at outside. There's a creeper, a white-flowering japonica, which smothers the end of the garage, a section of the roof and some of the side, and I wonder if she's looking at that. All the same, I'm glad of it.

She says nothing for a minute, but I know I can't get up and leave yet; she'd spring back at me. I can see how tightly wound she is and I hope I never grow to be like her.

'You'd like him, Mum,' I say. 'I'm sure you would.'

'I told you, I don't want to know.'

'Okay.'

Maybe I can leave. I stand and wait a couple of seconds to see if she'll notice.

'Peter who?' she says suddenly. She's turned away from the window and is staring at me as if I might be a stranger she's discovered in her home.

I hesitate and draw a long breath. There's an unmistakeable edge to her tone. 'Why? I didn't think you wanted to know.' Perhaps I've told her too much already. 'Why do you want to know?'

'I take it he does have a surname, a last name? That you've actually bothered to find out that much?'

Behind the coldness of her stare is an icy anger and it warns me she hasn't fully risen to her anger yet. Things aren't calming down at all.

'Of course I have. I told you, we met a –'

'Yes, a few weeks ago, so you say.'

'We did. Why would I –'

'Which is why you've been scuttling off to Angie Morel's like... well, like a bitch on heat, and why you haven't thought to bring him home before or mentioned him even once. Not that I'd want to meet him now, after –'

'How dare you! I hate you!'

She remains arms-crossed, pinched tight and frozen, and this makes me want to shout and scream even louder.

'I hate you!' I tell her again and head for the door, but in a couple of strides she's there before me and pushes the door shut. We're closed, the two of us, in this dark cage of a room.

'Of course you do,' she says. 'Although I'm not particularly proud of you at the moment either.'

I'm crying and I turn away, but she doesn't give a damn. I always get her wrong. I always think she's going to be nicer than she is.

'So, what is it?' she demands. 'I'm waiting. What's his last name? Do you actually know? I'll ground you until you've finished school; your father will take away your car keys if you don't –'

'Why? What are you going to do? You're not going to phone him or anything. I'm not going to tell you if that's what you're going to do. I won't.'

'Don't be ridiculous.'

'You promise? You have to promise. You're not going to wreck this for me.'

'I've told you once. Now stop being ridiculous. I have every right to know. You don't think for one moment, do you, that I'd let you go out again unless I know who you're with?'

I drag out my tissue and blow my nose. There's not much choice but to tell her. At least she'll have to accept that I'm serious about him and mean to keep seeing him. Maybe, when everything calms down and they're used to the idea, they'll even let Pete stay over. There are girls in my class at school who regularly sleep with their boyfriends, and their parents are fine with it.

'Lailer. His name's Pete Lailer.'

We're facing one another when I tell her, and it'd make my day if she swung everything about and said, 'That's a nice name.' But of course she won't. She's looking at me and waiting, as if she's expecting me to say something else.

'Peter Lailer?'

'Yes. He lives out at Mirton, on the other side of Lapishot. He's a computer technician – very clever.'

She's nodding and, stupidly, I think she's impressed, but she pauses for so long it seems she's thinking something else through, and that worries me. 'So he works does he?' She's too distant though, as if talking to herself rather than me.

I'm frightened I've told her more than I should. Even so, my relationship with Pete is the best thing that's happened and I've got to get through this if I'm ever going to bring him home. 'Only this year though. He's working so he can get money together and then he'll start uni next year. He's got a place, but he deferred.'

'And he works at Demlab, I suppose?'

'Yes. How do you know?' Momentarily, it occurs to me she might know his mother; that perhaps they're in the same embroidery group or something. Stranger coincidences have happened.

She shakes her head and says, 'I didn't. I guessed.'

It strikes me now I might have cost him his job. 'I'll bring him home,' I quickly offer. 'You can meet him. He wanted to come back with me today and meet you, but...'

She turns, begins to open the door, but shuts it again and turns back to me. She's even more agitated than before, but exhausted with it, and a speck of me might feel guilty at being responsible for this, until she raises a finger and starts wagging it in my face.

'Now you listen to me and you listen well. You will *not* see that boy again. Do you hear? He will never be welcome here. Not ever. You're going to tell him it's over between the two of you, and that'll be the end of it.' She pauses, but she's still got her finger in my face and all I can do is stand there. 'But, mark my words, my girl, if you go behind my back then I'll put an end to it myself. Do you understand?'

'No! You can't say that. You can't stop me. You can't stop me from having a boyfriend.'

'I can and I will. I am.'

'No. You can't decide who I see and who I don't see. This isn't the nineteenth century. You don't own me. You can't say that.'

'Oh yes I can. While you're living under my roof, I can. You're only seventeen and I'm your mother and I'm telling you here and now that you are not to see that boy again. Not under any circumstances.'

'I'm not a child and neither is he. Why are you being like this? Just because Dad's away —'

'I'll ground you. You won't go out without my say-so. Your father will take your car keys off you. He will. And you certainly won't go over to Angie Morel's anymore. I'll see her myself and make sure of it. I'll phone the Principal if I have to. You'll go to school and come directly home and that'll be an end to it. Mark my words.'

'No! Why? That's not fair. What have you got against Pete? What's he done to you? Nothing! You're just being mean, spiteful, because we're young and love one another, and you're... you're –'

'What? What am I?'

'I hate you. You're hateful.'

'One day, you'll thank me.'

'Like heck I will. For what? For wrecking my life?'

'For saving you from yourself. Because you're too headstrong to know any better.'

'Well, if that means ending up like you, then no thank you very much. I never want to be like you.'

'No, I know you don't.' She sort of smiles to herself and relaxes a little. 'But we're more alike than you realise.'

I swallow, look her in the eyes. 'I *will* see Pete. One way or another. We haven't broken any law and you can't stop us. You can't.'

The certainty of this makes me triumphant. Whatever else, I know she can't take this away from me.

She slaps me across the face then and I'm too stunned to react, but I refuse to run howling from the room, even if my face is stinging and my eyes are watering. I'm not going to give her the satisfaction. Instead, I make a point of holding my head up, jutting my chin out. 'Does that make you feel better, hitting me?'

She almost slaps me again. She tenses, holds herself rigidly upright and says, 'When did you stop being such a bright, clever thing and turn into a silly little tramp, I wonder?'

There are lots of things I could say and should say, but instead I snap back, 'When you stopped being my mother and turned into a miserable, old bitch.' This time I push past her and run crying from the room. I can't help myself.

'You come back here this minute, young lady, and apologise. If you think —'

But I'm upstairs and almost in my room before she finishes.

Sometimes it's our memories that haunt us. It's as if, instead of owning particular memories, we're owned by them. We might think of the past as dead and gone, and believe we should be able to bury it in the deepest grave without fear of it rising up, but we're wrong.

Some memories are so icy sharp in their vividness that the instant they touch us it's like being returned in the emotional flesh to the moment of their origin, and we're no longer free to do anything except act out each frame in each scene of that memory even as it burns at our skin. It doesn't matter how long ago they took place (like that shitty day with Gilbert or that perfect first time with Pete), our memory of the past becomes the present — the here-and-now. We might like to change what we did or what we said, or sometimes to stay completely with a moment, but we can't. Good or bad, these moments are hauntings that lock a part of us into the always-present of a particular time and place, so that it's always still happening even when we're not thinking about it and will always be happening, forever and ever, and from which we can't escape. We are our own ghosts.

There are other times, though, when the opposite occurs

and the immediate present thickens into a foggy swamp. The atmosphere is so dense and still that existence is like being trapped between layers of thick glass. You can try and move but you don't really get anywhere, you can try and speak but you don't really say anything; your remote actions and words belong to the detachment of the place rather than to what you were really hoping to do or say. It's like watching yourself in a film or sleep-walking through a script somebody else has written. The here-and-now is simply part of an act that belongs to a different being in a different age. Not you, not yours; not me, not mine.

It makes us almost innocent of our actions.

I slammed my bedroom door and wedged the top rail of my desk chair under the door handle. I'd never done that before.

Burying my face in a pillow, I replayed everything that was said – the entire scene – over and over in my head, wishing I'd said this or done that, and ready to storm downstairs at one point to start the argument rolling again so I could. But I knew she wouldn't listen. Whatever I said wouldn't make a blind bit of difference. Instead, I wouldn't say another word to her until I'd spoken with Dad. He'd listen to reason.

But what of Pete? I still had the smell and taste of him on me. The scent of his aftershave was tangled up in my hair. Of course we'd keep seeing one another. No one could stop us. It wasn't like he was a rapist or an axe murderer and, well, she'd just have to like it or lump it. It was simple.

I grabbed my mobile. There was a text message from him: **How's things? All ok?** And so I phoned back.

'What happened?' he asked. 'How d'you go with your mum?'

'We had a massive row,' I told him, and was about to share a few details, but decided to play it down. 'It doesn't matter what I do or what I want, it's never good enough for her. She's so out of touch with reality.' I looked at the posters around my room and couldn't help wondering why I'd kept them all this time. Two were of a band I'd once listened to a lot (action shots that captured the sweaty energy of the lead singer); one was a black and white photo of a model I once believed was beautiful and who, for a desperate month or two, I wanted to become; and one was a large, dog-eared print of Van Gogh's *Starry Night*, which I'd bought on a school trip to the National Art Gallery. They'd decorated my walls for so long I couldn't remember when I last properly saw them, but I certainly wasn't the girl who'd Blu-Tacked them there anymore. As for Albert, my one-eyed teddy in his green sweater, it struck me as infantile and embarrassing to have him lying next to me, especially with Pete on the phone, and so I opened the bottom drawer of my bedside table, scooped my knickers to one side and shoved him in.

'She called me some awful names,' I told Pete, 'and, well, I don't imagine we'll be talking to one another for a while.' There was no way I could tell him everything, otherwise he'd think my mother was an absolute nutter and he'd be too scared to come near me again. 'It's probably best if we cool things for a week or two, until Dad's back home and she's calmed down. Probably best if I have a couple of weekends at home and be the good little girl.'

'Really? Was it that bad?'

'You could always come and see me during lunchtime in the week, at school. I could get a pass easily enough. I'll fake the signature. And we could meet in town later, when classes are finished. My bus never leaves until after four —'

'But I'll be at work. I could probably get across at lunch for a short while, but not after school. I don't finish till five.'

'Oh yeah, I was forgetting that.'

'I won't see you properly for two whole weeks? Is that what you're saying?'

'It's probably for the best. But we can meet at lunchtime, can't we?' I kept my voice down in case she had her ears flapping downstairs or had sneaked up to listen outside my door.

'I guess. Although it won't be the same.'

'Well, of course it won't, but if the old dragon finds out I'm even doing that much she's likely to have me locked into a chastity belt and shut up in a tall tower, and you'll have to come and rescue me.' The idea brought a bitter and brittle laugh. 'Are you game for that?'

He didn't answer, so I said: 'Are you there? Pete?'

'Yeah, sure – sorry. I think my phone's on the way out. I dropped it when I was crossing the road. The screen's got a massive crack in it.'

I wanted to be with him more than anything. The weekend had made that clear. I didn't want to just talk to him on the phone with kilometres and kilometres of forest, paddocks and country roads between us. If only I could turn the clock back and fix it so she hadn't discovered us in bed; if only we could've enjoyed a whole unblemished day with one another, again and again.

We were like Romeo and Juliet, a pair of star-crossed lovers, and I nearly mentioned this to him. Instead I said: 'Did you ever read *Romeo and Juliet* when you were at school?'

'What? No, thank god. That's Shakespeare, isn't it?'

'What about the film? Have you ever seen the film?'

'No. Why would I?'

'No reason. It doesn't matter. I just wondered if you had, that's all.' He might understand better if he was with me. How I hated being stuck out in a hole like Three Creeks. But I'd phone Tess straight after Pete because she'd know exactly what I meant. I'd have to get in touch with Angie too, to word her up and warn her that Mother was on the warpath.

'I do love you, you know,' Pete said, redeeming himself. 'I meant everything I said earlier about us being together and all.'

'I know you did. Me too. Nothing can change that.'

After he hung up, I didn't have the smallest doubt that everything would work out between us. It'd all be okay. I had perfect faith in this.

I wanted to point the bone at Mother Dear, but Ice Queens are immune to such magic and, besides, she turned me to stone.

Grabbing my jacket, I crept downstairs. If the coast was clear, I'd take a couple of pieces of fruit from the kitchen and slip out the house, down to the river. I'd sit and think and clear my head and maybe I'd follow one of the tracks into the forest. But there was no way I was going to tell *her* where I was going. Let the old witch think what she would, and if she started worrying where I'd got to then so much the better. It'd serve her right.

Except the door from the hall to the kitchen was shut, which it never was, and I could hear her talking way too quietly on the phone in there now.

'There was nothing else I could do,' she was saying. 'That's easy for you to say, but you're not here, are you?' She may have been keeping her voice down, but I could make out the words well enough and could tell by her tone she was giving Dad an earful. 'You didn't have to see it or put up with her hysterics, did you?' Another pause. 'Don't you dare say that. Besides, she was hysterical and getting ruder by the second. She wouldn't listen to reason. You know what she's like sometimes.' Another pause. 'No, I didn't have any choice. It was for her own good. It was nothing more than a tap.' Long pause. 'Well then, perhaps you should have been here in that case instead of leaving it up to me. She can be so rude. Always so rude.'

I knew what she was doing. She was getting her version of our argument in first, so as to appear the much-maligned, under-appreciated parent, while I came across as the wayward, over-indulged daughter. Victim and villain.

Why hadn't I done that? I should've phoned Dad immediately.

Too angry to hold myself back, I threw open the kitchen door and shouted into the room: 'That's not true. She's lying. She's a liar!' Then I ran through the hallway, out the front door.

I was halfway down the path between the garage and the house when a car slowed on Rudely Road and pulled into our driveway, and I stopped and turned. For an irrational second, I thought it might be Victor returning to sort everything out, because the engine sounded similar to his, but then realised it couldn't be. He was on the phone and overseas. Maybe it was Pete, coming to make sure I was alright and to hell with the consequences. But a silver, four-wheel drive appeared and I recognised it straightaway; it belonged to the parents of Stella's friend, Verity.

From the driver's seat, Verity's mum waved at me and I nodded before stepping back out of sight. I listened to Stella say her farewells and to the slamming of a car door, followed seconds later by the shutting of the front door. The car reversed out the driveway and then there was the sound of it accelerating away from Three Creeks.

I knew what would happen next. I could see it playing out: Stella would ask where I'd gone and Mother would say I was in one of my moods and to steer clear of me. After this, she'd spend half-an-hour being syrupy-sweet to Stella, asking about her weekend, offering to make her a sandwich and a drink. She'd do everything she could – more than she ever normally does – to prove what a kind and considerate parent she was, because it'd discredit me if I decided to bring up the argument later or criticise her in any way. Stella would believe that the tension in the house was all down to me.

It wasn't fair.

Stella can be a bit naive at times. Always thinks the best of people. Too quick to believe what she's told. She's clever, for sure, and knows how to get what she wants, but she doesn't always think things through.

I knew how my mother would try and position Angie too, but I didn't fancy her chances there. Besides, not only had Angie met Pete already, but she invited me to use her house if I wanted it, and she knew what a bitch Mother could be because I'd told her enough times. No, Angie would be fine. All the same, as soon as I reached the river and had rolled a small log over to where I wanted to sit, I dialled her mobile, except a recorded voice told me her number was busy and that I should leave a message instead.

In the lee of the trees, where willows overhung the bank and old widow-makers had buckled long limbs into the water, the river seemed to brew its own dark stillness. A faint breeze stippled the surface elsewhere and each stipple caught a broken fragment of light before turning it back on itself. I watched a dragonfly dart and hover between the reeds, before dip-dipping across the water, but I lost sight of it amongst the reflections of the sky and so much borrowed height. I saw how the blackness of the water was not absolutely black, but shades of blue and the darkest greens, and I remembered the purple shadow cast by Betsy, my car, only that morning, although it had become too long ago already. Above the forest, a flock of kedamores screeched closer and closer, before wheeling into the distance again, and closer to I heard a softer cooing.

Twisting on my seat, I waited and listened and then noticed two pigeons strutting by the barbecues, pecking for scraps amongst recently-cut grass. I wished I had a handful of seed I could toss to them.

When we were little, Stella and I discovered a pigeon in Mum's cactus house. We were running through the garden and must've startled it as we ran past, because there was this sudden, thunderous crashing as it flew up at the windows, its wings beating against the glass, and we both shrieked. Then we laughed. The silly thing had got itself trapped inside and didn't realise glass wasn't thin air.

In a mess across the middle of the floor lay a broken terracotta pot, a pile of gravel and a prickly pear with a couple of yellow flowers snapped off. Worse for wear too was Mum's precious red pitaya – her dragon fruit. Stella pressed her nose against the glass and pointed to where the bird was, but it didn't go berserk again when she tapped on the glass or when I banged a little harder, and the funny thing remained in a dark corner underneath one of the benches. We could see it there, pretending to be invisible.

The cactus house had three thermostatically controlled windows in its roof, which opened when the temperature reached a certain heat and closed again when the day cooled. That's how the pigeon must have got trapped inside. It won't have been because Stella or me left the door open because we weren't allowed to play in there; not ever.

'I'm telling Mum,' Stella shouted, running into the house. She couldn't help herself. 'Mum! Mum!'

'No, let me,' I called, running after her. 'I saw it first.' But she was already in the kitchen, being told to take her shoes off, by the time I caught up.

'A big bird?' Mum said, after Stella told her about it.

'It's a pigeon,' I'm able to add.

She looked at us both and wiped her hands on her apron. 'You haven't been playing in there, have you? You didn't open the door and let it in, did you?' she said.

'No. We only just went out. It was already in there.'

She scowled and headed outside, and we had to run to keep up.

She put her hand against the glass to cut out the glare of the reflected light and peered inside. Then she eased open the door, pushing it back as wide as it'd stay. When she saw the broken pot on the floor, she shook her head. 'Are you sure you're both telling the truth?' she said.

'It's in the corner, under that bench. Isn't it Stell?'

Stella nodded the way she always did back then when she was a little kid, as if her head was about to fall off, and we both pointed.

Mum looked where we were pointing and glided slowly into the cactus house. As she bent down to pick up her prickly pear the pigeon flapped up again. It must have moved from under the bench while we'd been inside. It exploded from between two of her potted cacti, knocking one over and catapulting itself against the glass, where it must have stunned itself, because with the next moment it was on the ground, dazed, unblinking, its wings drooping.

If it had been me – an older me – I'd have left the door open and given it a chance to find its own way out, or I might have scattered a trail of breadcrumbs leading from the cactus house into the garden, like in *Hansel and Gretel*. However, I imagine it was a cold day and Mum didn't want her cacti to catch a chill because she was determined to get it out straightaway. Stella and I watched and it was marvellous to see at the time, how perfect she was with it.

She began by making soothing noises. Then, turning side-on, so she wasn't directly facing it, she edged cautiously towards it, tiny side-step by tiny side-step, freezing into a statue every once in a while, but gradually shrinking into a crouch as she got closer. It was magical how it worked. The soft, cooing noises kept the bird calm and the way she moved must have made her seem invisible, or as if she wasn't moving at all.

Stella held her breath and I held mine and I don't think either of us dared blink during this magic. We were as entranced as the pigeon.

When Mum was within an arm's length of it, and fully crouched now, she slowly turned and, in one swift but graceful movement, scooped the pigeon up in both hands and brought it against her chest, where she cradled it and cooed closely to it some more. She held it there against her and I could see its breast rising and falling, rising and falling, and one eye staring.

Stella laughed and giggled to see such a thing and I smiled and would have laughed out loud and clapped too, except I knew not to scare it again. It was the most wonderful thing to see.

'Can we keep it, Mummy?' Stella pleaded. 'As our pet?'

'No, of course not. It's wild. You can't keep wild things as pets.'

'Well, can we have a different pet then? A little kitty-cat or a puppy-dog? I want a pet.'

'You know what I think about pets.' Mum was firm, but her voice remained calm and soothing for the pigeon even as she said this. 'There, there,' she said, as if settling Stella or myself after a nightmare. 'There, there,' she was saying, and seemed almost hypnotised herself by the calmness of the moment she'd created and by the soft quietness of the bird. 'See, that's how it's done. It's easy really.' She had it tucked against her chest, holding both wings down against its body, stroking its feathers with her thumbs – that pacifying spot at the back of its head where the down is finest – and it made me want to close my eyes and sleep. Even though I wasn't tired, I could think of nothing better than being allowed to curl up with a blanket on one of those benches.

Instead, I took a couple of steps towards her, into the cactus house, and said, 'Can I hold it?'

'I want to have a go,' Stella whined, pushing forward.

That's when it pecked her and she said a rude word and let it go. The wildness of its flapping immediately swallowed up the small space and Stella and I ran out screaming as it smacked and beat against the glass in the roof, then it tumbled and fluttered and scrabbled against the windows above the bench. Chaos, the panic of terror.

Mum remained where she was, although she'd brought one arm over her head and held the other against her chest. The bench was a mess, with another cactus and a couple of pots of grit knocked over.

'Now look what you've done. Why did you have to do that?' She took a breath and surveyed the damage, looked to see where the pigeon was. 'Okay, you two, go away. I don't want you here. You're only making things worse. Go and play. You're scaring it, making it panic. Go and play in your room. Now. This instant.'

'It wasn't my fault,' Stella began to whine, but Stella always said things like that, so I took her by the hand and led her into the house. We'd just have to keep quiet and plays dolls or tea parties for a while.

Afterwards – it must've been half-an-hour or an hour later – when we'd had enough of being indoors and were bursting to be outside again, we headed into the kitchen. Mum was peeling and chopping apples, dropping the pieces into a large saucepan. She was standing next to the oven – the old-fashioned gas oven we had back then – and I noticed she'd changed her clothes. Instead of her skirt and cardigan, she was wearing slacks and a blouse. It was unusual to see her in trousers.

'Are we allowed outside now?'

It took her a moment to answer. She brushed a loose strand of hair out of her eyes with her arm. 'Yes, but don't keep coming in and out, for goodness sake.'

'Did you catch the pigeon?' I asked.

'The pigeon? Oh, yes, eventually. No thanks to you two.'

We stood a moment and she continued peeling apples.

'What's it doing now?' Stella wanted to know.

'What's what doing now?'

'The birdie. What's the birdie doing now?'

'Oh, it'll be with its friends, I imagine.'

'Back with its Mummy and Daddy?' Stella said.

'Probably. Yes, I imagine it will be.'

'Are you making apple pie?' I asked.

She stopped again and scowled. 'I won't be making anything if you two don't stop asking silly questions. Now go outside and play, or go and tidy your bedroom. One or the other. Now go.'

Outside, we peered through the glass into the cactus house as we passed, but there was nothing to see. Mum had made everything neat and tidy and there was no sign of a pigeon having ever ventured inside. Even so, I'd decided to write a story about it later. Maybe I'd let Stella draw some of the pictures. That way, we could use her pad of coloured paper and it'd look really good, but I'd have to show her what to do and I'd be the one who'd design the front cover.

'We'll call him Eric,' I said out loud.

'Who?'

'Our pigeon. We're going to write a book about him.'

And Stella laughed. 'Eric, Eric, Eric the birdie.'

Whether it was the afternoon of the same pigeon day or not, I don't know. I think it was, but memory is a slippery eel and it's hard to be sure what end you're holding onto at times. Neither do I recall what it was that made me think to do what I did. There must have been something about what Mum had said or done or hadn't done, or something I'd noticed in the garden, that gave me a clue and the craziness to uncover it.

We were sitting on the step of the front porch, pulling on our gumboots, and Stella said, 'What are we playing? Why do we need gumboots? I can't get mine on.'

'Ssh,' I whispered back. 'We're going to find buried treasure.' Except she got so bubbly and fizzy at this that I had to put my hand over her mouth. 'It's top secret and you have to be quiet. That's part of the game.'

'Otherwise the pirates will catch us?' she suggested.

'Yes, except we are the pirates,' I told her. 'These are our pirate boots.'

When she stood up, her boots were on the wrong feet,

but she could still walk okay and we'd be there all day if we didn't get a move on. Besides, although Mum was listening to a program on the radio, it could finish any minute.

We crept down the side of the house, ducking down and crawling under the windows, and Stella was fit to burst with giggles. Instead of running down the garden path to fetch our old beach spades from the shed, I made her squeeze through the hedge after me, so we could skirt round the outside edge of the garden and reach the back of the shed that way.

'No,' said Stella, who was teetering between laughter and tears now. 'I'm not allowed on the road. I'll tell Mummy.'

'We're not going on the road, silly. If we stay in the hedge, we're still in the garden. We're allowed to do that. Look, it's like a secret tunnel.'

She wasn't sure, but she still followed me, and it didn't take long at all to clamber between the thick, snaky branches from one end of the lawn to the other, where another, smaller hedge and the shed separated the lawn from the vegetable patch back then. When we climbed out again, and she recognised we were still in our garden, she was beaming.

'Again,' she said. 'Let's go in our secret tunnel again.'

But we were at the back of the shed and I pressed a finger against my lips. 'You wait here, Stell, and keep quiet,' I whispered. 'I'll get our spades. You mustn't move or the baddies will catch us and you'll have to walk the plank. Okay?'

'I don't want to wait here. I want to come with you. I don't want to walk the plank.'

'We're only playing, Stell. It's part of the game. We're pirates. I have to capture our spades back because they've been stolen by the baddies and you're the lookout. That's the best job. If I get caught, you'll have to rescue me. You can be the one who digs for the treasure, if you like.' Before she could argue, I slipped round the corner of the farthest wall and slid along until I was standing near the front of the shed. I peeped out to make sure Mum wasn't in the kitchen, else she'd see me, and then I sprang round the front, opened the door and dashed inside.

The reason we needed our gumboots was because the veggie patch had been turned over recently and the soil was sticky. However, there was a corner close to the path which had been even more recently dug and the soil here was a dark, chocolate colour. Moist chocolate.

I stood and pointed down at the patch with my spade. 'Here,' I said to Stella. 'This is where the treasure's buried.'

'Really?' she asked, and was laughing again. 'How do you know?'

'I just do. It was marked on a secret map.'

'Do you have the map? I want to hold it.'

'No, the baddies have it. I saw it before I escaped.'

'I made them let you go, didn't I?'

'We fought them off together,' I said.

She began digging straightaway. Small scoops, which sliced into the soft soil, but she was dropping most of the dirt back where she'd lifted it from because she wasn't holding her spade straight.

'Not like that, Stella. Like this.'

'No. You said I could.' And she stamped her feet and started a small cry until I stopped digging.

'I'm only trying to show you how it's done. It'll take you forever otherwise.'

'Let me do it,' she said. But a few moments later, she stopped. 'How far down is it?'

'I don't know. Do you want me to help dig too?'

She nodded and moved over a little.

Before long, we hit an unusual type of springy softness and I said, 'Hold on.' I scraped at the soil, revealing a strip of something white flecked with grey. I thought it might be paper – that it was wrapped in paper – until Stella pressed her spade down again and lifted soil and pinion feathers together. She'd caught the edge of its wing and it unfolded slightly when she lifted her spade.

'What is it? Is that the treasure?' she asked.

I was about to tell her, but was catapulted out the way with an abrupt force which threw me off-balance. Before I could stand up straight again, there came the sting of a cold slap across the back of my legs, followed by a second smack. Stella was crying, so I knew she'd been smacked too, and Mum was shaking me by the arm.

'What on earth do you think you're doing?' she was shouting. 'Pigeons are vermin; they spread disease. Now get inside, scrub your hands and go to your room – both of you – this instant.'

Stella ran off crying, down the path and across the lawn, each of her gumboots pointing outwards as she ran, and she wouldn't speak to me for the rest of the afternoon. I don't know whether she even realised what it was we discovered; all she knew was that she'd done something wrong and I'd made her do it.

Years later, when I reminded her about the pigeon, she claimed no memory of it. It's one of those memories she's left me alone with, and sometimes it irritates me that she could fail to remember the faintest part of it; either how we discovered it in the cactus house or how we dug up its body. Maybe she was just too young at the time.

SEVEN

SHOULD I PHONE DAD straightaway or wait until he returns home? By waiting and not playing Mum's game, there was every chance she'd annoy him with all her fussing and nuisance calls and that he'd end up being more sympathetic to me. On the other hand, if I said nothing, he might believe everything she said...

I didn't know what to do. I didn't want to talk to him about getting caught in bed with Pete, because really, when it came down to it, that was nobody's business except mine and Pete's.

Eventually, I consoled myself that Dad was reasonably broad-minded and I'd win him round. There's no way he'd stop me from seeing Pete. He'd appease Mum by promising to have a fatherly word with me, but all he'd really want was to meet Pete. After that, everything would be rosy and she'd have to lump it.

As for Angie, when I finally got through, she said, 'I'm so sorry, Meg. I feel as if I'm to blame because I said you could bring him here.'

'That's nothing to be sorry about. I'm glad you did. I'm

grateful for that.'

Even though we were only talking on the phone, the sound of her voice was a comfort. It soothed me. And the way she listened and spoke with me reminded me I was more of an adult than my mother treated me.

'Well, I didn't like to think of you taking risks in the back of a car. It shouldn't have to be like that. There's not enough room for two people *and* romance in the back of a car. That's not how love should be. All the same, I'll feel bad if it's put a wedge between you and your mum.'

I laughed. 'It's not a wedge, it's an iceberg, and it's always been there.'

'Well, don't worry, my lovely, it needn't come between us.'

After the call ended, I felt much better, more self-possessed. I knew Angie would help me find my balance again.

At school, on Monday, when I told Tess about the weekend, she thought it hilarious. 'What a bitch,' she said, and that made me feel better too.

During recess, I messaged Pete about meeting at lunchtime, but he messaged back that he was busier than usual and wasn't sure what time he'd get a break.

I replied: **Fair enough. Tomorrow instead? Phone later. M. xx**

When he didn't phone that evening and stopped returning my messages, I knew something was wrong. It wasn't like him. I stayed in my room and attempted to write an essay, but couldn't concentrate. Stella wanted help with her homework, but I had enough to think about. I just cleared the dishes when I was told, kept my mouth shut and closed my bedroom door.

In a year-and-a-half I'd be finished with school and could leave home. I'd go to uni and live on campus, or take a gap year and travel, or I'd get a job in Lapishot or the city or somewhere and rent a small apartment of my own, or find a room in a share-house with friends. I'd be free to be the person I wanted to be, free to spend time with whoever I wanted to spend it with, free to do whatever I wanted.

I shoved my text book and essay notes to one side and sent him a third message: **Phone me.**

Yet it wasn't until the following morning, as I was getting off the stale and steamed-up school bus, that I saw I'd just missed a call from him and had a new message: **We need to talk.**

There was a quiet spot at the back of the Art wing where I could phone from, next to where the bins and rubbish skips were lined up.

'What happened to you?' I asked. 'I tried calling you heaps of times last night.'

'Had a flat battery,' he said. 'Didn't find my charger until this morning.'

But his tone was flat too, and too matter-of-fact.

'What's the matter? You sound like something's up.'

There was a pause before he answered. 'I think it'd be better if we gave one another a break, like you said.'

'To let things calm down a bit? Is that what you mean? For a fortnight? That's what I said.'

Again, there was an overdrawn pause. 'No. Longer than that.'

A couple of Year 8 students walked past and I switched my phone from one ear to the other. How could he? After everything he'd promised. I waited until the brats were out of earshot, but heard him say, 'Meg?'

'You're dumping me. You are, aren't you? You're dumping me.'

'No, not as such.'

'Well, what are you doing then? What are you saying?'

'Look, it's not like I want to. It's just that I think it'd be better if —'

'You are. You're dumping me.' I closed my eyes and pressed my forehead against the damp, brick wall. There was a sheet-metal ventilation duct jutting out the wall a metre or so above my head and a series of large windows filling much of the length of the wall to the far end of the building. A phone started ringing in one of the rooms and I figured it was probably a teachers' office.

'Meg,' I heard him say, 'are you alright? Are you still there?'

That's when I hung up.

Two minutes later, a group of Year 7 students ran round the corner. I'd dropped my school bag and was squatting on my heels. A couple of boys yelled something and laughed as they ran past, but the last one — the one who was doing the chasing or being run away from — stopped and took a step towards me.

'Are you okay?' he asked.

'Go away. Leave me alone.'

He shrugged and ran off, and I redialled Pete's number.

'I don't understand. How could you? After everything you said. All those words and promises — didn't they mean anything? After... after everything...' But it was too hard to think straight and speak.

'Look, I'm sorry. Really I am, but... well, you know.'

I found myself leaning against one of the rubbish skips, next to several blisters of chewing gum and the foil top off a yoghurt carton that had been smeared and stuck there. 'No, I don't know.'

'Well, you know, your mum... well, she phoned. She talked to me.'

'She what?'

'Your mum, she called me. She got my number and, well, she told me how things were – you know.'

'No. Stop saying that. It doesn't mean anything. I don't know. All I know is what you're telling me: that the bitch phoned you and you're dumping me. What did she say? What did she tell you?'

'Look, I promised, but –'

'You promised! You promised what? You've got to tell me what she said.'

'She's frightened you'll get hurt, that's all. That's about it. She's just worried about you really. Seriously, she wasn't being a bitch. Not really. Not at all.'

'And you believed her? Whatever she said, you believed her. Her rather than me?'

'It's probably for the best...'

'No. No, it's not.'

I pressed my forehead against the cold, rust-pitted metal. I wanted to scream until I exploded, but all I had was a throat full of silence.

'Look, I better go,' he eventually said.

'Stop saying "look", will you,' I tried to snap back, but choked on the words.

'What?'

'Forget it. Just forget it.' I wished there was something else I could say to make him change his mind, so he could see how stupid he was being. I had an inkling there was something I might once have known to say, but I couldn't find my way back to it, and then even that feeling disappeared. It was too late.

'Anyway, I better go.'

I closed my eyes. 'Then go.'

'As long as you'll be okay.'

'Not that you give a damn,' I whispered, but it sounded like he'd already rung off.

<u>The Pointing of the Bone</u>
It's easy to mould a friend into being a happy, outward-going person, I reckon, simply by telling them it's these qualities you admire most in them. Even if it's not true to begin with, it makes them start to believe this about themselves and to become that happier, more outward-going person. It's equally possible to make someone angry or upset by asking why they're angry or upset or in a bad mood, especially if they aren't to begin with. And there's research that shows how people who believe they're lucky will go through life recognising their good luck in most everything they do. It's all about the power of suggestion and self-belief. I've looked this stuff up.

Some aborigines believe it's possible to kill a person by pointing a special bone at them and letting that person know they've been cursed with this death. It's powerful magic and, once cursed, most people die. There are recorded cases of this. They know they can't live and so they die.

In this way, my mother made me mad. She pointed a bone of her own.

She said I was unstable, hysterical, and she turned me into this.

She said I was mad and so she made me mad.

Her behaviour was no different to the bigots who used to lock women in lunatic asylums because they'd had a baby and weren't married, or because they refused to marry some ugly idiot they'd been told to marry, or because they were suffering from post-natal depression. No different at all. She couldn't stomach that I was in a good relationship, nor that, unlike her, I refused to see sex as something dirty and shameful. She couldn't stomach me being young and happy while she was middle-aged and bitter, so she did all she could to destroy it in me. I was sure of it at the time.

Events unfolded in front of me. It was like it was happening to someone else, not me, and all I could do was look on through glazed eyes.

Meg sits through Form Meeting and double Maths and barely hears what's being said. She's choked full of a foggy silence that's making her smaller and smaller as it grows and grows. The silence bleeds out from her and sticks to her; it grows around her, smothering her, numbing her and distancing her, and she can't think straight. Not one clear thought.

Tess finds her at recess. She's standing in front of the lockers in the Year 11 Common Room, but she's lost the sense to know what to do next. All she knows is that her mother contacted Pete – her Pete – and whatever she said was enough to end their relationship. It's a betrayal like no other.

Tess says: 'Meg, are you alright?'

Meg nods. She smiles. She pulls something of herself back and tears a hole in the sticky fog.

'Pete dumped me,' she says.

'I know. I just found out.'

It's enough to help her rip the hole larger. 'You know? How? How do you know?'

'He messaged me earlier,' Tess tells her. 'I phoned him back. I told him he was an arsehole. Are you alright?'

'What did he say? Did he say why?'

Tess rubs Meg on the back and says, 'Come on. Put your

books away. I'll shout you a sausage roll or pizza slice from the canteen.'

Outside, Meg asks again. 'What did he say? Did he say why?'

'Your mum's a prize bitch, you know.'

'What did she say? What did she tell him?'

Tess wants to get in the canteen queue, but Meg isn't moving. Meg stands and waits, and Tess hesitates, laughs and says: 'He said that your mum said you couldn't cope with a serious relationship, or words to that effect. That you were "emotionally vulnerable" or "unstable" or something. Can you believe it? He said she made it sound as if you were on the brink of a nervous breakdown or something. That if he cared anything for you, he should leave you alone. It'd be the kindest thing he could do. I couldn't believe –'

'What? She said that?'

'Something like that. That was the gist of it. He said she was worried about you, but I told him it was a load of bullcrap and he was an arsehole if he believed a word of it. I told him he was a cheap-skate loser if he could move on from you that easily.'

The silence has thickened around her again; quicker, denser. Her voice sounds muffled when she speaks and she's not sure how to break through. 'What did he say?' Meg asks.

Tess describes how she tore into him, and her outrage, but Meg looks on from the growing distance and notices her friend is enjoying the drama. She doesn't understand. Not really. It's a game to her, a bit of entertainment, and Meg realises she doesn't want to be with her anymore. Not even if she could break out of the fog. Not right now. She needs to be alone. Further alone. Not standing in the middle of the schoolyard with Tess speaking at her.

'It went downhill from there, I can tell you. He told me he wasn't being an arsehole at all, so I apologised and told him that, no, he was a piss-weak prick instead. I think the call ended at that point.'

Tess goes to the canteen and Meg goes to the toilet. She finds a cubicle with a lock on the door and stands there, leaning against the door.

After a couple of minutes, she takes out her phone and, when he doesn't answer, she messages him: **Need to talk. Phone me.**

She waits, and when he doesn't reply, she tries phoning him again, but this time the recorded message says his phone's switched off. She's leaning into the corner between the door and one partition, but she doesn't know what she's waiting for. All she knows is that she'll stay until the end-of-recess bell has rung. It's safer here. Some bogan has dumped a used tampon on the floor, next to the toilet, but there's nothing unusual in that. She pulls her jacket tighter, presses herself further into the corner, closes her eyes.

She's still clutching her phone. She wants to be sick, but she won't be sick. Not here. Besides, the sickness is too deep inside her, too much a part of her.

She scrolls through the numbers and selects 'Home'. She is crying now.

When her mother answers, Meg sniffles before she can speak and, even then, her voice is an inaudible whisper, so she repeats what she has to say until she knows she can be heard. 'I hate you. I hate you. I hate you. I hate you. I hate you!' She listens and expects to hear her mother say something – anything – but she doesn't hear a word.

Her mother will hang up on her. She knows it. Any second.

'Do you hear me?' Meg shouts into her phone, but each

word is rasped and raw.

'I hear you,' she hears her mother calmly reply.

Meg doesn't know what else to say.

Any second. She knows her mother will hang up on her. The bitch.

Her mother says: 'Now stop being hysterical. You'll make yourself sick.'

It makes her want to scream and scream until she explodes, but she's all choked up in sticky fog and, instead, she'll implode into the silence of herself. She'll become her own black hole.

If only she could scream and explode.

She reaches out and drops the phone down the toilet. It seems the only thing she can do. Then she pushes the cistern handle to flush it, but her phone remains unmoved in the bottom of the pan.

When Tess comes in and calls her name, she doesn't answer.

Once the end-of-recess bell finally rings, she closes her eyes for a few minutes before unlocking the cubicle door and stepping out. The place is empty. She washes her face, stares at herself in a clear patch of the graffiti-smeared and scratched mirror, before moving off to get her books for the next class. She doesn't know what else to do.

History had always been one of her favourite subjects, but she's late to class and Ms Perry, the Year 11 Assistant Coordinator, is filling-in for Mr Belescu, who is absent today.

'Why are you late?' Ms Perry says. She's finished taking the roll and has written Mr Belescu's instructions for the lesson on the board.

'I wasn't feeling well,' Meg says.

'Do you have a Late Pass from the school nurse?'

'I didn't go to Sick Bay.' A little quieter: 'I stayed in the toilets.'

Ms Perry adjusts the roll and takes off her glasses, waving them in front of her as she speaks. 'Next time, don't stay in the toilets, Meg,' she announces, so the entire class understands, 'but go to Sick Bay instead. And if you're not well enough to be in class on time, then get signed out to go home. You know the rules.'

There are only two spare seats and both are next to boys she'd normally avoid, but she's got no choice. She knows she shouldn't be in class or at school, not now, but she can't go home. How will she ever be able to walk through that door again? Her mother's a bitch and if she never sees her again it'll be a day too soon.

Maybe she can stay with Tess, except Tess would do her head in right now. She wouldn't help, she'd make things worse. And Angie – she can't ask any more favours of Angie, not after the last few days. She might lose her job if she got too involved. That bitch of a mother would go out of her way to see to it.

The only thing she understands with any clarity is that she can't go home. No way can she be in the same house as that woman. Not now.

Perhaps she could phone her dad. Tell him what's happened. Why didn't she think of that before, instead of throwing her phone down the toilet? She should have phoned him yesterday, straightaway. Not waited. Stupid Meg. Stupid, stupid, stupid.

She can't go home.

He'll probably still be asleep or in a meeting. What was the time difference? What was the time there? She can't even work that out now and she can't remember when he's due back. Stupid Meg.

Ms Perry is standing over her and the idiot boy next to her is smirking. Perry's saying something about day-dreaming and university, and she uses her surname to show she's annoyed. 'What are you thinking of, Miss Dapsy? You haven't even opened your book.'

Meg blinks and opens her book, tries to focus on the board to see what page she should turn to, but has to look at the book that Tyler what's-his-name has open in front of him.

'Don't look for help from Tyler,' Ms Perry says. 'Tyler's been on the wrong page all his life, haven't you, Tyler?'

Tyler smiles at this as though it must be a compliment, until the group behind him laugh and someone explains, 'She's laughing *at* you, Tyler, not *with* you. He doesn't get it, Miss.'

She shakes her head and turns back to Meg, opening the book at the right page for her. 'I don't know what's got into you today, or whether this is this way you always behave in History, but if you don't do your best in every class, there's no way you'll get a scholarship. Now, is there? There won't be any point in even filling out the application form.'

'Sorry,' Meg says, and makes a show of taking a pen from her pencil case and opening her folder.

'Your teachers can't help you if you don't help yourself. Can they?'

'No.' She shakes her head. 'No.' Hopes this'll make the woman go away and leave her alone, pick on someone else. On the other side of the room, two boys are screwing up sheet after sheet of paper and tossing them towards the bin, punching the air and giving a silent cheer every time one goes in, but the woman pays no attention to them.

'What was that? Don't slouch and mutter, Miss Dapsy. Sit up properly.'

Meg sighs and tries to change the way she's sitting, but she can't get comfortable in this school chair and one of its legs is uneven, so it wobbles every time she moves, and the desktop is covered with pictures – in ink, pencil and white-out – of penises and what she assumes to be a hairy vagina, although it could be an angry spider. There'll be chewing gum stuck under the edge of the table, and the whole place disgusts her.

She tries to concentrate, but can't, and several minutes later, Perry is standing over her shoulder again, waiting for her to write something.

'Come on, Meg, this just isn't good enough. I really am surprised at you. You've hardly done a stroke of work.'

Meg bites her lip and closes her eyes. The class is hushed and looking her way: the over-achiever who never gets told off being made an example of. If only she could curl up in a corner and sleep. When she woke up, everything'd be alright.

'Like I said before,' Perry goes on, 'if you're well enough to come to school, you're well enough to do your work. Now, stop letting yourself down and, if you can't care about yourself, do at least think about your parents. I know they want you to do well at school. If I don't see a bit more effort from you by the end of the class, I think I'll have to phone home, don't you?'

Meg understands that she has to open her mouth. If she doesn't get a few words out, she'll suffocate or implode. Already she's finding it hard to breathe. Short breaths. The tail of each half-breath begins to catch in her throat, along with the swelling silence, until she has to sick something up: a word, a scream, a noise.

'Leave me alone,' she says, but doubts she is heard.

'I beg your pardon? What did you say?'

She takes a quick breath and lets the words stream out. She has volume now and a tone that freezes every other sound into silence, and everyone is listening and everyone hears. 'Leave me alone. Get off my case. Pick on someone else for a change. Just leave me alone!' She's half-turned in her chair, twisting to stare at Perry, and following hard on the instant in which she wonders whether she's really said all this comes the instant when she no longer cares.

'How dare you?' Perry demands.

Meg pushes her chair back and struggles to stand, and the woman jumps out the way. 'How dare *you*? I told you I was sick!' she shouts back at Perry. There must be something else she can say, something that will explain, but at least the words have exploded out. Then she hears new words and wonders at first where they're coming from. 'You bitch!' the voice says and almost laughs to say it. The voice sounds like it's crying the next moment and her face is flooding with hot, angry tears, and her pencil case is spilling onto the floor with her books and Tyler's books. 'I hate you! How could you? I hate you!' Meg pushes past, is at the door trying to get out the room, and must run away from the terrible silence behind her.

She finds herself back in the girls' toilets, locked in a cubicle, pressed up against the door, leaning against the lock. There's a tampon on the floor, next to the toilet, but her phone is no longer in the pan.

There's a girl locked in the toilets and she won't come out. There's a teacher, the Assistant Principal and the school nurse outside, talking to her. She can't remember how she got there, but she knows she mustn't leave. It's too late to leave.

*

There's a girl sitting in the Assistant Principal's office and the nurse is sitting next to her, rubbing the back of her hand. The girl's head is bowed and she might be staring at her lap or the floor, but she's finding it hard to focus. What she'd really like to do is close her eyes and sleep. The Assistant Principal was sitting behind his desk, she remembers, but he's not there now and she wonders where he's gone. The door is shut and the room is cocooned from all the usual school sounds. No bells, no slamming of doors, no footsteps kicking along the floors of emptied corridors, no shouting, no crowded din, no raised voices, no announcements over loud speakers. The room is carpeted. Grey carpet. Her black school shoes are polished and her white socks are the regulation socks. She doesn't want to remember why she's here and she hopes this person next to her will keep stroking the back of her hand forever and ever.

There's a girl sitting in a parked car with her mother, except the girl only comes to realise this when the silence from the woman next to her grows so loud she's startled by it. It's like being woken from a deep sleep, only to find she's not in bed and that someone's staring at her. The car is parked and her mother sits in the driver's seat, staring at her, but she's not entirely sure where they are. It could be the Visitors' Car Park at school, or the Demlab car park, or the Netball Stadium car park; she doesn't immediately recognise it or know why they're there, sitting in silence, waiting.

She remembers a small, broken piece of dream at first. The bitter taste still lingers. Her head aches, her eyes and her throat are sore.

When she realises the dream is not a dream, she shouts 'No!' and reaches for the door handle. Somehow the car is moving now — how is the car travelling when it was parked a moment before? — and the door swings wide and there's the dizzy rush of bitumen and the squealing of tyres. 'You bitch! I hate you. I hate you! Let me out. Let me get out!'

The girl fights with her mother, but the door handle isn't where it was and she can't get out. There's glass and a window, which she wants to beat against and break through, except her mother's hands are on her, at her, her arms are locked round her with a strength she never imagined, and she can't break free. She's pinioned there.

The doctor's thick breath is too close to her face, but she can't move back. Something is holding her and her muscles won't work the way she needs them to. He shines a light in her eyes — first one eye, then the other — but the girl remembers not to blink. If she blinks, she'll never fly away.

The girl's father perches on the edge of a chair next to her bed and strokes her head. His left hand holds her right hand and his right hand strokes her hair; he brushes it back over the soft creases of her ear and across the side of her head. Every few strokes, his hand brushes back to the crown of her head and then caresses from there down to the small of her neck, before moving back to begin brushing over her ear again. As a child, on those occasions when she was over-tired and resisting sleep, she'd eventually close her eyes at this and drift asleep.

The first time he visits and strokes her hair, he appears tired and confused and, although he attempts not to show it, he cries.

'My Meggy,' he weeps. 'I'm sorry.'

The girl tries to close her eyes, but there's little difference between sleeping and waking in this place. She struggles to find the words that might describe what she feels, even if there's no way she can utter them, but her brain doesn't work properly anymore. Only later, weeks later, does a phrase surface that might have sufficed: *ineffably sad.*

She closes her eyes a moment and, when she opens them, he is gone. She closes her eyes then and, when she opens them, he has returned.

Once, when the girl's father is sitting by her side, holding her hand, stroking her hair, it fleetingly occurs to her that if they could stay like this for long enough, and if she could close her eyes and sleep the way she used to sleep, she might find her way back to a beginning, from which he and she might start afresh. They've addled her brain with drugs, though, and by the time she gets to the end of any long thought, she can't remember where it began, or why.

Afterwards, it seems to the girl she must have been like this for days if not weeks, but they tell her it was only a day-and-a-half at most. It seems that her father – Victor – sat and stroked her hair on two or three separate occasions at least, but he tells her it was only once. Their drugs addle time as well as her brain.

Slabs of sleep. Slices of half-waking.

Until then, I – that previous Meg – had never properly considered what a Psychiatric Unit might be like. If anyone mentioned the words 'mental hospital', what I'd picture was a composite image created from several films and a couple of books: *One Flew Over the Cuckoo's Nest*; *Girl, Interrupted*; *Rain Man*; *The Asylum*; *The Death of Napoleon...* The architecture would be decidedly nineteenth century (thick walls, high ceilings, barred windows, prison doors, dingy cells, green and cream painted walls, black and white tiled floors), while the grounds would comprise wide and lush lawns, dotted with wooden benches and circuitous paths, sweeping down under blue skies to a fringe of dark trees and a high, spiked wall.

I hadn't known that Lapishot & District Hospital had a Psychiatric Unit of its own, nor that it was both the most modern and most run-down wing of the hospital. I hadn't known there was a sad, little garden for patients to sit in, nor how bleak the dayroom overlooking it was. I hadn't known how cruel people could be.

Me. I had to find the I that was Me again.

It was easier to accept, or pretend to accept, that I was ill than to maintain my rage. Instead of believing me, they kept shoving drugs in me.

I poured a small portion of rage into the palm of my hand and closed my fingers around it. It became a handful of bird seed to clutch at. Lest I forget. When one of the nurses asked me what I was holding onto, I showed him my hand, unclenched it and shrugged.

'Nothing,' I said. They were the mad ones.

Mother had me committed – sectioned – but Dr Carmichael said I wasn't mad. I asked her. We talked about schizophrenia, bipolar disorder, psychosis, anxiety, personality disorders, Cuton's syndrome... all those words that get lightly tossed around in TV programs and magazine articles, as if they're the easiest thing in the world to diagnose. We'd even discussed them at school in Semester 1 Psychology. Dr Carmichael was confident, she said, that I was only depressed and emotionally stressed; my brain was absorbing serotonin too rapidly or something, but 'we'd soon sort it out'. She made it sound like the most normal thing in the world, although it can't be normal to drug someone up to the eyeballs and keep them in a locked ward with junkies and lunatics, can it?

It was too hard to believe.

I wanted to tell her how she'd be depressed too if her mother had her committed to a lunatic asylum. I wanted to ask what was so unusual about a person being upset, angry, furious, with their mother, or whoever, if she set out to destroy a perfect relationship... and succeeded. Wouldn't she, Dr Carmichael, be a tad peeved too? As for having been depressed before, but not aware of it because I was 'masking it', that sounded like baloney. I was never depressed before. I was over the moon because I was with Pete; I was as happy as a lark; I was as happy as Larry.

I couldn't see *her*, my mother, agreeing with the diagnosis either, although for different reasons. She'd rather I was straight-jacketed and dumped in a padded cell – throw away the key – and I knew it.

Dr Carmichael told me how the medication she was prescribing inhibited the reuptake of serotonin by the brain, which was apparently a good thing, and she talked about the side-effects of specific drugs. But it was hard to follow everything she said, even though she kept asking, 'Do you understand? Does this make sense?'

I wanted to tell her it might make sense and I might understand if only they'd stop stuffing me full of mind-numbing tablets. Instead, I leant forward, closer to her desk, in what I thought was a mock-conspiratorial manner and said, 'Sort out my mother and I'll be alright. She's the one who needs to be in here.' It was supposed to be a joke, sort of.

She smiled and let a minute pass before scribbling something down in her notepad, but I could guess what she was writing.

'While you're with us,' she told me, as if this was some sort of jolly Holiday Camp I'd signed up for, 'we'll get your dosage right and then you might feel better able to start talking things through. It can take a while. We'll start you on therapy and make sure you're comfortable continuing with this, so it's there for you after you've been discharged.' She looked across at me and smiled a bit too enthusiastically, pretending to be my friend.

'How lovely,' I replied and settled back in the chair. Sarcasm may be the lowest form of wit, but seriously, who could expect me to be 'chipper' about being there? How would I ever be able to return home again or go back to school? How could I face my friends or be in the same room as my mother? It was all too impossible. I'd lost my place in the world.

'You know, we all need a bit of time-out once in a while and someone to unburden ourselves to. There's nothing wrong with that, Meg. You'll be out of here and back home as soon as we think you're ready.'

I needed to clutch tight to my happiest memories too, for balance, even if they cut at me like a fistful of shiny new razor blades.

Pete and I arrive at Angie's house in the middle of a sunny afternoon. There's a razzle-dazzle glare to the light and the buzz of insects, the darting of dragonflies, the confetti of butterflies. The air is rich with forest odours: composting leaf litter, drying pine needles, resin. The air is warm on my naked skin.

Lulled, as we lie together, by the lazy tapping of the blind against the window, the shadows slowly sliding backwards and forwards with each hint of breeze, we're a tangle of happy limbs. I'm looking at him and he's gazing at me. We're entwined and no words need be spoken. I stroke his hair. His hand cups and strokes my breast.

I am new and the world is new and we float on the current of a gloriously long moment.

I would unhook the moon for him.

'Write everything down,' they said, 'the thoughts that crowd your little head.' Or words to that effect. 'Scribble it down in any old order, or as if it were a story, if you prefer. Change the names if it's easier. Better out than in.'

So I did. I began. Not that I'd let those nut-crackers see what I'd written. There's catharsis in the telling.

Ian is the therapy facilitator. First names only. He doesn't want to be called Doctor and doesn't want me to think of him as a psychotherapist or a counsellor, but as a *facilitator*. After all, it's a *partnership* we've entered into, apparently, and he's very particular about this even if, with his Cheap-Mart jeans and faded T-shirts, he's not half as particular about his appearance. Of course, he might deliberately dress down so all his junky and lunatic patients – "clients" – feel more at ease and ready to spill their addled beans to someone who looks as badly off as they are. Nonetheless, he wears an expensive watch and the four black-framed certificates hanging on his office wall confirm that not only is he a qualified doctor and psychotherapist, but has a surname too.

During our third session, Ian tells me that my parents are waiting in the next room and are here to support me if I want. They're keen to participate, he says, and believes their involvement will be very, very helpful. He tells me we discussed this during the previous session, but I can barely recall what day it is, let alone the details of yesterday or the day before.

I shake my head and continue shaking my head. 'No, no, no, no, no, no.' How can he not know?

'That's alright. That's perfectly alright,' he hurriedly tries reassuring me. 'They'll understand. Another day, when you're ready. They'll fully understand. They're here to support you, that's all.'

But it doesn't help. It's too late. Knowing what each session is leading towards wrenches me apart. It brings on a headache and makes me run to the toilet, even though I'm still constipated when I get there. I sit on the toilet, straining. I know what they're doing, how they've got their winkle-picking hooks into me. They won't let me out until I've done everything they want, think the way they want me to think, have recited the words they expect me to say. And the thought beats through my head that it would be easier to stay on Ward 8 forever than do all that. Within half-an-hour I'm blinded by the first migraine I've ever had, convinced my head's going to explode. I spend the rest of the day in bed with a hot flannel across my eyes.

If only, if only.

If only I could sick it all up and begin again.

Angie leaves a card and a bunch of flowers. The envelope has been opened, but the card reads:

DEAREST, DEAREST MEG,

TRIED TO VISIT YOU, BUT HEAR YOU'RE NOT RECEIVING VISITORS YET. JUST WANTED TO LET YOU KNOW THAT I HAVEN'T FORGOTTEN YOU, AM THINKING OF YOU AND MISSING YOU HEAPS.

GET WELL SOON.

ALL MY LOVE, ANGIE XXX

PS. THE PIANO IS LONELY WITHOUT YOU AND GUSTAV SAYS MIAOW!

The picture on the front of the card is a painting of a girl in a blue dress, seated at a white table. Sitting at the table with her is a white rabbit and a strange-looking brownish-grey creature. There's a large teapot on the table, a teacup and saucer, and a bunch of flowers in a blue milk jug. There's an eggcup on the floor. The floor is yellow, the walls are pink.

The inscription reads: *The pink Alice by Charles Blackman.*

When a nurse asks if I'd like a vase for the flowers, I say, 'Yes please. Do you have a blue one, like a milk jug?'

The nurse says, 'I'll see what I can do.' But returns with an ugly, red, plastic vase instead.

Five or six sessions in and I'm doing all I can to anchor myself tight: clamping my arms, clenching my teeth, pushing both feet down. Staring at the flecks of darker grey in the carpet, I'm holding onto several of the darkest flecks in particular, trying to stay with them. If I relax my grip, I'll stumble from the chair and run, run, run.

Less than a minute after stepping from the room, Ian ushers my mother and father in. He thought I might want to fetch them myself!

'This is a very good moment,' he says. 'Meg has done so well to get to this point, don't you think?'

'Definitely,' my mother says, pretending she's positively the fresh breeze.

'Hello, my lovely,' Dad says. 'We miss you so much. Stella sends her love. We can't wait to have you home again, can we?'

'That's right,' my mother says. 'As soon as you're ready.'

I force myself to look up. I force myself to smile.

'Excellent,' Ian says. 'Well, have a seat. Make yourselves comfortable. Would you like a coffee? Meg and I sometimes have a coffee while we're talking, don't we, Meg?'

I can't speak.

'Meg?' he says.

I briefly nod.

'Would you like to say hello to your mum and dad?' Ian suggests.

'Hi,' I mutter. I wish I had a long fringe. Something to hide behind.

'Coffee?' he asks.

I shake my head.

'"No, thank you",' my mother corrects me.

Bitch.

After a minute or two, Ian is rambling on. It goes more or less like this: 'I can't emphasise enough that this session isn't about making accusations or laying blame or feeling guilty; it's got nothing to do with guilt or fault. What each of us has to understand is that, while environmental or... well, a range of factors, can act as triggers, depression and anxiety disorders are complex health issues which are almost impossible to anticipate, let alone prevent. It's as much to do with the chemicals our brains need to function effectively and what happens when these chemicals are in short supply or when the brain absorbs them too quickly. I want to make this crystal clear.'

Besides his framed certificates, there are three posters on the wall, each one a labelled diagram of the brain, but there's nothing crystal clear about any of them.

'Nonetheless,' he concludes, 'it's also important to address any abiding anxieties and negative thinking patterns in order to achieve mental and emotional health, and we've identified this form of therapy as a key strategy in assisting Meg to do this. Does that make sense?'

He leads the discussion by referring to some of the

things he says I've said in previous sessions, seeking confirmation from me before inviting responses from my parents, but all I know is that I can't stop shaking. It won't stop. If I say nothing, but keep my arms like chains around me and both feet bolted to the floor, maybe the three of them won't hear me rattling apart.

They talk and occasionally, when there's no choice, I nod. It's not what he wants, but it's all I can give.

They're talking about emotions and I hear my mother use the words *brittle* and *vulnerable*, but although I'd normally rise to this, I shut it out and concentrate on containing myself. I am a tight box anchored to the floor.

Ian steers each comment towards an observation, paraphrasing and neutralising what's said at times, and I hear Dad mention *life experiences* and *adulthood*, but miss most of what he's saying. By the way the carpet is worn and discoloured, this room must've witnessed years of sessions like this, with the chairs in the same positions more or less, and it makes me sad. There are a couple of faded brown stains on the carpet, where coffee has been spilt and mopped up.

'Meg?' Ian says. 'Meg, are you with us? Did you hear what was being suggested?'

I look up, try to remember, and shake my head. 'No. Sorry.'

He pauses. 'The medication makes it hard to concentrate at times, doesn't it, Meg?' To my mother and father, he says, 'I did explain this is one of the side-effects, didn't I? That's why I believe it's better to have a few short sessions, rather than longer ones.' He pauses again. 'Perhaps if you try and express your feelings a little, Meg, it might help. After all, we need to hear what you're feeling in order to be able to understand and help you address those feelings, don't we?

We won't know otherwise, will we?'

'Yes,' I say, until I realise he's asked more than one question. 'No,' I add. Then: 'How's Stella?'

Dad smiles. 'Stella sends her love. She misses you. We all do. She thought you were coming home today and started baking a cake last night, just for you. To celebrate.'

'She misunderstood,' my mother says.

'We got our wires crossed,' Dad says.

'She'll bake another cake for when you *do* come home. You know how much she likes making cakes.'

'What happened to it?' I want to know.

'Happened to what?'

'The cake.'

Dad laughs. 'She threw all the ingredients straight into the bin. If you couldn't have it then nor could anyone else.'

This makes me smile. I'm happier because of this, but then it makes me want to cry too.

At one point, my mother says something which breaks through and shakes my anchored containment.

'I've always believed it's the responsibility of a caring mother,' she declares, 'to look out for the needs of her children, especially when their father is often absent because of work. It's not always easy doing the job of two parents, you know. It's even harder when you have to make decisions for them which you know they won't like.'

'It's an awkward cliché, but a matter of "being cruel to be kind," perhaps?' Ian suggests.

She pauses, considers. 'Well, no – no, not at all – but a matter of not always being very popular, perhaps. It's easy to make popular decisions, to let everyone do exactly whatever they want.' She glances at her hands, folded in her lap, and then back at Ian. 'Victor likes to make up for the time he's missed, I suppose.'

I watch Dad bite his lip, frown, and he says: 'Francine's had to do more than her fair share by herself because of the amount I'm away. It was particularly hard when the kids were little.'

'I managed,' she says.

Ian nods, smiles. 'It's a lot of responsibility being a parent, that's for sure. It's not an easy job at all, is it?'

I take a breath and want to speak, but the only words that come out are: '... about Pete.'

'Sorry, Meg, what was that?'

Another breath. This time, I work at pushing each word out slowly, carefully. 'She can't decide... who my... boyfriends are.'

'Ah. I'm glad you've shared that, Meg. Well done,' Ian begins. 'I know —'

'He was wrong for you,' my mother states, too emphatically, and the words hang there.

I can almost reach out and touch those five words, but don't know what to say in response. Then, after a great effort, I realise: 'You... never met him. How do you know... if... you never met him?' The sentence exhausts me.

Ian looks from me to my mother and waits. Dad closes his eyes and shakes his head. He rubs his face with his hands, but when he stops, he clasps them in front of his mouth. He looks at my mother and waits too.

'He was making you act strange,' she declares.

I grab a shallow breath and hope no one will speak before I say what I need to. I have to lean forward to help the words flow. 'I was happy. He was making me... happy.'

'He...' Mother jumps in, but stops. She shakes her head.

Ian waits. He gestures for her to carry on. 'This is an opportunity to talk all this through and bring it into the open. It's about supporting Meg and moving forward.'

But she shakes her head again and sits back in the chair. 'He was wrong for her. That's all. A mother knows these things.'

Ian slowly nods, half-smiles, clasps his hands together too. 'Forgive me, but you make it sound as if there's more to it than that. As if there's something else you want to share with Meg?'

She looks at him and purses her lips. 'Well, I'm sorry, but no there's not.'

I look to my dad, who pulls what might be a clownish face and shrugs.

I can't believe it. I begin shaking my head, but make myself stop. 'Then... I... don't... see... what... the... point... is.' Each word carries the weight of a breath. 'There's no point... in any of this... if she can't...' I struggle to find the words, but they elude me. '... if she won't.' I want so much to be sick. I've felt nauseous for days, off and on, but it sits there.

Ian holds up his hand. 'No, Meg, we're definitely making progress. You're making progress. You're doing very well.'

When he says, 'Let's go back a step to what we were talking about before, about parenting,' I close my eyes, can feel the breath die in me without a groan, because it seems he's erasing everything I've just said, about Pete and how happy I was, so it'll be as if I never even tried to say it. I only half-listen to him say, 'Is there a time, do you think, when, as parents, we have to step back a bit and let our children learn to take greater responsibility for themselves? When we have to expect that much of them?'

My parents are both sort of nodding and agreeing, although I haven't a clue what they're agreeing with. Then I sense a shift in my mother – a bristling hesitancy – and I try to take notice again.

'The job of being a parent gets even harder in a way, doesn't it,' he continues, 'because what we have to do is provide a safe environment in which our kids can take risks, take responsibility, and sometimes make mistakes for themselves? It can be the hardest thing, can't it, to let them do things differently to the way we'd do them, especially if we're frightened they'll get things wrong?'

My dad is still nodding, but my mother has become steely-faced. It slowly dawns on me where Ian has steered the conversation and I do my best to nod too. In a roundabout way, and while pursuing the argument my mother introduced, he obliges her to accept that, at seventeen, almost eighteen, I'm old enough to make decisions about boyfriends for myself. I hope that's what he's done.

I smile, but worry it might be seen as grinning. It's a small victory.

This is accompanied by a face-saving exercise too, though, and I'm alert enough now to understand what Ian is doing when he asks if I can accept that my parents have a responsibility to discuss such matters with me and to offer advice, and when he asks me to acknowledge how hard it can be for a parent to let go as their children become adults. I nod. I say, 'I do.' All the same, nothing can stop the bitterness I feel at losing Pete and the happiness we had together. You can't murder something so perfect and then bring it back to life again.

If only Pete had fought for me – for us. If only I'd meant as much to him as he'd claimed.

If only my mother had admitted what really bothered her instead of cloaking everything in gaps and silences.

If only Victor, in guessing what my mother was getting

at, had the guts to drag it into the open. If only he'd worried more about protecting me than appeasing her. Victor the Coward.

Either of them could've asked Dr Ian to leave for a few minutes, if they'd felt awkward talking with him there. I might not have broken into a million pieces, I might not have run away. They could've asked at least.

Or before. They could have brought the entire Pete Lailer business into the open any time before and settled it once and for all. There were years and years in which they could have resolved it between them.

If only, if only.

If only we could travel back in time and change every 'If only' in life.

Before Pete, there were other guys I played at going out with, but he was the only guy I'd ever longed to be with. It surprised me, but there were times when we were apart that I ached with missing him.

And I hate him. I hate Pete Lailer.

Bastard. Bâtard. Bastaard. Bastardo.

There is no word to save him.

Or Victor.

Or Mother Dear.

Dad and I are sitting in his car. He's switched off the engine, but I'd rather not unbuckle my seat belt. Not yet. He sits there too, waiting. I've only been in hospital a couple of weeks or so, but it's long enough to have become a stranger to this house. I'm no longer the person I was and this building, with its ridiculous little sign on the front gate – *Duparc House* – is no longer my home. I don't want the smallest part of it, especially its dark memories. It seems such a daunting feat, to walk from the car, down the path and across the threshold into the hallway, that I wish Dad could carry me.

'Victor,' I say. It's the first time.

He turns. 'Yes?'

'Can I call you Victor?'

'If you like,' he says and smiles. 'You always did when you were a little girl, before Stella was born.'

'Did I? Really? Good,' I say, and I make myself push open the car door. Stella will come running out any second, my mother will be waiting inside. 'Let's get it over with.'

I'll draw a line under this. Two thick, bold lines. It was the end of one life, the beginning of another.

EIGHT

I STOOD AT THE WINDOW and watched Stella head off to school. The world was pasty-grey, bedraggled, cross-hatched with rain, and it made me think of porridge slops. With one light breath, the glass misted from clear to greenish-grey and, spreading my fingers against its cold flatness, it reminded me of me. And yet, that first morning away from the ward, I didn't feel the slightest loss at waving goodbye to the school bus forever. As far as my anaesthetised emotions allowed, what I felt was free... or liberated at least. No more worrying about homework or exams, school uniform or school rules, the idiosyncrasies of teachers or the politics of the schoolyard ever again. Never again.

And typically, after shoving school, school, school, down my throat since I started Coddleston Primary, Mother now found it more convenient to believe that the pressures of school (coupled with flaws in my neurological make-up) were responsible for my emotional meltdown and for triggering my depression, rather than anything she'd said or done, or hadn't said and done. As if repetition carried its own conviction, she claimed several times that I'd always been predisposed to anxiety and even declared she'd been worried about whether I was coping since the start of Year Eleven. Ha! When Victor questioned this, she snapped back that he couldn't know because he was never around, and he backed off at that like a dog with its tail between its legs.

My mother was a liar and my father was weak. He was weakest when I needed him most.

Her willingness to let me leave school and sign up for a Horticulture-based course at Lapishot's College of Further Ed. was harder to fathom, but then suppressed guilt, like spite, can be a powerful motivator. When Dr Ian asked what I thought about continuing my education elsewhere – 'a less-demanding environment, perhaps' – and alternative career paths, the first idea to surface in my addled brain was landscape gardening. To be honest, I'd never thought about it before, but suddenly there it was. All those hours of working with Angie in her garden must have sown the idea.

It was hard to believe. Me, working outdoors with plants and soil, rocks and timber, doing practical stuff, and not studying to be a doctor or a lawyer, or whatever it was she had me pegged out to do. For the first time in my life, I couldn't think of anything I wanted to do more and, after all her dreams for me, it was like getting control back of who I was and who I might become. I couldn't wait to tell Angie.

Victor dropped me off at Angie's place because I wasn't allowed to drive while on medication, and Angie drew me inside and hugged me like she'd never let me go. Outside, it had grown colder and bleaker, with rain slashing down, whipping the driveway into muddy puddles; the wind was blowing the rain across the verandah, against the front door, but inside it was warm and snug, and Gustav strutted up and rubbed his body against my legs. She embraced me and squeezed me tight and I felt awkward at first, but after a moment I relaxed and gave in to being held like that, and it surprised me how much I needed to be held.

I know my brain was woolly, but I had a vision as we stood there that the world would be a safer, saner, more sheltered place if everyone had someone, or several people, to hug them tight every day and to mean it. With Angie's arms around me and her body pressing against mine, I couldn't help but think: Forget shaking hands and kissing cheeks, the world needs to learn how to hug and be hugged. Not short, superficial hugs, but long, blanketing hugs. She held me tight, pulling us firmly together, and I surrendered to being held like that until I was completely holding her too.

'Oh, Megsy,' she said, 'it's good to have you back. It's so good to see you. Welcome home.'

When she stood back and placed her hands on my shoulders to look at me, she stroked my hair briefly and smiled and kissed me on both cheeks. She might have been crying, which made me want to cry too, but I couldn't. Not so soon.

What else must I remember of the time between then and now? Apart from how completely Pete Lailer vanished from my life.

The Blackness, I guess. Mustn't forget the Blackness. It was the main hiccough. I made a mistake and it became my punishment, even though it wasn't totally my fault. Apart from that, they were four years of relative calm (no pun intended).

I got a job with *Hoekman Landscaping & Gardening*, which allowed me to study and work at the same time, like an apprenticeship, and there was a brittle truce between my mother and myself, even if it was eggshell-thin and quivered with tension at times. Its fragile nature highlighted that nothing had changed for her and that she had no intention of changing herself; there was the act she put on towards me, and then there was the way she'd always been and would always be for everybody else. It made me realise we'd never be close, the two of us. Our relationship was dead; she just needed to embalm it so it looked alive to other people.

As for the hiccough, I'd had enough of shoving antidepressants and other medication into my body, and genuinely believed I could stop taking them when I felt ready. This wasn't my fault. They should have explained, at a time when I wasn't drugged up to the eyeballs, that you have to be weaned off the things, lower dose by lower dose, and can't suddenly stop them or The Blackness will get you.

And it got me. The Blackness rolled in and took over my life.

I won't dwell on it – I can't – except to say it was a big, black swamp that sucked me in and fed off me. Like a nightmare I couldn't wake from, it grew so big it drowned every thought I had and every speck of light until it became the only element of existence, reducing me to a dark, miserable, saturated shadow – worse than being nothing. The only thought I could half-find my way towards was how to cheat The Blackness out of its hold on me.

That became my focus. It was easier to think about ending it than being drowned by it.

I thought about all the different ways it could be done, but decided the best way would be to take some pills and sling a rope from a tree in the forest. I figured the rope from the old swing might do, or the old washing-line coiled in the shed, but neither was any good (too frail, too short) and I had to buy a few metres of better quality stuff (just right) from the hardware store in Lapishot. I hid it in my old school backpack, deciding that if anyone saw me with it they'd just think I was going for a long walk. I'd wait until a weekday when Stella was at school, Victor was at work and Mother had gone into town to meet her cronies, and then I'd head into the forest and follow an animal track I knew. I'd find a tree with a strong, horizontal branch about three metres off the ground, but there'd have to be something underneath like a large rock or a fallen tree for me to climb onto, to drop from.

This was how I'd escape. I researched how to do it. I planned it methodically. I thought about all the other people who'd vanished into the forest.

On my second outing in search of the perfect spot, I found it. After that, I took to going for a walk, to my spot, almost every other day.

'I wouldn't mind a walk myself,' Stella said once. 'Can I join you?'

I allowed her to come the first time she asked, in case she grew suspicious. The second time, though, I said no.

'I need to be alone,' I explained.

There was something ritualistic and calming about sitting in my chosen place and thinking about what I was going to do. For a while, it made things better, less weighted-down and was enough to keep The Blackness at bay. It was a peaceful, timeless place I'd found, with the distant raucous of ravens and the primordial screeching of kedamores strangely adding to that timeless peacefulness during the day, while at night there'd be the creaking of branches, the rustle of leaves, the warbling of a coodylark or two.

When those waves of Blackness got too high, all I had to do was write a note – the things I needed to say – and grab my bag.

Dear Stella was the one who sensed something was wrong. She noticed the sickness of my shadow and how it was eating me up; how I avoided speaking if I could, or how I'd abruptly swing into being over-cheery. While Mother steered clear, it was Stella who phoned Victor and told him to come home, and it was Victor who hurried back to be with me and who gently explained and accompanied me to the doctor.

Months later, when they properly got me free of the medication, it was the sweetest joy to be able to think clearly and be alive again; to consider playing Chess and Scrabble, of all things, without having a brain clogged with soggy sponge, and to lose the extra weight I'd put on, because the drugs made me fat, fat, fat. I began to know who I was once more, who I'd once been, and what it felt like to be me. There was no way I'd ever let anyone put me in that other place again. Not ever, not ever, not ever. I made that vow to myself then and there.

I celebrated by nick-naming myself Mad Meg. It was my private joke and sometimes I'd answer the phone by saying, 'Hello, this is Mad Meg speaking.' Angie would laugh if she was on the other end or might ask if I could escape my padded cell for five minutes to come visit her, while Stella or Victor might respond with something like, 'You're the sanest one of all of us, Meg.' But Mother hated it. She'd purse her lips and want to spit at me. I could tell she did.

Also, so as not to forget, two things happened last year, which might've properly messed me up if I was the brittle basket-case my mother made me out to be, except they didn't. Of course they didn't. I wouldn't let them.

The first was when Graham Hoekman, my boss, announced he was giving up his landscaping and gardening business. He'd had enough of it, was ready to retire and wanted to move closer to the city where his kids and grandchildren lived, he said.

I was devastated. Graham was a good boss, he'd taught me a lot and I doubted there'd be any other landscaping and gardening business in the district willing to take me on. One of the Lapishot sawmills had closed down, taking a transport company and a couple of other firms with it, so heaps of workers had been laid off and times were tougher than they'd been for years.

The prospect of being unemployed and stuck at home or working as a check-out chick, serving kids I'd been at school with, filled me with dread. I didn't know what to do and, in the space of half-a-day, the future shifted from bright to dark again.

Worse still was that it put everyone's eyes on me – Mother, Victor, Stella – as if they expected me to have a breakdown on the spot; as if there's no difference between being fed up and being depressed. I sensed them watching me, waiting for the storm to break, and I wanted to shout at them to stop and to cover their eyes or look the other way, but instead I had to make light of things. I learnt to pretend, to smile when I didn't feel like smiling and to disguise my feelings better than ever before.

Victor came to my room one evening and sat down next to me. I was listening to music and reading a book.

'You okay?' he said.

'Yeah,' I said.

'Really?'

'Shit happens,' I replied, and turned a page.

This seemed to reassure him and he smiled, nodded. 'Maybe it's meant to be and something else'll turn up. Something better. Who knows? Sometimes it's like everything happens for a reason, isn't it?'

He'd said things like this before – they both had – but I don't think he really believed it. It was a silly, comforting thing to say to Stella and me when life hadn't gone the way we wanted. I didn't like that he said it, not anymore, especially if he didn't believe it, and it seemed like a weak thing for anyone with a gram of logic to say, let alone a research scientist.

I looked up. 'Part of a bigger plan? Like fate, destiny?'

'Yes. Exactly,' he said, brightening.

'I doubt it,' I said.

He shrugged. 'You never know. We can never tell what's round the corner. Clouds with silver linings and so forth.'

I shook my head, preferred to return to my book than be disappointed with Victor. 'Maybe.'

As it turned out, I needn't have worried. He and Mother must've talked it through, made a few enquiries, cooked up a plan, because a couple of days later she got me as soon as I arrived home from a job at Cowley Bend. I was in the laundry, kicking off my boots, about to wash my hands, and I noticed Dad's car was already in the garage. It was unusual for him to finish work before me.

She opened the laundry door and said, 'You're back then?'

'Yes.'

'How was your day?'

'Good. How was yours?'

She looked nonplussed as if mine was a silly question, then looked down to make sure I hadn't brought mud in on my boots. 'When you've cleaned up and changed,' she said, 'your father and I want a word with you.'

My heart sank.

They were in the sitting room, with a couple of booklets

and several documents spread out on the sideboard, and appeared conspiratorial and pleased with themselves. Stella came into the room straight after me and she looked as perplexed as I felt.

'Have a seat,' Victor began.

'What's up?' I said. 'What's happened? What have I done?'

'Nothing's up,' Mother said. 'Why should it be?'

'This decision of Graham's to retire...' Victor continued.

'Yes?'

Broad smiles.

'We have a proposal for you.'

'You do? What?'

'Well, we wondered whether you'd thought about taking on the business yourself? Not working for someone else, but being your own boss?'

'What, like starting a business from scratch?' Obviously I'd thought about it, but knew I couldn't afford the sort of set-up Graham had, with his truck and trailer, ride-on mower, push mower and various tools, and I'd learnt how hard it was to attract new clients, let alone establish enough regular clients to make it worthwhile.

'No,' he said. 'Have you thought about buying Graham's business from him, as a going concern?'

I shook my head. Graham regarded himself as a self-employed gardener with an assistant, rather than a business owner, and he liked a fuss-free life. He'd told me he didn't think they'd be any takers and that, anyway, he couldn't be arsed with the mountains of paperwork associated with selling a business. He'd looked into it and the only people who'd make any money out of it, he reckoned, would be the solicitors, the agent and the tax man; certainly not him.

'He's not selling,' I said, 'and I wouldn't be able to afford it if he was,' but then I'd already told them the whole story.

'Forget that second minor detail for the moment,' Dad began.

'What if we told you he'd sell it to you?' Mother asked. 'Your father's been on the phone to him, had a chat with our solicitor.'

I looked at Victor and he nodded, raised his eyebrows and grinned. 'You can buy it as a going concern: the equipment, customer-base, all the goodwill he's built up across the years. What do you reckon?'

I didn't know what to say. I looked at Stella, who seemed impressed, and she shrugged. 'How much?' I asked. 'Where will I get the money?'

'We'll loan you the money,' Mother said. 'We've talked about it and we've decided we'll loan you the money.'

I looked back at Victor.

He smiled. 'We will. If it's what you want. It'll be an interest-free loan. You can pay us back when you can afford to, but it'll be your business.'

'There are evening courses you can attend on running a business. We looked into it for you.'

'There's lots of information to help people set up small businesses. You can even apply for a Government grant.' He paused, took a breath. 'It's up to you, Meg.'

Which is how *Dapsy Landscaping & Gardening* began.

The second thing that happened, shortly after we signed off on the business, was when Angie applied for a teaching position at an International School in Malaysia and was appointed. I wouldn't see her for twelve months.

Angie and I had become even closer since I'd left Lapishot High. In fact, it didn't take much to realise that, of all my friends, she was the only one who stuck by me when

I was 'sick' and the only one worth keeping.

I know my spell on medication wiped me out of circulation for a few months, but, no two ways about it, my oldest friends dropped me and scuttled away quicker than you could say 'Psychiatric Unit'. Maybe they were embarrassed at not knowing how to be around a certified loony girl like me and so found it easier to avoid me altogether. Or maybe they felt guilty for allowing a small time, without getting in touch and asking how I was, to grow into too long a time, and then didn't know how to bridge that gap. All the same, I wouldn't have given up half as easily on Tess, Katie or any of the others, if a similar thing had happened to them, and I'd certainly stood by Tess when she'd rubbed life up the wrong way at various times before. On the whole, most people are shallow, self-centred and gutless when it comes down to it, and you soon learn who your friends are when the poo hits the fan.

Apart from Angie (and Stella, who doesn't count the same), there wasn't anyone else left. She was my dearest friend and my refuge, and I think I was hers.

'Take me with you,' I said, the way people do, knowing it can't be done.

'I'll make room in my suitcase,' she replied, but then stopped as if struck by a new idea. 'Orrr,' she said, drawing the word out for extra emphasis. 'Or you could fly out in my school holidays and we could explore Malaysia together. That'd be a great thing to do. Yes, definitely. How about that? You could stay with me in Kuala Lumpur and I'd show you around, and later we could travel up into Thailand and Cambodia. Seriously, we could do it.' She was beginning to bob up and down on her heels, waving her hands around, the way she did when she was excited. 'We'd have the best time together. We should, you know. We seriously should.'

How I wished I could say yes, but of course I couldn't.

'Why not? It'd do you good, Meg. Look, I'll show you on the map.'

I didn't move. 'The business,' I pointed out. 'It's going to be tight for the first couple of years. I won't be able to afford it. No way.' And before she offered to pay the airfare, I added: 'Neither the money nor the time.' Except I wasn't sure it was true about not taking time off. Maybe I was afraid that, if I left for a short while, it'd be too hard coming back. Everything I'd made good, or thought was good, might seem sour afterwards. It might highlight the life I wasn't having – how the people I'd been at school with had since left for university or taken gap years to travel the world. How would I ever settle down again?

She'd stopped bobbing. It was worse than if she hadn't suggested it in the first place. Perhaps she thought I could do it if I really wanted to, or perhaps she accepted I couldn't.

I was too deflated to ask what would happen with her house and Gustav. I didn't want to know. I imagined he'd either go with her or that one of her relatives would look after him, and I imagined she'd rent out her house or shut it up for the year. Life would be too dull without her, but it'd force me to spend my time making the business work and, well, anything could happen in a year. I might meet someone else, I might win the lottery. There was a one-in-fourteen-million chance either way.

During the afternoon, when I was back home feeling sorry for myself, she phoned and was all excited again.

'Meggy!'

'What's happened? Are you alright?'

'How would you like to live in my house for a year? To be my house-sitter when I'm away?'

'What?'

I sat with my mobile pressed against my ear and couldn't think what to say. The words bobbed around in the same way I imagined she was. It was too wonderful an idea. There must be a reason why it couldn't work, why it wouldn't happen, but if Angie was offering this... well, it would be like being part of Angie, being part of her life, and it'd get me away from home at the same time. Two birds with one stone.

'Are you there?'

'Really?' I said. 'Do you mean it?'

'Yes, really. Of course I mean it. I've been thinking of nothing else since you left.'

'Aren't you going to rent out your house, get some money for it?'

'Even if anybody wanted to live all the way out here, the thought of having strangers in my house, having to put the Bechstein in storage, dealing with estate agents... yuk! That's one of the things I've hated thinking about and I'd almost decided I'd rather sell up than do that. However, if you were to house-sit for me, it'd solve the problem and you could even look after His Royal Highness too. Would you mind taking care of Gustav for a year? Say you'll do it, Meggy. I'd love it if you would. You'll be doing me a huge favour.'

I felt like I'd won the lottery already. 'Oh yes, yes, I'd love to, Angie. Of course I would. Thank you, thank you. As long as you're sure? As long as you trust me? I promise I'll look after it.'

'Of course I do. I know you will. There's no one else I'd rather have here than you, Meggy. I just wish you could come with me, or at least visit me, but this'll be the next best thing.'

*

Together we strapped her suitcases into the back of my truck – *Dapsy Landscaping & Gardening* – which was a heap more reliable than Angie's old bomb (although not so unreliable that a colleague of hers wasn't happy to buy it for a song), and I drove her to the airport. It was a six-hour round trip, but before we left the house she went through her written notes (vet details, how to regulate the hot water service, what mail to forward, which bills to pay) and triple-checked she'd got her passport, her ticket, her wallet, and that she'd handed me the right bunch of keys.

'I'm certain there's something I've forgotten,' she said.

'It'll be alright,' I told her. 'I can easily get in touch if there's a problem.'

'Well, it's all yours then.' But she glanced back at the house several times between climbing into my truck and us pulling out the driveway. 'I can't believe I won't see it for a year. Or you.'

'Nor me. I'll try not to burn it down,' I laughed.

At the airport, I waited in the queue with her as she checked in, and afterwards we sat in a crowded, messy café and ate lunch together, but I couldn't say what I wanted to say and her focus was elsewhere. She talked about her new school and I tried to sound interested, I described the work I'd be doing for a new client and she nodded in all the right places, except neither of us were really hearing the other.

Not until we were outside the Departures Hall and it was time for her to go through Security and time for me to stay put did I find the courage to tell her the best I could.

'I'll miss you,' I said. 'You really don't know how much I'll miss you. Really.'

She hugged me. 'I'll miss you too, Meg.'

I wondered whether she'd understood me and I looked for some sign that she knew she was my closest friend, my only friend, and how fiercely I meant it.

I waited. I needed to know. And then I saw it: she bit her lip and struggled to smile and nodded.

'Good,' I said.

I tried to hug her the way she'd hugged me once, and then I stood back. I had to let her go.

'There are times I wish I wasn't going, you know. Especially right now.'

I smiled at that. 'Send me a postcard whenever you visit somewhere special.'

'I'll send you a postcard every month. At least once a month,' she promised, before leaning forward and kissing me goodbye.

It was a brief kiss, but a proper kiss on the lips, not the cheek. It was the first time I'd been kissed by another woman like that and I didn't know how to respond.

She looked at me a second – inquisitively, perhaps, to see how I'd taken it – but then hitched her flight bag onto her shoulder, clutched her coat and walked towards the automatic doors. I watched her walk away and, although it was only twenty paces or so, I was afraid she wasn't going to turn and wave, and that she'd said her last goodbye. They were long seconds of watching and brought with them the bitter flavour of being alone again, but at the final moment, when the doors slid open, Angie turned and gave me the brightest wave and blew me another kiss, and I waved back.

That was then. Before.

Two more lines.

NINE

Friday. Two days after the fire.

Keep busy, I kept telling myself. Much better to carry on working than to dwell on things. Much safer to have a routine.

Except I couldn't get the stink of smoke out my nose. It was everywhere. When I boil the kettle over breakfast for a peppermint tea, the steam has a smoky taint and my drink is bitter. When I let Gustav out the back door, the morning has the sharp, tangy smell of wet ash about it. Could it really have drifted all the way from Three Creeks, over the paddocks and through the forest, across the previous day and night, to saturate Angie's place? Or was I imagining it? I lifted my arm to sniff my clean work clothes, but it wasn't on me. It might have been in me, but it wasn't on me.

It wasn't going to be a good day. I could tell.

I got halfway across the lawn to the garage before realising I'd left my packed lunch on the hall table. Then, as I pulled the front door shut for the second time, the sound of two cars heading down the road towards Angie's place halted me. It was unusual to hear more than one solitary vehicle at a time on Nine Mile Road and so I waited, listening for them to accelerate into the distance, but they slowed as they approached the driveway and pulled in.

A marked police car and a dark blue sedan.

Breathe, I told myself. Breathe.

Mick Droyler got out first. He smiled and walked around the car, up onto the verandah.

I drew a long breath, exhaled slowly, but didn't move.

'Hi, Meg. I phoned to see if you'd be in, but couldn't get through. Looks like we caught you just in time.'

Caught me?

'Hi,' I said.

He hesitated. 'Everything alright?'

I nodded. Wanted to see who was in the second car. 'Have you found Dad?'

The door to the blue sedan opened and, with his balding head and brown suit, I recognised the arrogant prick who'd searched my truck and given me a hard time the day before.

Mick shook his head sympathetically. 'No, not yet. Meg, this is Detective Steven Earles. He's —'

'We've met. What's he doing here?'

Brown suit walked over and nodded a curt greeting, but remained on the path between the gravel of the driveway and the grass.

Mick said, 'I just need to have a quick chat and thought I'd see how you were, and this fella here is tagging along, getting to know the area. He may want to ask you a question or two as well. Like I said, remember?'

The phrase *kid gloves* sprang to mind. Mick was treading warily and handling me with kid gloves. Through Tess, if not from somebody else, he'd have heard the rough story of my breakdown and that I'd spent time on Ward 8, and it's possible he thought I was vulnerable, precariously wired, likely to blow a fuse at the slightest strain. Although maybe, for old times' sake, he was simply being friendly and sympathetic – going out of his way to be kind. Maybe he was that type of copper. Either way, no one likes to be considered a cripple, emotional or otherwise, and I was tempted to let him know that I was stronger and more resilient than most, thank you very much.

Or maybe they were up to something. What if they'd decided I was a prime suspect and they'd driven out here to spring a trap?

'Nice house,' Earles said, but his eyes were on everything. He took in the front of the house, glanced across the garden, looked a little longer in the direction of the old timber garage.

'I have to go to work,' I told them. 'I'm late.'

'That's some garage,' Earles said, but I wasn't fooled. 'Must be a hundred years old at least. What was it originally, a stable or something?'

He was such a fake. That's what irritated me most.

'I don't know. I wasn't here then.'

Mick smiled, but Earles said, 'Mind if I take a look?'

It's not as though he gave me much choice. I had half a mind to ask if he had a search warrant, but Mick was still smiling and so I shrugged. 'Whatever turns you on,' I said.

When he'd crossed the lawn and was about to go inside, I called out, 'Watch out for snakes. There was a copperhead in there the other day.'

He hesitated and Mick chuckled, but then carried on regardless.

Pulling out the front door key again, I said, 'You want to come inside?'

Mick shook his head. 'We won't keep you. I take it you still haven't seen or heard anything either?'

'From Dad? Nothing, no. I was about to phone and ask you the same thing. Is he okay, do you think? Why haven't the Animal Action mob claimed responsibility? Won't they want a ransom or something? Do you think he's alright? What will I do if they contact me? Or do you think they'd contact Demlab first?'

He ignored my questions. Why do the police always do that? Pretend-cops do it in films all the time too. They ask questions, but they never answer them.

'He hasn't drawn any money out of his bank accounts, Meg, and he hasn't used his credit cards, not since he arrived back from America. Do you know whether your parents kept much cash in the house?'

'I wouldn't know. Don't think so.'

Pulling out his notebook, he flipped it open and flicked through a couple of pages until he found what he was looking for. Meanwhile, Earles came out the garage, walked round the side and peered into the tangled undergrowth covering the back. What was he up to? I'd planned on clearing all that mess for Angie while she was away, although I reckoned it was the binding of creepers that held the rotten timbers and rusted-out roof together.

Perhaps he was looking for tracks or soil samples or something to do with my truck. It had to be that. Mick Droyler would keep me talking while he snooped around. Why else would the two of them come all the way out to Angie's? It was enough to make me think twice about Tess's dad.

'What's he looking for?'

Mick briefly glanced in Earles' direction and said, 'Meg, we noticed there's a small safe in one of the ground floor rooms. Would you know what the combination is by any chance? Otherwise we'll have to get a locksmith in.'

I'd forgotten about their safe.

'I don't. Dad probably told me once. It's only a fire safe, that's all, in the study, where they keep... kept passports, insurance documents, those sorts of things. I think my passport's still in it. Stella might remember the combination; she's good at remembering numbers.'

Earles emerged from the other side of the garage, stood on the lawn and brushed himself down before heading back toward us.

'It's not like they owned the crown jewels or anything,' I added. 'Or had piles of cash stacked in it.'

'No,' Mick said.

'That's old,' Earles said, smiling.

At first, I thought he said, 'That's odd,' and I wondered what he'd found?

'What is?' I said.

'The garage, or whatever it was originally. It's probably older than the house.'

Mick and I were on the verandah and Earles was looking up from a rectangle of morning brightness on the lawn, until he stepped up to join us.

'You don't often see timbers cut like that. Have you noticed them? They're old tree trunks sawn in half, lengthways, without any planing back.'

I glanced at Mick and Mick shifted his weight from one foot to the other.

'Meg was telling me about the safe at her parents' house. Is there anything you need to ask, Detective?'

'No, I don't think so. Not at the moment,' Earles said and smiled again.

Mick waited a moment and cleared his throat. 'Now, Meg, we have to ask this,' he began, and I immediately tensed. 'We have to look at every possibility.'

I tried to nod and say 'Okay,' but no sound came out. He was about to ask if I did it, if I set fire to the house. This was their test, their trap.

'About your dad. You might not want to think about this, but do you know whether he was having a relationship – an affair – at all? Or your mum for that matter? Was there any suggestion of this or... or anything whatsoever? Anything strange? Any quarrels?'

Hadn't he already asked about that stuff? I opened my mouth, but stopped and relaxed a little. I could sense Steven Earles staring at me, probably trying to gauge my reactions, trying to winkle-pick his way into my head. Perhaps they'd got wind of something and were trying to throw me off my guard.

What to say? I remembered what my mother told me about Victor's old girlfriend, and wondered now if it'd be worthwhile telling them how he might've still been seeing her, regardless of what he'd claimed. *Abby, short for Abigail.* But I couldn't see how that'd help. It couldn't possibly. It'd make things worse.

'An affair? I don't think so,' I said. 'No. Not that I know of.' But they noticed my hesitation and so, to cover it, I said, 'Why? Why do you ask? Have you found something suggesting he was?'

'If he left of his own free will, then someone must have given him a lift, or he wouldn't have left his own car behind. There's no record of him ordering a taxi.'

It seemed nonsensical, this line of enquiry. Instead of pursuing the A.A.R. they were going off in this weird direction. The thought made me shudder. Perhaps that's why they were looking behind the garage.

'You don't believe the Animal Libbers have got him, do you? You wouldn't be asking otherwise.'

Earles acted as if he knew everything. 'Groups like the A.A.R. don't keep quiet if they've done something like this. Believe me, they'd want the publicity – as much as they can get – while the media's still interested, otherwise it's pointless for them. So you see –'

'What about the graffiti?' I blurted out.

He almost sprang at me. 'What graffiti? How do you know about that?'

Too late to un-say it.

I looked at him, I looked at Mick.

'What graffiti?' he repeated.

'The graffiti on the front of the house,' I said. 'Like last time. That word.'

'When did you see that?'

'Yesterday,' I told him, 'when I came to the house.'

'You couldn't have seen it,' Earles snapped back at me. 'You were only at the back of the house. I didn't let you go any further.' At which Mick Droyler stood a little straighter.

I shook my head. Had to think fast and tell it right. Otherwise it'd seem I knew more than I should. Otherwise it'd look like I did it.

'That was in the afternoon,' I explained. 'I stopped by in the morning too, on the way back from the hospital. That's when I saw it. All the neighbours were milling around.'

I breathed easier again. Besides, even if I hadn't seen it, I'd have heard about it soon enough. News travels fast in a place like Three Creeks. Sinister details and juicy titbits of gossip travel at the speed of light. That's the nature of such a place.

He looked at me and said nothing, and I decided not to volunteer anything else.

'You'd have had to catch a taxi back from the hospital, wouldn't you, Meg?' Mick said, confirming my story as much as anything, and shifting his weight from one foot to the other again.

'That's right. After you dropped me off to see Stella.'

'What time was that?' Earles wanted to know.

'In the taxi? Shortly after eight, I think. Around then. It could have been earlier.' Out of habit I looked at my watch; I fumbled with my keys and almost dropped my lunchbox. 'That's why I thought it must be those animal liberation nuts again. After last time. Who else would do that... write that?'

'Things aren't always what they appear to be,' Earles said. As if I didn't know.

Mick said, 'We have to explore every angle, every possibility, Meg. That's all. And it is a possibility your dad left of his own free will – that he wasn't hurt or kidnapped.'

I nodded, felt easier again. Mick was alright. He really was. 'I know,' I said. 'I understand. I appreciate what you're doing. Really I do.'

There was a noticeable pause, as if we'd got to the end of official police business, and Mick smiled (warm and genuine, unlike Earles' fake smile). 'You're heading back to work already, Meg?'

'It's easier to keep busy,' I told him. 'It'll take my mind off things. There's nothing else I can do.'

'Fair enough. I think I'd be the same. Nothing to be gained by sitting around stewing over things.'

'No.'

'Anyway, Tess sends her love. She asked to be remembered to you and to tell you she's thinking of you.'

It took me aback. 'Thanks. I appreciate that.'

Earles said, 'We'll let you know if we have any news.'

'Okay. Thank you.' It was the politest I'd been to him. I had to be careful. I doubted he was as foolish as he seemed.

'Or if we need to ask you any more questions.'

After Angie left for Malaysia and I began house-sitting for her, it was enough at first to unpack my suitcases and boxes and to find places for my things amongst her belongings. Sometimes I'd walk from room to room, stroking a hand across the timber furniture, sensing the solidness of it, or needlessly plumping up the cushions on the settee. In moving from one house to another, from one world to another, it was like shaking off the remnants of childhood and its hold over me, to embrace something more vibrant and vital and full of promise, even if it left me anxious and uncertain too.

I'd tentatively open drawers and cupboards to discover what they held (tablecloths, Angie's winter jumpers, spare bed sheets, dresses and skirts, shoes, knick-knacks), or I'd pick up and examine ornaments I'd seen a thousand times before. I'd sit and stroke Gustav as he dozed, bury my face in a bath towel, or simply take a deep breath whenever I detected Angie's scent on something. All this exploring and discovering, all this seeing and touching and smelling, helped confirm the certainty that I'd really left the past behind and was living a new life.

But while being surrounded by so many intimate reminders brought Angie back to me, and sometimes reminded me how she'd kissed me, it also highlighted her absence. She was someplace else, a long way away, and would be for a whole year. What's more, the knowledge that she'd rarely write emails and hated the idea of posting photos online made the distance seem greater. How I longed for her first postcard, to see the words she'd write for me.

It arrived at the end of that first week, and though the picture was a bog-standard, touristy photo of Kuala

Lumpur's twin towers, the realisation that Angie must've written and mailed it within hours of landing cheered me. I was her first thought.

> Dearest Meggy, Good flight, although last stretch a little bumpy. Torrential rain on journey to KL, but steamy now. Very humid. Hope you had safe journey back and that you settle into house quickly. Haven't been up Petronas Towers yet, but saw them from bus — maybe tomorrow. I wish you'd been able to come with me and that we could explore this city together. Please change your mind about visiting if you possibly can. Look after yourself and have fun. Love, Angie xx

Her second postcard arrived two weeks later. It showed a bustling street market at night, full of bright, contrasting colours, with street-vendors cooking food in the foreground and a mass of stalls and people filling the street behind. Hanging from racks and spread across benches were scarves, hats, T-shirts and jewellery, and I imagined Angie squeezing through the crowd, wandering from stall to stall, buying a silk scarf, trying on earrings, tasting spicy dishes. I pored over every detail until I could almost taste the flavours of the place myself, hear the raucousness of the market, smell the rich, distant exoticness of that world.

> Dearest Meggy, Have settled in and begun to make friends. School is good — better resourced than I'm used to — and the kids are amazingly well-behaved. Not quite used to that yet! Colleagues and students are from around the world, although mainly Malaysian. Struggling with humidity, although am told will soon get used to it. The monsoonal rain is

She wrote nothing about the market, or anywhere she'd visited, but at least she'd sent two postcards in three weeks. I pinned them up in the kitchen, on the big cork board next to the fridge, but had to rearrange things to fit them in.

I'd examined Angie's collection of cards, photos and tiny newspaper clippings hundreds of times before, almost every time I'd been in the kitchen with her (having a cup of tea at the end of a session on the piano, grabbing a glass of water when we'd been working in the garden, all those meals she'd cooked for me), and I'd inspected them again after moving in because occasionally she replaced old ones with new favourites. Strangely, it wasn't until I rearranged them that I realised one of my long-standing favourites — a card of Chagall's *The Green Night* — was a birthday card I'd sent her. I had no memory of buying it, writing in it, or giving it, and couldn't remember what present accompanied it, but sure enough it was my handwriting inside: *Happy birthday (belatedly) to the best friend I could ever have, and thank you. Hope you had a wonderful day. All my love, Meg xxxxx*

I couldn't remember what I was thanking her for, but guessed from its lateness that I'd probably written it shortly after being released from the Happy Farm.

That Friday, the second day after the fire, turned out to be another bright, clear, still day, although the sun didn't have much warmth to it. Nonetheless my head remained in fog.

I was wrong to think keeping busy would help, because even as I trimmed hedges, raked lawns, tidied edges, I couldn't stop thinking about the fire, what had happened, why it had happened and where the police were going with their investigation, or rather where they *weren't* going. I was slower getting round my clients because I couldn't stop figuring what I had to do next. It was like trying to plan ten moves ahead in a chess game: considering all the different ways to position an opponent while anticipating every potential response. I really had to be careful not to tell the police too much, but was beginning to think they needed pointing more firmly in the right direction. I'd already told Mick Droyler the story about the car and white van parked next to each other at the campsite shortly before the fire, but apparently that wasn't enough.

In the middle of the afternoon, once I'd cleared as much as I could on a new residential job where the grass and shrubs were spectacularly overgrown, I made my decision. I stowed my tools in the back of the truck, loaded the ride-on mower on the trailer, climbed into the cab and closed the door. Part of me was still tempted to start the engine and move off, but I knew I wouldn't be easy until I'd spoken to Mick again. I had to do it. I'd rehearsed the conversation over and over, looked at it from every which way, so I took out the card he'd given me and tapped out his number.

He answered straightaway, but sounded busy.

'It's Meg Dapsy,' I said.

'Hi, Meg. What can I do for you?'

He was more formal on the phone, which worried me, until I reminded myself that everything had turned to shit and I had no choice but steer a way through. There was too little left to lose. I had to do whatever I could.

'I feel silly phoning you,' I said.

'You've remembered something? That's alright. That's fine. I'm glad you've called.'

It sounded like he was about to say something else and I waited, until he prompted me: 'What is it, Meg? What have you remembered?' If anything, he sounded impatient.

'It's about the A.A.R.'

'You've heard something? They've been in touch?'

If only.

'No, it's nothing like that.'

'What then?'

'Look, this is going to sound bad. It might sound as if I'm saying this out of spite or anger, but I'm not. Honestly.'

'Okay.'

'In fact, I decided not to say anything this morning when you and the detective called, simply because of how it might sound and because there's probably nothing in it.'

'What is it, Meg?'

'Okay, well, you probably heard from the other officer – your colleague, Officer Aitkens – that Stella was seeing an ex-boyfriend of mine?'

He said nothing.

'Pete Lailer,' I reminded him.

'Go on.'

'Well, I never thought of it before, and there's probably absolutely nothing in it... I don't want to get him in trouble if he's got nothing to do with it...'

Still he remained silent and it was putting me off. I should have waited until I'd gone into the station because I could've gauged his reactions more accurately, except I thought it'd be easier over the phone.

'When we were together, when I was seventeen,' I hurried on, 'he was right into Animal Rights. The A.A.R. Even though he worked in Demlab.'

'He worked at Demlab?'

'Yes, he was a trainee computer technician or something.'

'Why didn't you mention this before, Meg? After the graffiti was scrawled on your parents' house?'

'Because I didn't know he was back in town. He quit Demlab and he left Lapishot a couple of months after we broke up. That was more than two years ago – no, almost four years.'

'Four years?'

'Almost.'

'It was when I was still at school and so I didn't make the connection. I had no reason to.'

'Okay. Go on. You thought he'd left the area? Where did he move to?'

'He travelled overseas and went to uni, I think. I didn't even know he was back until I saw him from a distance a few weeks ago. I thought he must be visiting his mum or something, but Stella told me he's working in town again and he's been back for two or three months now.

'Okay. Okay. So, this lad –'

'Peter Lailer.'

'Lailer? How do you spell that?'

'L-A-I-L-E-R. He's the one Stella... But that's not the reason.'

'Yes, anyway, what you're saying is that he would have known your dad was the manager of Demlab and he'd have known where he lived?'

'Yeah. It was no secret.'

'And did he tell you, when he was your boyfriend, that he was a member of an Animal Rights group?'

'Well, he didn't actually show me a membership card or anything –'

'No, well –'

' – but he made it clear he didn't much like animals being used for research and he definitely thought it was good what groups like the A.A.R. did. He showed me their website, a couple of videos, that sort of thing.'

'Yet he worked for Demlab?'

I shrugged, the way you do even when you're talking on the phone. 'There's never that many jobs to choose from, not around here.'

'That's true,' he said.

It was getting stuffy in the cab, so I wound the window down, enjoyed the rush of fresh air. Our conversation was going better now.

'He laughed about it,' I said. 'Told me they needed people working on the inside.'

'He said that? Are you sure?'

'Something like that. Words to that effect. It was a while ago and he might no longer think it, of course. Even then, it seemed more like a joke than anything else. He was only nineteen at the time.'

'But you think he could have been involved with the graffiti and –'

'No. I don't know.'

'What then?'

'I'm not sure. Why would he have done any of that – be responsible for that – if he was going out with Stella? No, I don't think... I just thought... Well, you said if I thought of anything whatsoever and I couldn't help wondering if he – if Pete – might have any contacts with the A.A.R. who would know what's happened to Dad. That's all. It might be a way...'

Taking a deep breath, I glanced out the window and at the rear-view mirror. A small flock of sparrows were pecking at the lawn I'd just slashed and cleared.

'A way of what, Meg?'

'A way of finding out whether they did it... where Dad is... if he's okay. That's all.'

Another silence. I'd said too much. Perhaps I shouldn't

have said anything the other day about the car and the white van. When they checked up on him and found out he had a bluey-grey car registered in his name, maybe it'd be too obvious I'd described Pete Lailer's car. I wasn't sure anymore. It was too hard to know.

'Are you in Lapishot now?' he asked.

'Yes. I am. I'm in Walcott Avenue. Why?'

'You said you'd call into the station to have a look at some pictures of vehicles, to identify the make and model of the ones you saw parked at the campsite recently. I meant to remind you this morning. Maybe now would be a good time?' It was as if he'd read my mind.

'I guess I could,' I said, and I wondered now if I shouldn't pick out a different model to Pete Lailer's, or be deliberately vague, so all they'd have was the colour – nothing too specific. 'I was about to go to another job, but I guess I could call in first.'

'If you could.'

'You won't let him know I told you this, will you?'

'We'll see you in a few minutes, Meg.'

I waited a moment in case he had anything else to say. 'Okay.'

Everything was tied up in knots, thanks to bloody Pete Lailer. There was no way I could let him and Stella stay together.

My sense of Angie's presence ebbed and flowed, waxed and waned. There were times when the house was brimming with her, as if she might walk from one room to another at any moment, and this made me wait anxiously for the post. But after a few days, when no postcard was delivered, the house became so empty it echoed with her absence, and I felt more like a ghost haunting it than her house-sitter. I'd walk from room to room, cupboard to cupboard, drawer to drawer, picking up and examining her belongings, reminding myself that we were, after all, sharing this house together.

Then, when a postcard finally arrived, it reminded me how intimate and close the two of us really were, regardless of the kilometres. At first, I'd be able to hear her voice behind each word she'd written, could visualise her squeezing each compact sentence into the limited space there was on the card as she sat in a Malaysian café somewhere, sipping strong coffee, and I could smell the monsoonal humidity of the place, the sweatiness of the people around her. She'd transport me to her. Until, as I re-read the words over and over, searching each phrase for extra nuances of meaning, and began to think about what I might write in reply, my sense of her proximity would fade and I'd realise how separate we were.

Her third postcard arrived one month after the second. Disappointingly, instead of the tight lines of microscopic words, there were only five lines in her usual-sized handwriting:

> HI MEG, TOOK STUDENTS TO SEE EXHIBITION WITH THIS PIECE BY GIACOMETTI. VERY GOOD. THANKS FOR YOUR LETTER. IT MADE MY DAY AND MADE ME REALISE HOW MUCH I MISS YOU TOO. WILL WRITE MORE NEXT TIME. LOVE ANGIE XX

Two postage stamps, illustrating different Malaysian spiders, obliterated half my surname, but that didn't matter. The front of the postcard was a photograph of Alberto Giacometti's sculpture *The Palace at 4am*.

The figure of a woman stands in one 'room' of a structure that might be the frame of a house or a cage of sorts, or the palace itself. There's a large pod shape, like a crude boat, mounted upright on a wall, with a round object at one end, which might symbolise a baby in a cot, although the more I look at this the less I'm sure. In another 'room', in a cage within the house-cage, is what looks to be a long spinal column – longer than the woman is tall – and above this, framed by a window space at the top of the building, is a skeletal bird. The bird's wings are stretched wide in frozen flight and its lethal beak is frozen in a primordial scream, except the entire scene is haunted by silence.

I propped the card on my bedside cabinet and wrote a reply.

Stella would come and stay with me straightaway, as soon as she was released from hospital. Or so I imagined. She'd have my bedroom and I'd move into Angie's room, which Angie wouldn't mind at all. It'd only be until we'd sorted out what was happening to Duparc House; like whether it had to be bulldozed and re-built, and whether we wanted to sell it or not. We wouldn't know what our options were until the insurance claims were submitted and worked through. Not that I thought anything would happen in a hurry. In the meantime, we'd keep each other company and I'd help her get through the rest of the school year and her exams.

Except Stella had other plans.

After calling at the Police Station, where – surprise, surprise – I wasn't able to identify the specific model of the bluey-grey car, while I could pick out the white van as a Mercedes-Benz Sprinter Van, I returned to the hospital. Stella was still in bed, waiting to see the doctor. Neither of us mentioned our argument, nor Pete Lailer, and I certainly wasn't going to tell her where I'd just been or what I'd told Mick Droyler about lover-boy over the phone. Instead we were guardedly polite with one another, which made me wonder even more about Stella because she'd never been like that with me before.

'How was your day?' she asked. Then, noticing my overalls: 'You haven't been working, have you?'

I said, 'I wanted to take my mind off things.'

'Oh, I suppose so. Did it work?' she asked. 'You look exhausted.'

'No. Haven't been able to think about anything else. How are you feeling?'

'I've felt better.'

'I thought they'd have discharged you by now,' I said. 'I've been expecting you to phone all day, asking me to pick you up. They're not keeping you in for another night, are they?'

'I don't know. I hope not. I think the doctor's been caught up in some sort of emergency. You go on home – back to Angie's, I mean. You don't have to stay here. Besides, you look like you could do with a proper sleep.'

'You'll phone me when they say you can leave? Or tell me what's going on if they want to keep you?'

'Yes, of course.'

Perhaps she hesitated. Perhaps there was something else in her tone I might have noticed, but that's pretty much the way the conversation went – strained – and what we agreed.

Driving back to Angie's, I slowed as I passed the house in Three Creeks, where a van and a car were parked in the driveway. They hadn't been there earlier, I don't think, but I noticed them now. The sun was a low blob in the sky, sinking into the furthest horizon of trees, and it wasn't a good light, but I could see that the van was much like the one I'd described to Mick Droyler, except this was light blue and had *Forensics* or *Pathology* or something painted across the rear doors, and alongside that was Detective Steven Earles' dark blue sedan.

When I got to Angie's, someone had left a casserole next to the front door – meat, carrots, peas and potatoes, by the looks of it, in an earthenware dish – and I was glad I'd been out when they called. I picked it up, but before I got the key in the door, my phone rang. Balancing the letters from the mailbox and the casserole with one hand and sorting through my keys in the other, I couldn't get the phone out my pocket quick enough to answer and the missed call listed a long, unfamiliar number. I wasn't sorry because I didn't want to talk to anyone else right then, but that's when I found the front door was already unlocked.

I'd used my key to get back in that morning, after forgetting my sandwiches, but I'd gone back inside again after the cops left, because I needed the loo, and maybe I'd pushed the latch up without thinking. It's not the sort of thing I'd usually do, leaving the house open all day, but my head was messed up and I couldn't be absolutely sure either way. It rattled me, though. Anybody could have got in and snooped around; even the person who'd left the casserole. What if some random nutter had found their way out here, or someone who had it in for me? They could still be hiding inside for all I knew.

All sorts of possibilities rushed through my mind.

Maybe this person, whoever it was, was the same person who'd just phoned me and hung up. Perhaps they were lurking in the shadows on the edge of the forest, phoning me to spook me and check out my reaction. I'd watched a film with a scene like that once.

I was exhausted, like Stella said, and I wasn't thinking straight, but I locked the door behind me now, put everything else down on the hall table and grabbed one of Angie's golf clubs. It was only after I'd gone through each room, checked all the windows were fastened and assured myself that no one was inside that I started to relax, which is when my mobile rang again. I answered it this time.

'Hello, Meg Dapsy Landscaping and Gardening.'

Nothing.

'Hello?' No answer. Not even the crackle of a weak signal. It sounded like someone was listening, but I couldn't hear a whisper of them.

Then the call ended.

I was even more spooked now. That's how tired I was. I decided it wasn't some casual nutter, but Pete Lailer. I was sure of it in the same way I sometimes knew Stella was ringing, or Victor, or Mother, before I'd answered. It certainly wasn't a customer asking me to quote on a job. It had to be Pete Lailer. He'd got wind of what I'd said to Stella or Mick Droyler and the bastard wanted to give me a hard time. It didn't make sense, but I was so jumpy I couldn't help myself.

I needed to sleep or keep busy. One or the other. I should have stayed with Stella until it was time to bring her back to Angie's.

A couple of minutes later, I realised it was probably Stella trying to get in touch because she was ready to come home. She said she'd phone.

I rang the hospital switchboard and asked to speak to her.

'Has the doctor seen you yet? Do you know when you're getting out?'

There was a moment's hesitation before she said, 'Yeah, now. I'm just getting dressed. The doctor finally got round to me about fifteen minutes ago and she says I'm okay to leave. I was about to phone you.'

'You didn't try phoning a few minutes back? Twice?'

'No. Why? The nurse has only just taken out the drip-thingy.'

'It's nothing. Doesn't matter. Someone tried ringing and I thought it might be you.'

'No.'

'Okay, well, I'll come and get you,' I said, and felt relieved even though it meant doing the thirty-minute drive back into Lapishot. 'I'll grab a bite to eat and I'll come and get you.' It'd be good having company again.

'No. That's alright. You don't need to. I'm staying with Jasmine.'

'Jasmine?'

'Just for a few days. Really, it'll be too hard getting to school and back from Angie's place and I've got final assessments coming up next week. I can't afford to miss any more time. Besides, it's all sorted. Jasmine visited me straight after you left and her mum invited me to stay. Until we get a few things sorted.'

'But it's Saturday tomorrow – the weekend. Isn't it? Look, if this is –'

'It's got nothing to do with him – with Pete – honest. I'm staying with Jasmine, not Pete. For the moment, anyway.'

For the moment? I didn't believe her. She was fobbing me off, treating me like I was stupid. It was exactly the same lie she'd used on Mum. She was probably all set to move in with Peter-bloody-Lailer now.

'You mustn't see him again, Stella. Really. You mustn't.'

'No, Meg, don't. Don't start that again.'

'I mean it, Stella.' I had to do something. 'Look, you wait there, at the hospital. I'll come and get you. We need to talk. We really need to talk. Urgently. I thought you were coming here and then, well, I was going to –'

'Stop it, Meg. I know you're upset, and... and... I know that.'

She was beginning to cry again. I could hear her.

'I didn't mean for it to happen and I'm sorry,' she carried on, 'but you can't help who you fall in love with. You can't, can you?'

'It's not about that – about me. It's not. Look, I'll come in. Stay there.'

'No. I won't. I won't. Jasmine and her mum will be back for me soon. I don't want you to, Meg. I don't want you here.'

I could've told her everything that our mother told me two days before, but I had to be careful and it would've been too difficult saying it over the phone. Instead, I said, 'Stella, the police think he could be involved.'

'What?'

'It's true, Stella. They know he's into all that Animal Rights stuff. Don't you know what they sprayed across the front of the house before they set fire to it?'

I'd pressed the phone hard against my ear until it hurt, and I squeezed my eyes tight shut. It was all I could do to stop blubbering again too.

'No, that's not true,' she said. 'You know it isn't. It's not true.'

'It is,' I told her. 'I'm afraid it is.'

Then she said: 'You're mad. You are mad. I don't believe you.' And she hung up.

After all I'd done for her.

Twenty minutes later, I was lying on the settee with a cushion over my head, wishing I could stay like that forever. I'd begun drifting away from the meanness of Stella's words when my phone rang yet again. I wanted to ignore it, but figured it might be Stella grovelling an apology and a change of mind.

Except it was the same new number as before and so I answered it, but played them at their own game and didn't say a word. I listened to whoever was listening to me, until Angie spoke.

'Hello, Meg – Meggy? Are you there? Can you hear me?'

'Angie, it's you. I didn't know who it was.' I sat up properly on the settee. 'Did you phone before, earlier? I couldn't hear you.'

'Yes, it's me. I've been trying to get through to you. At last.' She sounded distant, as if the telephone satellite was about to break from orbit and drift away into the empty universe. 'Can you hear me?'

'Yes, just.'

'Oh, Meggy, I heard what happened. Someone at school... I'm so sorry. Are you okay? Is there anything I can do? Anything at all?'

I didn't want to cry again, but I didn't want to talk either. Not with Angie. Not then. Hearing her voice reminded me of everything she'd written in her letter. It was sitting on the mantelpiece, where I'd propped it on Wednesday.

'There's nothing you can do,' I told her. 'There's nothing anyone can do.' How I wished I'd gone with her to Malaysia and that we were sitting somewhere exotic talking about something completely different. How I wished she'd phoned me every week and just talked to me. How I wished she'd never left. How I wished Wednesday had never happened.

'Is there any news about your dad?'

'No. Nothing. No news.' I couldn't think what else to say.

'I wish I could come back and be there for you, but... '

She paused and I hesitated. Even though I didn't want her here, seeing me at my worst, none of this would've happened if she hadn't gone away. Maybe it wouldn't have happened if she hadn't written that letter.

'It's alright. There's no point,' I said. 'You've probably got exams to mark or reports to write or something.' They were the words she'd used.

'I do. That's right, but I'll get away if you want me to. I'll come back for the weekend if it helps.'

'No, there's no point.'

There was another brief pause before she said, 'I can't believe it. I really can't believe it. It's terrible, Meggy. I wish I could do something.'

'There's nothing you can do,' I told her again. 'The police are doing everything they can.'

'Do they know how it started?'

'It was Action for Animal Rights, they reckon. Arson.'

'No.'

I wanted the phone line to die, for the call to end. I wished I'd never been born.

'How's Stella? Is Stella okay?'

'Stella's fine.'

'You sound exhausted, Meggy. I wish I could be with you.'

I wanted to tell her I'd received her letter and to ask what it meant. I wanted to tell her what my mother said about Pete Lailer and how Victor said it probably wasn't true – it very likely wasn't the case at all – but I couldn't. I didn't want to lie to her, not to Angie of all people, but things were different between us now and always would be; they had to be. Nothing could ever be the same again.

'I am. I'm exhausted,' I said. 'It's been a nightmarish couple of days.'

'Well –'

'Look, sorry, Angie, but I have to go. I'm expecting another call. There's a lot to sort out. I'm sorry, but... '

'That's alright. I understand. You make sure you let me know if there's anything I can do, though.'

'I will, yes. Thanks.'

After she'd hung up, I noticed the battery in my phone was almost flat. I muted it and plugged it into my charger, then took the envelope off the mantelpiece and unfolded the sheet of paper inside.

DEAREST MEGGY,

I'M SORRY IT'S TAKEN ME SO LONG TO WRITE A PROPER LETTER TO YOU, BUT THAT DOESN'T MEAN I HAVEN'T BEEN THINKING ABOUT YOU. I CERTAINLY HAVE. MORE THAN YOU CAN KNOW. ANYWAY, BEFORE I GET BOGGED DOWN IN MARKING EXAM PAPERS AND WRITING REPORTS, AND INSTEAD OF MERELY SCRIBBLING A FEW LINES ON THE BACK OF A POSTCARD, HERE'S A PROPER LETTER AS WELL AS A POSTCARD. HOW HONOURED YOU MUST FEEL. NO ONE ELSE GETS BOTH!

EVERY TIME I SEND A CARD, I IMAGINE YOU PINNING IT UP IN THE KITCHEN ALONGSIDE THE OTHER CARDS, AND SOMETIMES IT FEELS AS IF I'M ALMOST THERE WITH YOU, WHILE AT OTHER TIMES IT ALL SEEMS VERY FAR AWAY, AS IF THAT PART OF MY PAST BELONGS TO A DREAM.

I'VE SENT YOU THIS PHOTO OF KLCC PARK, WHICH IS AT THE BASE OF PETRONAS TWIN TOWERS, BECAUSE IT'S SOMEWHERE I'VE GROWN QUITE FAMILIAR WITH, AND HAVE HAPPY ASSOCIATIONS WITH. I'VE WANDERED THROUGH AND SAT IN THE PARK SEVERAL TIMES, SOMETIMES MEETING A FRIEND HERE, AND IT'S ALWAYS A POPULAR SPOT. MORE THAN THAT, AND AS WITH ANY PARK OR GARDEN I VISIT, IT ALWAYS MAKES ME THINK OF YOU. THERE ARE SO MANY EXOTIC PLANTS AND TREES I'VE NEVER SEEN BEFORE — BRIGHT, LARGE

FLOWERS AND STRANGE-LOOKING FRUIT — AND I KNOW YOU'D LOVE IT. YOUR GARDENER'S THUMB WOULD BE TWITCHING OVERTIME.

THINGS ARE GOING WELL FOR ME — VERY WELL. I'VE MADE A NUMBER OF GOOD FRIENDS, WHO I WISH YOU COULD MEET, AND I ENJOY TEACHING MORE THAN EVER BEFORE (IT MAKES ALL THE DIFFERENCE WORKING WITH STUDENTS WHO ARE INTERESTED IN LEARNING AND BEING IN A SCHOOL THAT HAS THE RESOURCES TO HELP THAT HAPPEN).

MEG, I DON'T KNOW HOW TO TELL YOU THIS APART FROM JUST SAYING IT, BUT I HAVE SOME EXCITING NEWS: I'VE MET SOMEONE!

I AM SO HAPPY.

WE MET ON MY FIRST DAY AT THE SCHOOL AND BECAME GREAT FRIENDS STRAIGHT AWAY. SHE SHOWED ME AROUND, INTRODUCED ME TO HER FRIENDS AND HELPED ME GET SETTLED AND FEEL COMFORTABLE HERE, BUT — WELL, YOU KNOW HOW THINGS CAN HAPPEN — SOMETHING ELSE CLICKED BETWEEN US. FOR THE LAST FEW WEEKS, I'VE SPENT SO MUCH MORE TIME STAYING AT HER APARTMENT THAN AT MY OWN THAT WE'VE DECIDED I MIGHT AS WELL MOVE IN. WE'RE GOING TO SEE HOW IT GOES, LIVING TOGETHER — ONE STEP AT A TIME — BUT I'M SO EXCITED, MEG, AND I HOPE (I REALLY, REALLY HOPE) YOU'LL BE HAPPY FOR ME TOO.

ANITA IS DUTCH AND SPEAKS FOUR LANGUAGES, AND I TEASE HER BY SAYING I'M ONLY WITH HER SO I CAN HAVE MY OWN PERSONAL TRANSLATOR. SHE ARRIVED IN MALAYSIA TO TEACH MATHS AT THE SCHOOL A COUPLE OF YEARS AGO, AND IS THE SAME AGE AS ME. I'M NOT SURE WHAT ELSE TO TELL YOU,

I'm not upset by Angie's letter. I'm not. Just sick of my own company, that's all. The postie delivers it Wednesday morning, the day after Stella's argument with Mum, and maybe it's half the reason I decide to finish work early that afternoon; partly to cheer myself up and partly to cheer Stella up. It'll be a surprise if I meet her from school and take her out for coffee and cake. We'll have some prime sister-time together, might even look in a couple of her favourite clothes shops afterwards – she loves doing that stuff. She can off-load the details of her argument and we'll see if we can sort it out, get her back home, and she can ask me the special favour she was after. She can tell me about this latest fella of hers and I won't think about Angie or her new friend at all. If Stella still insists on staying another night with him, then I might even get to meet this stunning guy who's bowled my little sister over.

There's no parking to be had out the front of the school and it's almost three-thirty. I'd forgotten how busy it gets here – streams of cars, buses, and soon it'll be teeming with kids – and if I don't get a park quickly, then dash round to the school gates, I might miss her. Now I've gone to the trouble of being here, I want to enjoy the pleasure of surprising her.

Fortunately there's a couple of spaces in a side-street, although in my haste I almost break my wing mirror against the tree I park too close to. London plane – *Platanus x hispanica*. Grabbing my phone, I slam the door and run down and across the street towards Hallett Road.

I'll message her in a minute, tell her I'm here. Knowing Stella, she'll turn her phone on the moment she finishes class. It'll still be a surprise.

It's busy, busy, busy. The pavements are filling already and a few parents are standing next to their parked cars, taking in the low, afternoon sun while they wait.

Walking briskly towards the crossing against the first flow of students, I keep scanning the main gates and the pavements on the opposite side of the road in case Stella's out before I get there, and I take out my phone. She might be with Jasmine and that group or she might head towards the bus loop if she's decided to go back to Three Creeks and weather Mum's storm.

That's when I spot him.

Pete Lailer.

I see him standing, leaning against the bonnet of his car; a different car to the one he used to have. I'd heard he quit Demlab and left Lapishot to travel overseas, before starting uni, but it seems he's returned. Even though he has his back to me, I have a sense of him before I properly recognise it's him and it's this which stops me.

Groups of noisy school kids, swearing and laughing, straggle past as I stare across the road. There's something about the way he stands. I'm still gripping my phone, but that's all.

He shouldn't affect me and maybe he doesn't. I'm not given long enough to find out because, as I'm watching, he looks as if he's seen who he's waiting for. Though he remains leaning nonchalantly against his car – it's a bluey-grey colour and has a hubcap missing – he straightens his back, waves and beckons to someone.

Following the direction he's looking, I see a group of eight or nine Year 12 girls, with the tell-tale 'senior' stripes on their uniform, heading out the gate together. I might have known. What a creep. Still chasing schoolgirls. I can't believe I ever saw anything in him. Yet suddenly I'm glad I've experienced this moment because it helps me realise all over again what a shallow and vain creep he is and how I've been better off without him.

Three or four of the Year 12 girls wave back at him and then there's laughter and they all wave back. They're calling out to him, but I can't tell whether they're mocking him or teasing him because I'm a distance away, on the other side of this wide road, and there's the constant rumble of traffic, the grinding of gears from a late bus.

I flip open my mobile and am about to call Stella when I

see her amongst this same group of Year 12 girls. She does this playful hop and skip thing, which separates her from her friends, who wave goodbye to her, and she saunters (as deliberately nonchalantly as he was sitting) up to Pete Lailer.

No.

I step back across the pavement, away from the road, onto the boundary of someone's driveway; shielded by their stout gatepost and a hedge of red photinia. Can only stand and watch.

No.

He pushes himself off the car at Stella's approach and the first thing they do is kiss. Not the greeting-peck of friends, but the most intimate of kisses, and this time I hear the cheer from Stella's crowd, who are standing, watching, where she left them. Jasmine is there too. I recognise her.

Even while she's still kissing him, Stella adds to the spectacle by raising her middle finger in the air at them, and her friends laugh and begin walking away. My Stella.

When she steps back, and while they appear to talk, he strokes her hair, brushes it behind her ears, and then she leans in close to him again. They kiss some more, but this time I see her slip one hand into the back pocket of his jeans and he places both his hands on her bum, drawing her even closer.

I can't move. I can't breathe. They mustn't know I'm here. I look behind me, across the driveway and garden to the front door of the house, and for a frightening instant the only possible escape seems to be to dash inside that house. I hope no one's watching me from inside, about to open a window and shout at me to move on. When a bunch of students walk along the pavement towards me, I turn out in front of them and, keeping my head down, stride quickly back to the corner of the side street. I half-expect to hear

Stella calling after me, but the pavements are busy, the road is busy and it's clear her mind is on other things.

I'm adrift. I'm sitting in the cab of my truck, but I'm adrift.

It seems like forever, but it's probably not even fifteen minutes. I get my breath back, try to clear my thoughts. To think one clear thought.

So this is what she wanted to talk about. She wanted to make sure I was okay about her being with Pete Lailer. As if I ever could be. No wonder she wouldn't tell me on the phone. She's obviously staying with him, sleeping with him. He's the one who wants her to move in with him. The bastard!

The bitch!

I slam both hands against the steering wheel.

Can't believe it.

I have to get out of here. Have to turn the ignition on and drive, but don't trust myself. Not yet. Have to concentrate.

The only thing I'm sure of is that Stella can't be with him. She can't. Anyone else, but not him.

Why should she?

He can't be with her. My own sister.

Why should they have one another?

Breathe, I tell myself. Think about breathing.

It's not right and it's not fair. Besides, she's too close to her exams. He'd fuck everything up for her. Like he did for me. Everything.

I don't know what I feel or want anymore. Except not this. I can't take this.

Breathe.

I loosen my grip on the steering wheel, sit back in the seat and try concentrating on breathing. Exhale slowly, push each breath out; let my lungs fill by themselves; observe the sound of each breath, the fall and rise of my ribcage, the passage of warm and cool air. It's an exercise I learned from Dr Ian, but it's not always as easy as it sounds.

Exhale. Inhale.

I have to get Stella back home. That's what I have to do. The first thing is to get her away from him and back home. I'll call in on my way through Three Creeks and I'll talk to Mum. She has to end her argument with Stella. She'll stop Stella from seeing Pete Lailer as soon as she knows about it. She better had.

I take a deep breath and then push it out.

At the back door, I'm tugging off my boots when she arrives in the hallway and peers into the kitchen. I can tell I've surprised her.

'Oh it's you,' she says, 'I thought I heard the door being opened.' She picks up a tea towel that's draped across the back of a kitchen chair and folds it in half, end-to-end. 'I didn't hear you drive in.'

'I did. My truck's right there,' I tell her. 'Were you having a snooze?'

'Hardly. I was tidying the bathroom.' Then she says, 'I wasn't expecting you.'

I pull off my second work boot and place both side-by-side on the doormat. 'Thought I'd call in on the way past. See how you are.' I do my best to sound nonchalant.

'I'm fine,' she says. 'Shouldn't I be?'

I shrug, smile. She thinks I'm being over-solicitous because Victor's away. It's the sort of attention she'd crave and then enjoy resenting.

'Your socks have got mud on them. I don't want that traipsing through the house. I've just cleaned.'

I breathe out. 'I wasn't planning on traipsing through the house. Just sitting in the kitchen over a drink. Thought you might like some company, what with Dad away and –'

She looks across at the kettle. 'You want a drink?'

I push out a breath and remind myself that I have to get Stella back here, but Mother's in one of her prickly moods. 'You're not making this very easy.'

'Making what easy? Are you here for something in particular? Something you want? I thought you said you were just passing.'

I place one hand against the wall to steady myself and pull off one sock and then the other, dropping them on the mat.

When I move to fill the kettle, she crosses the kitchen and wipes the wall where I've leant, and when she sees me glaring she says, 'Your hands are dirty. You'll leave a mark.'

Why does she have to be like this? I put the kettle down and hold my hands out for her to see. 'They're clean,' I say. 'I didn't mark the wall. I washed them before I left my last job.'

'They don't look clean to me. The dirt's ingrained,' and she takes the kettle and puts it under the tap. She nods at the tea towel as I pull a kitchen chair out from the table. 'Put that across the seat.

'What? Why?'

'Those overalls,' she says.

'What about them?'

I leave the tea towel where it is and sit down. There was a time when I wouldn't have dared, but not anymore. I should tell her she's being rude and leave, but I can't. She still has some power over me. Besides, she has to know about Stella.

'They're filthy.'

'No they're not. I've only been cutting lawns. And it's a

wooden seat, for goodness sake.'

'Have it your own way,' she says, and puts the kettle down. She doesn't switch it on, I notice.

Everything I'd rehearsed, about Stella needing to be at home if she was to study properly for exams, is messed up. The order of the words is gone. She does this to me. I can't just blurt out about Pete Lailer either.

I say nothing and she continues: 'This is my house. I take pride in the way it looks. I don't think it's too much to expect other people to respect that.'

I stare at her. I shouldn't have come.

'Nothing else matters, does it? People just make it dirty. Appearances are everything.'

She purses her lips and says, 'It wouldn't hurt if you took a bit more pride in your appearance.'

Pushing the chair back, I stand and point to myself with both hands. 'I'm a landscape gardener, remember? You expect me to wear a twin set and stilettos?'

'You could at least do something with your hair.'

'You're rude.'

'I'm your mother. If I don't tell you, who will? Your friends?' And the last is a sneer. Unmistakably a sneer.

There's the scrape of chair across floor tiles as I push it back under the table and then I'm at the back door, struggling to pull on my socks.

'So now you're going, are you? That was quick. One home truth too many, I suppose.'

'This isn't a home,' I tell her.

'Then have the decency to act like a guest.'

I can't believe it.

I pull off the sock I'm half-way through putting on and shove it, along with the other, in my overall pockets, and I stand to face her. 'Why did you kick Stella out? How do you expect her to study if... if she's got nowhere to stay, if she doesn't have space to think? She'll fail her exams. It'll be your fault.'

'Ah, that's why you're here, is it? She sent you. I might have known. Well, you can tell Stella she made her bed and she can lie in it. If she's ready to apologise and accept a few ground rules – to behave in a civilised manner – then... well, she knows what to do. You tell her that.'

'Do you even know where she is? Do you even care?'

'I know exactly where she is. And I don't have the slightest doubt she'll soon outstay her welcome there.'

'With Jasmine? Is that what you think?' I shake my head. 'I don't know why I bother. It's pointless –'

'Well, let's face it, Meg, you don't really bother, do you? Not really. Isn't that the point?' She stares at me a moment and absently picks up the teapot, takes the lid off, glances inside and puts the lid back on again.

I shake my head. 'I don't have to listen to this.' I pick up my boots and grip the door handle, but I stop and turn back to her. 'You spoil everything, you know. You can't bear to see other people happy, so you do everything you can to destroy it. That's all you've ever done. You're like a black hole sucking the life out of people.'

She's still holding the teapot, but she refocuses on me now. 'What nonsense. You're talking nonsense. You know you are.'

'You're trying to wreck Stella's life in the same way you wrecked mine. Aren't you? Don't you want her to go to uni? Is that it? You want us to end up bored shitless like you. Is that why you're doing this?'

'Doing what? I wish you'd stop being so melodramatic. And don't you dare use that sort of language in this house. Grow up a little. You're supposed to be twenty-one. All you'll do is make yourself... you'll make yourself sick again.'

She's a bitch. My mother's a bitch. I hate her. I want to throw something at her. I want to hurt her in the same way she hurts me. All the things I wish I could say.

I look her in the eyes and I tell her. 'She's with Pete Lailer, not Jasmine. Did you know Stella's staying with Pete Lailer, my ex-boyfriend? The one you... That's who she's with right now. That's who she's staying with, sleeping with. Did you know that? Do you even care?'

'Don't be ridiculous.'

'It's true.'

'You're being ridiculous. I thought you'd got over all that nonsense.'

I shake my head and want to laugh. It's too thin a victory. 'I saw them together. Very cosy. Have been for a while, by the looks of things. She told me she was staying with her boyfriend the moment you kicked her out, and he's her boyfriend.'

'Liar! You spiteful girl.' She pushes the teapot down onto the bench and strides towards me. She looks mad, crazy, and for a second I consider running upstairs to my room, until I remember I'm no longer the child; she doesn't have that power over me. Not anymore. She can't hurt me.

'Why would I lie? About that of all things. I saw them. She told me. I don't care what you say.'

She grips me by the shoulders and tries to shake me, and for a brief instant I'm unable to stand back and make her release me. Her power returns. She digs her fingers into my shoulders and says, 'It's not true. You tell me right now, Margaret Dapsy, it isn't true.'

'It's Meg, not Margaret,' I tell her, and I twist my shoulders until she lets me go. I make her let go. 'And it *is* true, thanks to you. Why wouldn't it be?'

'She can't. She mustn't.' She takes a step back and turns away from me. 'I don't believe it,' she says, but she's addressing herself, not me. 'I *won't* believe it.'

It stops me. The abrupt shift in her tone is too marked and I suddenly see things I never saw before: the things that never made sense. It's a revelation. 'What are you talking about? What's wrong with him?' It isn't just that he's some bloke she's sleeping with, but that it's Pete Lailer. I move to the side of her, want to see her expression and what she's hiding. Four years ago I couldn't see it clearly enough, but I can now.

She's not listening to me, though. Her face is contorted and it looks like she might be crying, but her eyes aren't moist; they're angry and bitter and dry.

'What's wrong with Pete Lailer? Tell me.'

Mother sees me and shakes her head. 'Go away.'

'Tell me.'

She says nothing.

'Tell me.'

She shakes her head and says, 'It's none of your business. Now go, I don't want you here.'

'Of course it's my business. It's obvious it is – and Stella's too.'

She's going to refuse, but I won't let her. She can't do that.

'Unless you're making it up,' I continue, to goad her. 'Like you made everything up before. Because you don't want Stella and me to go to uni, and don't want us to enjoy life.' But my words too quickly become a torrent and I barely breathe to measure what I'm saying, letting the words spill out as they will, until I think I might be screaming. 'You couldn't bear to see me having fun and being with someone who meant something to me. You couldn't, could you?

You'd rather pretend I was sick and couldn't think for myself than that. But that's you, not me. It's all you. You're the sick one. Making it up out of spite and jealousy, because that's who you are. It is. You always have been. A black hole. You're just spiteful and jealous and you always will be. Spiteful and jealous... spite and jealousy.'

She stares at me and, for a moment, I think she's scared of me. When I stop and see her staring, my boots are on the floor and my fists are clenched. My jaw is clenched and there's an ache in my head which wasn't there before.

'Jealous?' She mutters and sounds genuinely puzzled. 'What could I possibly be jealous of? You're twenty-one, you didn't even finish school and... Is that really what you think? Why would I be jealous of you?'

'For one thing, I'm not dried-up and bitter. I'm not a bitter, middle-aged, used-up, old woman. I'm young. I've got my future ahead of me.'

She doesn't move. She stands and looks dispassionately at me, as if I'm an insect she can't be bothered with, but her eyes look tired and her face is drawn and pale, and my head is throbbing.

'You better go,' she says. 'I've got nothing more to say to you. Go. And make an appointment to see Dr Carmichael while you're at it. I think it might be time you saw her again, don't you?'

'You bitch. Is that your response to everything?' I grab my boots and am glad of the dirt that falls onto the kitchen tiles. 'I knew you were making it up. You just couldn't bear to see me happy. It wouldn't have mattered whether it was Pete Lailer or some other boy, you couldn't stand the fact that I was happy when you've spent your whole life specialising in misery. And now you're about to do the same to Stella. I know you are.'

My neck is stiff and I know she's done this to me. I won't stay a minute longer. I don't think I've sorted out what I came here to do, but I can't remember what that was anymore, not at the moment. If I never set foot in this house again, it'll be too soon.

I'm turning the handle and opening the door when she speaks.

'You want to know about Peter Lailer?' Her voice is calm, but her words are too measured.

I look at her, but don't say anything. I don't believe she's got anything to say.

'He's your brother, if you must know... your half-brother – very likely. He is.'

'What?'

'Yes. If you must know. Almost certainly. Your precious Peter Lailer... he's the son of Abby Lailer –'

'Abby Lailer? Who's Abby Lailer?'

'His mother. Your darling father's... mistress.' She laughed at that. A dry, mirthless laugh. 'She was his girlfriend before we were married, but the weak fool couldn't help himself; went back to her while we were engaged... nine months before Peter Lailer was born. I'm sure you can work the rest out for yourself, you silly girl.'

'What?'

She says nothing.

I work it out.

'No.'

'Oh yes. Some things never change. Yet I'm the one that gets punished, over and over.' She closes her eyes and pauses. 'You and he... together –'

'No. My brother? Is that what you're saying? No. No.'

'Half-brother. Very likely. But then your father will never admit it. He'd be mad to.' She stares at me. 'But that house in Mirton they live in... he helped her get that house, the moment she moved back here. And why on earth do you think the boy got a job at Demlab the moment he left school? You don't know half as much as you think you do.'

I shake my head. Her words pass around me, over me, but won't settle. I won't let them. I try to see a different shape to what she's said, to rearrange them so I might have a different idea to hold onto, but she's defeated me.

'There, you have it now.'

It's ridiculous. But it's too absurd not to be true. It accounts for everything. Suddenly, the words and the idea are locked in place.

Breathe. Breathe.

'That's a lie. An absolute lie. You're lying. You're a liar!'

She takes the tea towel off the table and starts to fold it again.

I'm sitting in the cab of my truck, clutching my work boots on my lap. My socks are in my pockets and I may have taken the skin off a few toes as I ran. My head is raw and there's a blinding ache behind my eyes; coloured dots floating in from my peripheral vision. I have to get away from this place.

By the time I reach home – drive to Angie's – my head is pounding. All I can think about is swallowing a few pills and crawling into bed. I spill food into Gustav's bowl, drag myself upstairs.

Pushing shut the bedroom door, tugging my curtains closed and clambering out of my clothes is a blind struggle, but the pills are strong and I sink into a deep pit of sleep within seconds of drawing the blanket over my head. Total escape.

*

'It's a beautiful day,' I say. 'I wish every day was like this.'

We kiss, with me pressed up against one side of my truck (not Betsy, my old purple car), and there's a delicious urgency in our kissing. When my bag slips off my shoulder and I drop my keys on the ground, I notice there's something strange stretching out in the shadows beneath the chassis. It's something to be scared of, whatever it is, but I ignore it, pretend it isn't there, in the hope it'll disappear.

At the front door, Pete pushes his hands through his hair while I fumble with the key, knowing there's something behind us. Yet, as soon as I shut the door, we tumble into an urgent, uneasy kissing again. His hands steal their way inside my T-shirt, I have one hand in the back pocket of his jeans and one hand fumbling with the buttons of his shirt. As if this will save us and keep us together.

We tumble into the lounge, next to the piano. Except the French windows are already open and I'm afraid that whatever was outside is now lurking inside.

'Quick,' I want to say, 'help me shut the doors,' but no words come out, and I'm so tangled up with Pete I can't move.

My waking is abrupt. There's no gradual rising to the surface. Sharp awake. I open my eyes to the black of night, push the bed sheet away, and remember every detail of the afternoon: Stella and Pete Lailer outside the school, the way my mother was, the things she said. Disgust, horror, a poisonous anger.

I remember further back, to Pete and me, and what we did with one another. The nakedness we shared, the sex we had, the feel of him inside me.

But Victor – how could he? Never saying a word about

it. How could he? Unless she's lying.

I have to speak to Dad. This can't be the way it'll always be. Even if things can't be unsaid. But what will I tell him?

I close my eyes. Crave a longer, deeper sleep. Concentrate on lying still, on listening to the sounds of night, the feel of darkness, the touch of cool air on my face, my shoulders, my hands, but then I snap back to what my mother said and... and nothing can ever be the same again.

Twisting the alarm clock round on the bedside cabinet so I can see it, it's only a couple of minutes after midnight. All the same, I've been submerged in sleep for several hours and I know that's the end of it. My brain won't stop churning it over. No more escape.

I'm awake and yet it's more like a bad dream than the bad dream I was having.

What she said, even if it was a lie – cruel, malicious bitch – or an insane, deranged mistake, there's no undoing this undoing. How can there be? Our family is finished. I feel empty, hollow, broken, and realise this is the way I've been for almost four years.

But if Victor knew what she thought, what she believed, why didn't he put an end to it? One way or another. Too passive, too gutless, too damned accommodating? He should have divorced her years ago. None of this would've happened then. I'm angry enough to hate him for this – I'll never forgive him – but I hate her more, even more, for making me feel like that.

I need to know. To hear the words from him.

My phone's in my overalls, my overalls are on the floor next to the bed. I pull them onto the bed and scrabble through the pockets to retrieve and unmute it. I try to remember how long he said he'd be away: another two or three days, until the weekend. Damn him.

It'll be mid-afternoon over there, I think, but it's hard to focus on such details with so many other thoughts rushing and crashing about. Maybe he won't be in a meeting and he'll answer his phone and I'll tell him everything she said. I'll make him talk about it, I'll make him answer. No more dirty little secrets.

He'll tell me she's wrong, that she's got everything mixed up – badly mixed up – but he'll get Stella home again, where she belongs. I'll tell him it's not me but our mother who needs to see a doctor and how worried I am about her. If anyone should be locked up, it's her. I'll phone the doctor, I'll drive her to the hospital, I'll visit her once or twice in Ward 8, and everyone will realise it was her – it was always her – not me. It's what I've had to put up with. Then they'll be sorry.

Victor's phone rings only three times before a recorded message cuts in: 'This phone is currently turned off or unable to obtain reception. Please try again later.'

Damn. Damn him. He should be here. None of this would be happening otherwise.

I have to do it myself. I have to put my pieces back together again. I have to get up. I'll drift further apart otherwise, until everything is lost forever. I'll go crazy lying here.

It's not true, what she said. She's making up stories. That's what she does.

'Likely,' she said. Not *definitely*. Although even that...

You slept with your brother. Half-brother. What if it's true?

I'm shivering, frozen brittle and I want to SCREAM! I can feel myself spinning, but I'm not going to let this happen to me. Not again. She's not going to do it to me a second time.

If only I could drive a knife through the past. Chop it off and let a fresh one grow. Sick it all up.

I have to get Stella away from him.

She's mad, despicable. I hate her.

TEN

A figure in overalls and a brown, woollen beanie steps out onto the verandah of an unlit house at night and down onto the lawn. It is me, but it isn't me.

She is agitated and yet remote at the same time, as if she might be half-awake and half-locked into a bad dream. The night is colder than she imagined it would be, but the darkness is thinner, less dense. There's the faint glow of a quarter-moon veiled by slips of cloud and a long, wispy scarf of mist at the edge of the forest. She carries an angry plan of sorts, a sack of resentments and, from a box in Angie's studio, a can of fluorescent green spray paint. These things propel her forwards, like a sleepwalker with a single focus. A powerful, nocturnal logic dictates what she should do, and it's this that prompts her to shove a pair of disposable latex gloves in her pocket.

By the same strange logic, she tells herself that if her truck shows the slightest hesitation in starting – it's sometimes sluggish in cold weather – she'll put the spray can back and go for a night-walk instead, or return to bed. She tells herself she'll turn the engine off if it sounds so loud it might wake the distant neighbours, and she unwinds the window to listen. But it starts first time with the calmest of purrs.

She reverses slowly and tells herself that if she can't see well enough without lights (because she'll need to turn them off in Three Creeks) then she'll drive back into the garage and leave both the truck and her scrap of a plan right there. But she can see well enough and so carries on. She dares herself to carry on. She steers gently onto Nine Mile Road, cruising with barely any acceleration, and travels four, five hundred metres before gradually pressing harder on the pedal and carefully changing gears, although it's another five hundred metres before she flicks on the lights.

A cream and green truck with a wheelbarrow in the back, a fork and two spades, a hoe and a rake, a pick-axe and hatchet, rope, tarpaulin, a brush, secateurs, hedge-trimmers – the accoutrements of a landscape gardener – trundles along an unsealed forest road at night. Not too fast.

On the edge of Three Creeks, half a kilometre or so before the Wallan River Road meets the Rudely Road, the lights of the truck are turned off and, a few hundred metres later, it slows and is steered onto the verge, alongside a hedge of rambling wattle *(Acacia perambulare)* where it stops.

Duparc House.

A figure in overalls and a brown, woollen hat, waits in the cab of her truck a minute before climbing out and pushing her door shut with the most subdued of clicks. It's always me and it's never me.

She knows what she must do. There's no other choice. Her mother needs to be shaken awake and made to be sorry. She must scare her into telling the truth. It's the only power she has left.

Without Victor for company, Mother will be desperate to have Stella home. She'll do everything she can to get her home. Then, tomorrow, she and Stella will make her acknowledge her schemes and her lies, revealing herself for what she is. Stella will be her witness and everything that's been said will be unsaid; she'll make her take it all back.

If anyone needs to see a doctor, it's Mother. They'll call the doctor if they have to.

She walks alongside the hedge until she arrives at a certain spot and pushes through the outer, most recent growth of wattle; leaves that would be luminous green in daylight, even at this time of year. She feels her way slowly forward, arms reaching in front, until she comes to an unexpected, invisible barrier of tangled branches. She pats down her pockets to use her phone as a torch, but then remembers leaving it by the side of her bed. Standing there in the dense, leafy blackness, she almost comes to, but her eyes gradually adjust until she rediscovers the hidden path and she carries on.

Breaking out at the side next to the shed, in what's always been one of her dad's patches of garden, she treads through the undergrowth and raises the smell of bruised nettles and lemon balm. *Urtica dioica, Melissa officinalis.* All five senses are more attuned to the night now, than when she entered her secret tunnel, and she inhales the scents of the plants until they fill her. Ahead looms the house. How she hates the place and everything it represents. Its bones are a cage for ill thoughts, sick memories, and she can feel them sticking into her.

Her gaze focuses on the two windows of her parents' bedroom. All is quiet. Her mother has probably swallowed one of her little sleeping pills. Knowing her, she'll have shrugged off the memory of her meanness and be sleeping without a care in the world. As snug as a bug in a rug. Not a second thought.

The girl wishes her father was here and not overseas, because then she wouldn't have to be. Either way, he isn't blameless for the way things are. Far from it. She knows that more than ever.

Taking a few steps across the lawn, her boots leave footprints in the dew. It probably won't matter, not once daybreak arrives in several hours, but she steps back, walks around the rear of the shed, between it and the weed-infested compost heap, and onto the concrete path that divides the lawn in two. She follows this to the back of the house, then along the side to the front.

It'll be simple. She remembers how her mother reacted last time, a couple of months back, after the nutters from Action for Animal Rights sprayed graffiti across the wall and slashed the clothes on the line. It'll serve her right too.

Except she should've shaken the can when she was in the truck. She forgot about that. Careless, careless, careless. So now she tilts it gently one way and then the other, shaking it slowly, making sure the ball-bearing inside the can doesn't rattle and clatter the night apart.

If she hesitates, it's because there are older, softer memories waiting to ambush her, but she knows these are her weakness too. They'll destroy her if she lets them. Instead, she draws on the bitterness of her anger, which has become forged and tempered into a hard, blunt weapon.

A section of wall close to the front door has recently been re-painted. There's a large patch that's a cleaner, sharper white than the rest, and it's glistening with moisture from the night air. But she resists stroking a finger across it, even to check how damp it is. She must be clever and careful.

Breathe in. Breathe out. She instructs herself to take her time, to breathe slowly and deeply. What she does is slowly exhale before allowing her lungs to fill by themselves. Once, twice... six times she does this, and each time she observes, more acutely than before, how the scent of night rises from the grass and how it clings like cobwebs to the house.

The slow breathing begins to distance her from her anger, though, until she remembers her mother is comfortably sleeping inside: a mass of bitterness and vitriol that's lurking inside. She pulls on the pair of latex gloves, holds the can at a point that approximates the height the letters were scrawled last time and presses the nozzle.

She presses the nozzle and draws a single vertical line in fluoro green – the downstroke of *K* – and stops. The spray is more *whoosh* than *hiss* and resonates too distinctly against the stillness of night. Perhaps she should have brought a tin of paint and a brush instead, but it's too late now.

She'll spray faster instead, and then she'll be away and back to bed.

She finishes the *K*.

Next the *I* and the first *L* are accomplished, but the spray nozzle begins to splutter and she wonders whether there's enough to finish the job. She'd thought it was almost full. There's some streaking of the *K* and she wishes she'd brought a rag to wipe the wall dry first, but it's too late now. Except, someone who'd done this before would be better prepared.

It's at this point she realises a different way of doing things and how much better it'll be. And easier. So she sprays the second *L* and leaves it at that:

KILL

There. Even more threatening than *KILLER*. It reads like an escalation from the A.A.R.'s last visit. The thought of them prowling around at night will send her mother into a frenzy. It'll scare her witless and shitless. She'll be screaming for Stella to come back home. She'll be screaming for both of them.

A figure in overalls and a brown, woollen beanie stands back and attempts to admire her handiwork. (Red or black paint would've been more dramatic.) She bites at the gum on the inside of her mouth and is torn between giggling and crying. It's done, but it's not her fault. It's not. She looks down at her boots and remembers that afternoon in the kitchen.

She should leave now. She needs to return to her truck and leave, except she's more lost and alone than ever. If her mother had been a real mother, instead of betraying her time and time again, she wouldn't be standing here, haunting this place in the empty hours. Even so, what the girl's done... it doesn't seem enough. It's cost her everything and her mother nothing.

She really should leave. She'll have to stop on the way home and bury the paint can and gloves in the forest. And she fully intends leaving until, in clutching the can and holding herself together during this moment of night, she turns and notices her mother's precious winter roses (*Esther Lee*) and hellebores *(Helleborus niger)* in full bloom. They glisten gloriously. A whole damned bed of them; so neat and tidy, formal and controlled. The moisture on their petals and dark leaves reflects the light of the quarter-moon, despite the clouds, and she understands what else she can do.

Anyone could find their way to the garden shed. It'd be an obvious place to snoop if you were an Animal Rights activist bent on vengeance and looking to see what's what.

After all, they found their way to the washing-line last time, right next to the shed, where clothes are hanging even now, inviting attention, but she'll leave those alone. She has no taste for shredding clothes.

She places the can in the centre of the garden path, so as not to forget it on the way out – that wouldn't do – and cautiously turns the door handle. It's old and dilapidated, this shed, and her dad has been promising to replace it for donkey's years, but she remembers how the tarnished and dented brass handle sometimes separates from the spindle, how the bottom hinge of the door is almost broken, and that she'll need to slightly lift it at the same time as pulling it open. However, she knows what garden tools will be hanging against the walls from rusty hooks and crooked nails, what will be scattered across the surfaces of the old potting table and bench, and it's best if she uses these instead of her own.

As she opens the door, there's the sound of a small creature dropping from the lawn mower and scurrying to the back of the shed. It slips behind shelves that are stacked with two decades worth of rust-ridden paint tins, almost-empty bottles of mineral turpentine, methylated spirits, oil, petrol, mouldy boxes of slug bait, weed-killer, jam jars half-full of assorted nails and screws. Probably a bush rat, she tells herself, and takes comfort in knowing that not everything's asleep. She's not completely alone.

Her eyes are accustomed to the darkest of spaces now, but she could find her way about here blindfolded if needs be. She's always loved the smell of the shed and breathes it in: dry lawn cuttings and petrol from the old, Budding Classic two-stroke mower; oily rags; the tanginess of corroded metal; the sweet mustiness of rotting timber.

She doubts the hedge trimmers will be sharp enough and

suspects they'd make too much clickety-clack; a spade might do damage quickly, but the thrusting and chopping would create as big a racket. She reaches out into the scatter of dark shapes with the tentativeness of a blind woman — pliers, two spanners, a tangle of wire, a matted rag, a garden trowel and a screwdriver — before alighting on two pairs of pruning shears. One has short blades and the other has long blades. She brings the short-bladed pair closer to her face and turns to the door for better light. They look and feel almost new. Both pairs are sharp and will do the job, but she holds on to the long-bladed shears because their longer reach and larger bite will make for faster work, safe from thorns. Besides, her mother once argued she should only use short-blades for pruning roses ('Any gardener worth their salt knows that'), so decides on the long ones. They'll do nicely, thank you very much.

It's not in her nature to destroy nature, but there's little natural about the regimentation of her mother's rose garden. Too tidy and twee, too precisely-spaced and colour-coded, too ordered and unimaginative. As for the bloody cactuses in the glasshouse, maybe she'll give them a drink of weed-killer before she leaves.

When she's standing in front of the flower bed, facing the house, she knows she could stop, and the thought occurs for half-a-second that she should stop, but the hurt has gone on for too long and so she squats down to stab at a few hellebores. It's experimental, the way she does this, to see how it feels, but it's too slow, too unsatisfying, and she stands again and tries snip-snapping at an *Esther Lee*, which is much better. Snip-snip.

Flowers and stems topple, petals fall. They land at her feet and add a new, perfumed scent to the night. She smiles and continues. It's surprisingly easy to do this damage.

There's no refinement in destruction.

When she's finished, she straightens her back and looks about; not at what she's done, but at the landscape of night: the shades of dark growing from the garden and the house, from the trees and the sky above. Night has even more shadows than day, she realises, once you take the time to look for them, and it strikes her as odd that she feels at ease in this nocturnal world, but there's definitely comfort in it. There are no bogey-men when you are the bogey-man; there are no other ghosts. She looks about and observes. There's a faint night-shadow of tree thrown across the darkness of lawn – an additional layer of darkness – and, perhaps from the same tree or a neighbouring one, the sporadic warbling of a coodylark (*Lullula nocturnes*). The air has grown cooler since she arrived and so maybe the mist is creeping out from the forest and up from the river.

For some reason, she remembers an old French lesson from school: that the French words for 'sun' and 'day' are masculine, while the words for 'moon' and 'night' are feminine, and it strikes her as quite telling and, again, comforting.

The moon is a hook in the sky tonight.

I would unhook the moon for you.

A figure in overalls and a brown, woolly hat, shivers, adjusts her grip on the shears and slips round to the rear of the house once more. This time, she stops at her mother's cactus house.

She should leave now, she really should, but this will only take a minute or two. Mother's weeping prickly pear – *Opuntia dolorosa* – is begging a drink of *Weed-All*. It's exactly what those Animal fanatics would do.

She turns the door handle, but it doesn't open. It's

padlocked. It's never been locked before. There's a new clasp and hasp screwed in place, probably because of their last 'visitors'. Shiny brass. A brand new padlock. Damn. She crouches down to see how easy it'd be to force off, but tells herself it doesn't matter; she's done enough.

Which is when she becomes aware of a sound or movement behind her – a new layer of darkness, perhaps – the movement of a night-shadow. She turns and stands and torchlight blinds her.

'What...' he begins to say, and stops. 'Meg. It's you. What the hell are you doing here?' He pushes out a long breath, sighs, drops his shoulders. 'For goodness sake. I thought we had those Animal Rights morons back.'

The cold sweeps over her.

'Dad. You're home. What are you doing home?'

He swings the torch beam away, steps to one side and shines it on the padlock. 'Yes, I am,' he says uncertainly. 'We finished early. A couple of meetings were cancelled. I managed to switch flights.' He stares at her with an intentness that's unusual for him. 'Meg, what are you doing? What are you up to? Do you know what time it is?'

Her pause is too long. 'I couldn't sleep,' she tells him. She wants to tell him more, to accuse Mother and berate him, but it's harder now he's actually here and has discovered her here too.

He nods. 'Okay. Me too – jetlag. But what are you doing... here... now? Why are you trying to get into Mum's cactus house? At this time of night. Is everything alright?'

She looks away, across the garden, which, against the yellowing rim of torchlight, seems darker than it was, and she feels suddenly awkward wearing latex gloves and clutching pruning shears. Her thumb rubs against the snib of the blade lock and pulls it up, pushes it down; up, down, open, closed. The beam of light lands at her boots, and when she notices this and looks down at it he turns it off.

She looks around. Beyond this borrowed perch of land on which Duparc House and its gardens sit, and beyond the broad emptiness of paddocks, there's a dark edge to the world, formed by the black river and the endless forest. It's all there is. Nothing more. There's no real purpose to any of it, it seems. Not anymore. She realises she's on the brink of losing everything.

He coughs, clears his throat; exhales a breath of mist. 'Thought I heard someone moving around out here. Thought it might be a fox or a deer at first, but then realised it could be those idiots come back. Was going to phone the police, but thought I'd feel a bit silly if they found a deer eating the parsnips. Didn't want to be the boy who cried wolf, in case they *do* come back.' He hesitates. 'That wasn't you, was it, Meg? That business we thought was the Animal Libbers, that wasn't you?'

His question sends a shiver of prickly heat through her now, followed by another cold shadow. All the same, she protests: 'What? You think –'

'No, of course it wasn't. Of course I don't. Sorry. It's just – well, seeing you out here tonight, it made me wonder. I don't always think my best at this time of... in the middle of the night.' He laughs, almost. 'Anyway, it's as well I didn't call the police, isn't it? Otherwise *they'd* be asking you what you were doing fiddling with the padlock to your mum's cactus house at one in the morning, instead of me.'

She closes her eyes and tries to think. Is numb now. He'll never believe her. If he sees what she's done, if he sees the graffiti, he'll never believe her. They'll lock her up again. Unless, when he's returned to bed and thinks she's left, she sneaks back, gets some turps from the shed and cleans that word off the front of the house. *KILL*. She'll scrub and scrub until it's gone, but she'll be quieter this time. Maybe she'll find the tin of white paint among the shelves and she'll paint over it instead. As long as he doesn't see it first. Not now.

Not that she doesn't have every right to be angry. But he won't understand. It's going to be bad enough when he sees what she's done to the roses. She can't undo that. And why should she? She has every right to be angry. Her mother's been an absolute bitch and, as for him...

'Meg?'

There are many things she needs to tell him, but they're all tangled up in anger and hurt and disgust – with her mother, with him, with herself – that she needs to shout them, not speak them, and they're so knotted together she can't find a beginning.

'You were away,' she tries, but falters.

'You're not alright, are you?' he says. 'It's not alright, is it? Your mum told me you'd been acting... that you've been a bit unsettled these last few days.'

These words bury her further, until she gasps and pushes through. 'She said that? Is that what she told you? And you believe her? No, that's not it. It's not like that at all.' Panting, she steps towards the back door of the house, ready to have this out with her. She'll have a shouting match with her, make her admit the things she said, and then he'll understand. 'Did she tell you what she said? Do you know she's kicked Stella out? And... What you did? Pete Lailer? About me and... I hate her. I wish she was dead. I really do.'

'Ssh, Meg. You don't mean that. You know you don't.' He puts an arm out to hold her from heading inside. 'Don't say that.'

'I do mean it. I do. Let's go and ask her.'

'She's asleep, Meg. You know she's asleep.'

'Well, let's wake her. I'm sick of this. I want to hear her say all those things again in front of you. She's a liar. She has to be —'

He shakes his head and attempts to put an arm round her back, to steer her towards the garden bench next to the lawn. 'We're not going to wake her, Meg, are we? We'll let her sleep.' He smiles, but it's a lop-sided smile. 'We couldn't if we tried, I don't think. She's taken one of her little pills. Snoring like a trooper.' He sighs, shrugs, lets himself droop a little. 'It's been a hell of an evening, a hell of a night, but it'll be alright. You'll see, it'll be alright.' His voice is subdued – measured and mellow – and she realises he's talking like this to calm her. He thinks she's hysterical and needs to be calmed.

'It won't be alright. It can't be alright. Not ever again.'

'It will be,' he says. 'You'll see.' He sits down on the seat, places the torch on the ground and tugs at the sleeves of his thin jumper, stretching them over his wrists. He motions for her to sit next to him.

'I don't want to sit,' she tells him.

'It's not as bad as it seems, Meg. Your mum told me what she said to you. About your old boyfriend – Peter Lailer – Abby Lailer's boy.'

'She told you that?'

'I wish she hadn't mentioned it to you, but, like I said, it's been a hell of an evening. I was beginning to wish I'd stayed away.'

Meg stands in front of him, waiting for more, but he doesn't say anything at first. He motions at the bench again. 'Won't you sit down, Meg? You're giving me a crick in the neck.' He smiles, wants her to smile too, but she won't.

She needs to shout, but the momentum of the last hour

has abandoned her and reluctantly she sits down.

He puts an arm around her shoulders and she says, 'Don't.' He shrugs, folds his arms instead.

She opens and closes the secateurs, places them in her jacket pocket and takes them out again.

'You're upset,' he observes.

'Of course I am. Is it true?'

'Is what true?'

'What she said. That Pete Lailer's my... our half-brother? That's he's your... that you're his father?'

'Oh, Meg. No, of course it isn't.'

'But she said —'

'You're mum's always had a thing about Abby Lailer. It doesn't matter how many times I've told her, somehow she refuses to unconvince herself. Even if I were to give her proof — a DNA test, for goodness sake — I still think she wouldn't believe it.'

'You haven't had a DNA test?'

'No. And it's not going to happen.'

'So he could be?'

'No. Look, no. He doesn't know anything about it, and he doesn't need to. His mother — Abby — she's sure he's not, and she should know. The only person who's got a bee in her bonnet about it is your Mum, but then your mum's always had a bee in her bonnet about Abby Lailer full-stop.' He sighs, places a hand on Meg's knee. 'She's not as confident as she seems, your mum. I know you two don't always see eye-to-eye, but that's partly because you seem full of confidence to her, whereas she's never had that.'

Meg stands. 'She said I slept with my brother. That's what she said. That's why she broke up our relationship, told lies to him, and had me locked up —'

'That's not true, Meg. You weren't well. You were

depressed. The doctors could see –'

'Because of her. Because of what she did.'

He stands and places his hands on her shoulders, and he smiles and shakes his head. 'No. It would have happened anyway, my love. That's no one's fault.'

'No. You weren't here. You don't know. How can you say that? How can you take her side?'

He bites his lip and calmly says, 'Let me tell you about Abby Lailer, Meg. She was the first girl I ever loved. Can I tell you about Abby?'

He shuffles and stamps his feet and waits for her to answer, and Meg notices he's wearing slippers. She wants to be angry with him – she is angry with him – but he looks out of place standing in the garden in his slippers in the middle of the cold night, so she shrugs and, when he sits down on the bench again, lets herself sit down with him.

'I had a relationship with Abby before I met your mother. At university. We were very close, even though she was one of the prettiest and most popular girls around. We were together for several months, but when she broke it off I wasn't really surprised. To be honest, I wasn't sure what she saw in me. Anyway, I had other girlfriends after her and then, a couple of years later, I met your mum – the usual story.' He pauses, closes his eyes, leans back. 'Do you really want to hear this?'

Meg shivers and nods.

'Well, one thing led to another and eventually your mum and I got engaged. Except, we had an on-again, off-again relationship for a while, what with me doing research on a meagre grant and then having to apply all over the place for jobs. Anyway, things were a bit bumpy to say the least and there was a time, shortly before we were married, when I thought it was all over. We'd had a blazing row and… and I didn't think I'd ever see her again. I thought it was all over.'

'And you got back together with Pete's mum? With Abby Lailer?'

He nods. 'Sort of. That's about the size of it. We'd kept in touch, remained good friends, and she phoned me one night when… after her partner left her. She was upset. She'd been with him longer than I'd been with your mother and it was all over. Well, it almost seemed like Abby Lailer and me… we spent a few days together again, nothing more, on the rebound, I guess.'

'What happened?'

In the distance, from one of the neighbouring farms, a dog barks: a short ripple of excited yaps, then silence, followed by another couple of half-hearted yaps.

The silence washes out and washes in again.

'What happened?' she repeats.

'Your mother found out, and she was… not in a good way.' He coughs. 'She wouldn't want me to tell you this, but under the circumstances… and I want you to promise not to say anything about it to her. Okay? Anyway, she thought she was expecting, which is why she'd been so moody, she said, or something similar, although, as it happened, it was a false alarm. Well, the wedding was suddenly back on and everything was organised double-quick, and that was the end of Abby Lailer and me.'

'And you got married.'

He smiles. 'To cut a long story short.'

'But nine months later, Abby Lailer…?'

'More or less.'

She feels the disgust rising in her again. Can't believe he denied it a few minutes ago. 'So you *are* his father? Is that what you're saying? That Pete Lailer —'

'No. No. Although it's what your mother believes.

Refuses not to believe. But look, I even asked Abby about it once and she was absolutely certain that Peter's father was the bloke she'd broken up with. He left her because he found out she was pregnant with Peter, who apparently is the spitting image of him. No doubt about it, she said. Nothing to worry about. It's just that when your mum found out how Abby had moved to Mirton with a baby shortly after I got the job at Demlab, she... she made her mind up.'

There's nothing Meg can think of to say. Not straight away. It's all too mixed up. Mixed up and messed up.

'Why didn't you tell her that? Why didn't you make her see? Don't you realise what she did to me? Don't you care?'

'Of course I care. You know I do. Don't say that, Meg. You weren't well, you really weren't. Besides, when your Mum found out that Peter Lailer was working at Demlab, and that I'd put in a word for him, as an old friend of his mum's –'

'He's with Stella now.'

'So I hear. It was all I could do to stop your mum from launching into Stella about him, but we've put that one off until tomorrow at least.' He smiled as if he'd achieved something. 'Ironic, isn't it? Quite a coincidence. Oh, the joys of living in such a small pond. But you'll meet someone of your own, I guarantee it.'

'Is that all you can say?'

He says nothing for a moment, but looks at her before looking away, towards the back of the house. 'It's the middle of the night, Meg. I'm jet-lagged and tired and... it's been one thing after another since I got home.'

He's weak. Her father is weak. He used to be such a tall man.

'To cap it all,' he continues, 'I find you trying to break in to your mum's cactus house at one in the morning.'

'I wasn't –'

'Give me some credit, Meg. And, for goodness sake, take off those gloves. They give me the creeps. Why on earth are you wearing them?'

His tone has become abrupt and remote, and this sudden shift throws her off guard. It reminds her why she's angry.

'She's been a royal bitch. She really has. She loves those bloody cacti, those bloody roses, more than she does Stella and me. Always has done. She should never have had children if she didn't want us.'

'Don't say that. You mustn't. Not ever. We've always...' He stops, looks across at the cactus house and then at Meg. 'Her cacti? You were going to destroy them? Is that what you were trying to do?'

'No, not all of them. Just one of them. That big ugly one – the prickly pear – I was going to give it a drink of weedkiller. Payback, to see how she likes it. Make up for some of the hurt...'

She places the secateurs in her pocket, peels off both latex gloves and is surprised by the cold touch of air brushing against her fingers. He closes his eyes and she looks away, and when she looks back he's staring at her.

'But the secateurs, Meg. Why have you got secateurs? Have you already done something? Her roses? Your mum's roses?'

He quickly stands. He's going to march round to the front of the house and he'll see the massacred roses and he'll see the graffiti too. After that, he'll never believe it wasn't her the first time.

'No!' she calls, reaching for his arm. 'No, you mustn't!' She has to stop him. 'I hate her. You don't know how much I hate her.' If only she could curl up and cry, and if only that would be enough to make everything alright, but instead she's stretching tight towards the brink of a scream, and the screaming will swallow her. She teeters, but holds herself back and wails instead: 'You never stopped her. You weren't here.'

'Stop it, Meg.'

'It wasn't me, last time. The graffiti wasn't me.'

'Oh no, Meg.'

'I'll clean it off. You mustn't see it. You mustn't go round there. You mustn't!' She almost feels relief now, for having told him.

He stands there and he's staring at her.

'Oh Meg.'

'I had to. I had to. For Stella. It was the only thing... You never answered your phone –'

He shakes his head. 'Let go of my jumper, Meg. Let go now. Calm down. For goodness sake, calm down.' He prises her fingers free and takes both her hands in his. 'Just stop it, Meg. Stop it now.' He pauses, hesitates. 'Now, listen.' And he proceeds slowly, weighing his words too carefully. 'Whatever you think, you really do need to see someone, Meg. You do. We can sort everything else out later – all this mess – but you really need to see Doctor Carmichael. Don't you? You don't have to feel like this, you know. She'll help, won't she? How about we phone her in the morning, my love? Or Ian, that other doctor? Everything seems worse at night. What do you say? Let's give it a go, eh, shall we? For your own good, Meg. Things can't go on like this, can they?'

She shakes her head.

'You can stay here tonight,' he continues. 'Just like old times. In your old room. Don't go back to Angie's. You don't need to. We'll sort it all out together, in the morning; in the light of day. It'll be alright, you'll see.'

He moves to put an arm round her shoulders and she takes a step back, buries both hands in her jacket pockets.

'That's not fair,' she manages to say. 'No. You can't do that. Why do you always take her side? Why do you always...' No one's going to shrink-wrap her brain again. It'll be back to Ward 8, the pills, the fog, but thicker fog this time because they'll turn it up, until she can't find herself anymore. That's what her mother wants and he's playing along. The bitch has tricked him. She always wins. 'No. I hate her. You can't. That's not fair.'

'What are you saying, Meg? You're muttering. What are you trying to say? Are you feeling okay? Do you want to go in now? It's cold out here.'

No. No, no, no. But no words come out. Only night.

'Hells bells, Meg, let's go inside, shall we? Between you and your mother, I don't know. But it's no big deal, it really isn't. You'll see. Come on, Meg, take my hand. Poor old Meg. I can call the hospital now, if you want. They're bound to have a doctor on call. We could drive over there now, or in the morning. Whichever you want, Megsy. Really, it'll be for the best.'

He has her by the arm and he's leading her across the lawn — the damp, dew-covered lawn — and she knows they shouldn't be standing on it, but doesn't remember why. She doesn't know much at all, except she won't go back to Ward 8. They won't do it again. She won't let them. She's not stepping into the house and she's not going to let him take her to hospital.

'No,' she says, and her voice sounds strange, even to her. It's a whimper and she's crying, and he turns and draws her to him and hugs her.

She doesn't want this hug. Not from him, not at this moment. There's a betrayal in it, because of where he's leading her. She can feel his hands on her back, but her hands remain clamped at her sides.

'Poor old Megsy,' he coos. 'Megsy, my love. Do you want me to phone now or in the morning? What would you prefer? It's your choice.'

He lifts a hand to stroke the hair poking out the back of her beanie, at the nape of her neck, and she has to make him let her go.

She doesn't want this.

She pushes away, but he's determined to soothe her into a helpless child.

'There, there. Calm down, Meg. Everything'll be fine. Relax. I'll give them a call.'

'No! Stop saying that! I don't want to. There's nothing wrong with me. Let me go.' Her anger is black and dizzying.

He pulls her closer, binding her to him and she tries to push away. She'll drown otherwise.

'Let go!'

He holds her tight. Too tight. He won't let go of her.

Black and frenzied. Beginning to drown.

She panics furiously; frees her arms. Has to prise him off. Clutch at anything to lever him off. Break to the surface. She beats out.

It isn't her. It comes from somewhere outside her.

A whirlpool of half-spun impressions, fleetingly observed: *she beats and beats against his back... the warmth of his jumper, the hardness of steel, the cold of night... once, twice... maybe three times... all too fast... he gasps, is gasping, then stumbles, releases his grip... she's free... he pushes against her, leans into her, holds onto her, stares at her... she's holding him now, struggling to keep them both on their feet, buckling under his awkward, lanky weight... still clenching the open secateurs in her fist... their sticky, wet handles... and she can't let go.* She can't let go.

It happens all too quick. And from too far away.

Black and cold, she sees what she's done and feels the leaking warmth of it, but from a distance and detached, as if inhabiting a body she's watching from another world. She feels the shiver of him and needs to lower him to the ground – has to let him go – except they remain standing, buckled together.

His breath gasps, 'Oh Meg.'

Who'd have thought flesh so soft? Painfully, she thinks of the time she smacked Stella on the nose: *Smell cheese.*

'Sorry,' she says from the distance. 'I didn't mean to. Dad?' She makes herself close the blades and drop the secateurs.

There's the shallow warmth of his gasp against her neck, the side of her face, but she can't hold him much longer, even though she's holding him under the arms and is clinging tightly to him now. She'd like to lift one hand to stroke the back of his drooping head, except she can't do both.

'Dad?'

He shivers, pants and grows heavier, and she has to bend her knees and sink lower, lower, onto the damp grass.

'It's alright, Dad – Victor.' She doesn't know what to call him, but she lays him on his back and kneels at his side.

His eyes are wide open and staring. He tries to sit up, but gasps and sinks down again.

'Get her, Meg. Get Mum.'

She looks at him, puts an arm round his shoulders. He doesn't know what he's asking.

'... be alright,' he whispers. 'Just... get her. Quick... Call Stella.'

He gurgles and flinches; there's blood in his mouth. She

wants to believe he must've bitten his lip. She must've made him bite his lip when she hit him, but she remembers the deer and she knows.

'Meg.' His voice is a faint rasp.

She sits with him a few minutes while he lies there. The cold wetness from the grass soaks through the legs of her overalls, as if she might have pissed herself, but she ignores this and nods, smiles, stroking his hair.

'I'm sorry,' she hears herself saying, but it doesn't feel like she's speaking.

'Oh, Meg.'

It's the last thing he says.

His breathing comes harder, more laboured, like he's struggling up-hill, or has almost drowned, which is ridiculous because there's no water here, only dew. Eventually, he slips into too-deep-sleep and she feels as if she should sing something.

It takes an age to fully find her way back to this place, this moment. Too late for an ambulance.

She understands she can't stay kneeling on the grass all night, waiting for the world to wake and find her. Should she phone the police and tell them? Give herself up?

It was an accident. Self-defence, at least. He wouldn't let her go. He shouldn't have done that. She didn't mean it to happen. She wasn't in control. It wasn't her. Even so, they won't believe her. They'll ask what she was doing here in the middle of the night. But whatever she says, her mother will tell them she's mad.

She could clean off the graffiti, but she can't stick the roses back together, and for that they'll lock her away and drug her up to the eyeballs forever. Those nut-cracking doctors and nurses, they'll break her apart and steal who she really is and they'll lock the best of her deep into a place she can't find her way out of. Like they did last time. Like *She*, that woman sleeping upstairs, persuaded them to.

They'll extinguish her completely if she lets them take her again.

It's all *her* fault. Everything. None of this would have happened if it wasn't for her. She can't let her get away with it a second time. She won't let it happen.

She has to think.

Think clearly.

Think, plan, act. Survive. Survive and live

What's done is done.

She glances at Victor, notices his eyes are half-open, as if he's watching her, half-resting, and briefly hopes. But when she waves her hand in front of his face, he doesn't blink or flinch and, besides, there's no pulse.

She smoothes his eyelids shut so he can't see her, then gives him three kisses: one on each eye and one in the middle of his forehead. Kiss, kiss, kiss.

He's still warm, but she has to survive, so she wipes the blood from her hands on the grass and pulls on the latex gloves once more – clammy and cool now – and gently rolls him onto his stomach.

He's gone and nothing will bring him back.

For being dark, night is infinitely bigger than day; it stretches and spreads into the farthest reaches of the universe... and beyond. And this tiny instant she inhabits isn't even a speck in a miniscule particle of all that. Who she is and what she does counts for nothing. Not really. There's no all-seeing eye, no divine judge.

She needs to shower and get rid of her overalls, her jacket; she must remember to scrub behind her fingernails.

But later – that'll have to be done later – for other things have to be done first.

What things? What else?

The graffiti and the roses. Together, they'll make it look like the A.A.R. were here, which is good now – it has to be that way now – but she has to get Victor away. He'll tell too much of a story. Deep in the old forest maybe, where no one will disturb him. Where she can grieve him later and where he won't turn against her even more. A bed of peat, a blanket of moss. A pleasant spot.

She knows the perfect place. A remote area of beech trees, near a massive boulder.

There's a roll of hessian weed-mat in the back of the truck, and the wheelbarrow of course. Or she could use the tarpaulin instead of weed-mat. Either will do. Something to wrap him in and carry him in. Snug as a bug in a rug. She mustn't forget the secateurs or the paint can. No, she mustn't leave anything of herself behind.

A figure in overalls and a brown, woollen hat, shrouds the body of a man in blue tarp. She drags the dead weight of him onto a wheelbarrow, which is almost impossible to balance at first, and teeters along the garden path and behind the shed towards her truck. When she stops and realises what she's doing, who she's carrying, she begins shaking and blubbering until the wheelbarrow almost topples over again, but she lowers the handles, takes slow breaths, stares up at the vast sky and finally navigates her way through the gap in the wattle.

She swings from cold logic to angry hysteria and back again, and has a thousand different thoughts, but the one she keeps returning to, the thing that maddens her most, is the absence of natural justice. If there was any natural

justice in the world, her mother would be dead and not
Victor. It should have been her. It really should. Everything
would make more sense then.

She's exhausted.

For the umpteenth time, she considers using turps or
petrol to rub off the graffiti, but doesn't know what else she
can do with Victor. If only he hadn't grabbed her and sided
against her, nor held her like he did. Why should she be
punished for that? It's her mother who should be punished.

If only she could set it all – the graffiti, the vandalism,
Victor's disappearance – firmly at the door of the Animal
Rights mob. If only she could silence her mother.

She's next to the rusty frame of the old swing and she
leans against it for a moment. The mist has fully crept up
the paddock to the edge of the garden now and the quarter-
moon is masked by clouds. She vaguely wonders at what
point in her childhood the swing seat was taken down, and
it's while she's half-thinking about this that she understands
what she must do next and why there's no other choice. Do
or be done by. She's gone so far that there's no turning back.

There's petrol in the shed and there'll be matches in the
kitchen.

She remembers how her mother had the gall to wipe
invisible marks off the wall and tried to make her cover the
seat of the kitchen chair with a damned tea towel before she
sat down; how she treated her like dirt. It was like being spat
at. She hates every brick, every stick of furniture in the
house; she hates all it stands for, all the memories it contains
and the way it reduces her. She hates her mother.

There's no point crying, but she's crying when she unscrews
the lid from the metal tin and pours petrol across one end

of the table, over the newspaper folded there, across the floor and down one wall. No more crumbs, no more dirty fingerprints.

She wipes her eyes with one arm of her overalls, stands at the open kitchen door and lights a match. It splutters in the draft and dies.

She steps back into the kitchen, closes the door and lights another match. As soon as she tosses it towards the glistening petrol on the floor, it goes out.

She looks around and, noticing the calendar on the wall, tears off a month. Lighting a third match, she sets fire to the page, opens the door in readiness to escape and tosses the burning paper to the floor.

Like a huge intake of breath: a single Whoosh!

Night-night, sleep tight.

ELEVEN

I watched the high beam of headlights cut an arc across the wall, listened to the crunching of tyres on gravel. The car engine was switched off and I peered at the clock – 4:07. There was a moment of quiet, the slamming of car doors and footsteps heading towards the house. Seconds later, came the knock on the door.

I hadn't been asleep. Hadn't long been in bed. One job after another. I'd just been lying, waiting, going over and over. Too rigid, too tense. Knowing, anticipating.

I stood on one side of the front door, swallowed hard and said, 'Who is it?'

'Police. It's Senior Sergeant Mick Droyler. I have Police Officer Wendy Aitkens with me.' He switched on his torch and shone it at himself, and I could see something of a distorted face and a uniform through the crazed glass.

'What do you want?' I said. 'Do you know what time it is?'

'We need to speak with you, Meg. I know it's late, but this won't wait till morning.'

The cold and dampness of mist swept in with them, and

I allowed a shiver or two as I shut the front door. I told myself to say what I'd say if I didn't already know, to play the part and not miss a beat. A matter of twitching the right strings at the right time.

'You're bringing bad news,' I said. 'At this time of night. What's happened? Who is it? Is it Angie?'

He turned his cap between his hands, looked at it, then stopped. 'Can we sit down, Meg?'

'Someone's dead, aren't they? Or there's been an accident. That's why you're here. Who is it? What's happened?'

'There's been a fire,' he said.

TWELVE

I muted my phone and plugged it in to charge after speaking with Angie, but an hour or so later, during which it had grown dark and the blunt stillness of the last couple of days gave way to a knife-edge of wind, it began vibrating across the coffee table like a demented wasp.

'I hate you!' Stella screamed. 'You told the police that Pete was with the A.R.A. didn't you? I know you did. Why did you do that?'

I closed my eyes. 'You mean the A.A.R.? All I told them is what he told me four years ago, if you must know. Actually, what I said was that he probably wasn't involved, but that he might know someone who was. So they can find Dad. That's all I told them.'

'No! Why did you have to tell them anything? They took him in for questioning, gave him a hard time. They took his laptop, his computer – all that stuff. They treated him like he did it, like he set the fire, and they asked me again why I was home and when I got there, whether Pete drove me back, how long I'd known him, as if I –'

'I had to tell them so they can find Dad. He's missing,

Stella. Those Animal Rights nutters have got him. They've kidnapped Dad and we need to get him back.'

'I knew you –' she began, but couldn't finish for crying.

'I tried to tell you, Stell, but you wouldn't listen. There's other stuff you have to know too.'

'What other stuff?'

'Not over the phone. I can't tell you over the phone.'

Gustav nudged the door open and strutted into the room. He paused, walked over to me and brushed against my leg before turning about and brushing his other side against me.

'What stuff?'

'Not over the phone.'

'About Pete?'

'And Dad.'

'Tell me. Tell me now!'

She wasn't giving me time to think about it. 'It's about why Mum bust up my relationship with him. It's why you mustn't see him either.'

She said nothing and I tried to carry on.

'A few days ago... a while back, anyway...' I stopped. It was too quiet on the other end. I couldn't even hear her breathing. 'Stella? Are you there? Are you still there?'

'Tell me. Just tell me.'

I had to tell her. All the same, they were hard words to say. 'She told me... Mum told me that Pete Lailer... that he's probably, more than likely, our half-brother. She told me how Dad had a fling with his mum – Pete Lailer's mum – nine months before he was born. It was just before Dad and Mum got married. They'd had a bust-up or something, but then got back together again. So there, that's why. That's why you mustn't see him. You mustn't. You understand? He's our half-brother, Stella. Possibly. Mum was certain of it. That's why she did what she did to me. Now do you see? It wasn't me, it was her.'

The silence from Stella's phone was emphatic, like an exclamation mark, and then she hung up: the inevitable sting.

I held my head in my hands, could hear the wind whistling a high-pitched note across the chimney. All I wanted was to sleep and for everything to become right again.

Victor haunts me, but not her. He haunts me when I'm awake and he haunts my dreams.

In my dream, I set out to visit him and make sure, during day-light, that everything's as it should be and that he's sleeping tight. Except his resting place isn't as deep into the forest as I was certain it was. Instead, I walk behind Angie's ramshackle garage, burrow through the overgrowth, which is thicker than I remembered, hop the broken fence and I'm there. Too quickly.

The forest is a strange, confounding place in this respect. Not just in dreams, but in actuality. Often, it turns you around, disorientates you, until you find, after hours of marching towards the unknown heart of it, that you've ended up only a few metres from where you started. Sometimes, you can't find your way back to a peaceful clearing you've discovered, or a secret cluster of rocks or an unmapped cave, no matter how hard you look, and yet, on another occasion, you'll come across it again without searching for it and it's somewhere else much closer or much further away than you originally thought. As if the forest can shift its shape at will.

When I notice how easily I've arrived at this area of golden beeches, I tell my dream-self that at least now I'll be able to visit and talk to him regularly, even though I'll need to be more careful about covering my tracks. It's far from ideal, but there's nothing I can do about it, unless I move him and make his bed someplace else. Then I start worrying about how I'll move him.

However, there's something wrong. The big rock, which is fringed on two sides with bracken and briar, and which I've climbed and sat upon several times, is exactly where it should be, so I know I'm in the right spot, but instead of there being a mound of leaf litter and moss to mark Victor's resting place at the lowest point of the dip, there's an empty hollow. He's gone.

'Dad!' I shout, and in shouting jump out of sleep. Almost.

It's night and freezing cold, and the house shivers against the wind, and I'm brittle with panic. In that half-awake world where dreams and actuality overlap, I'm terrified by Victor's disappearance.

Where can he have got to? Has he crawled from his shallow grave to the back of Angie's old garage, or has someone unearthed him? Maybe he was only unconscious after all and I buried him alive, which means I didn't have to set light to the house. Why did I have to set fire to the house? He'll be mad with me; he'll definitely want to lock me up. Maybe the police know what I did and they're on their way to arrest me; they're creeping up on me, waiting to jump out at me.

I listen.

The wind cuts through the trees and stabs at the house, slicing between the boards and joists, making the timbers tremble and wince, as if someone's moving from room to room... until I realise they might be, they actually could be. In fact, they are. The noises are masking someone's movement downstairs, opening a cupboard door and closing it, moving across the hall from one aching floorboard to the next, rattling at the French windows.

It's Victor or Steven Earles or Mick Droyler or Angie or…

I know I'm imagining things. I know I'm half-asleep. And I tell myself to reach out and turn on the bedside lamp, to pull off the remaining layers of sleep and let my dream scab over, but there's familiar comfort in the scritching and scraping of the buddleia's bare branches along the edge of the verandah roof. There's nothing to be frightened of, I try to tell myself, there really isn't. Sleep, sleep, there's no one there. Besides it's too cold to be awake, and I can't help but slip away again.

Away to the bare bones of a house in the murky depths of the forest. My parents' house, but not my parents' house. In essence Duparc House – our house – but different in appearance and location.

A narrow, confined path winds through thick undergrowth, but when it squeezes a route around that landmark boulder of mine and suggests a clearing up ahead, I realise straightaway where I am, and am relieved it's much further from Angie's house and deeper into the forest after all. I expect to find Victor's grave in this dark dell, but the house fills it instead. Not the complete house and not the charred wreck either, but something much less and much more.

Although I understand it's our house, the burning of it has reduced it to something similar to Giacometti's *Palace at 4am*: a cage-like structure of posts and beams tied together. The peaty earth is the floor, the broken sky is the roof. I know there should be people or objects inside the framework of rooms, but I can't remember exactly who or what, and I move from one defined space to another, searching for them. I like the way the trees press up against the house and help clothe the walls with their leaves, and I wonder how I could have ever disliked living here.

It's then I notice a long chest positioned in the centre of the main room, drawing me magnetically towards it. How did I miss it before? It wants me to lift the lid, but every instinct warns me to run away.

I know what's inside. I know whose body is inside.

I can't help myself. I can't resist.

I place my fingers against the edge of the lid, ready to raise it, when, from right behind me, someone coughs. A real, wide-awake cough.

And I'm fully awake in an instant. Back in bed. Absolutely sure I've heard an actual cough. Deep, like a man coughing. Not something that's grown out of my dream, but that's broken through it instead; too close and too loud.

I'm lying rigidly still, staring into the darkness, trying to see who's there, waiting to hear a floorboard betray them. Reaching an arm out, trying not to make a noise until the last possible moment, I find the bedside lamp and click it on.

Light! There's no one in the room. No remnant of fleeing shadow across the far wall. No sound at all.

Maybe they heard me. Maybe they're holding their breath, just outside my door, standing on the landing, rigid, still, and waiting too.

Victor, or Steven Earles, or Pete Lailer.

'Who's there?' I shout.

Silence.

Nothing.

You're a silly goose, Meg, I tell myself, but keep my eyes

fixed on the doorway. I probably dreamt the cough, or it was the sound of the house creaking or the crashing of a tree; a sound that translated poorly in my dream.

I mustn't go to pieces. I can't. What happened with Dad was an accident. It was as much his fault as mine. But I couldn't have told the police, not after everything else. There was no point. It wouldn't have done any good. And she would have made things worse. Like last time. No one would have understood. I did what most people would've done, under the circumstances.

Not everyone gets caught. I know they don't. Not if they're careful. Not if there's no evidence, no motive. Not if the finger clearly points in a different direction.

I mustn't let myself go to pieces. And it's too cold a night to be sitting up, staring at the dark landing. My bed is losing warmth, my feet are growing icy and I'm desperate to pee.

Turning on the electric blanket, I swing out of bed and move swiftly to the door where I flick on the main light and grab my dressing-gown, keeping one eye on the landing all the time. There's nothing to arm myself with – no golf club in my room, no baseball bat – but at least I can switch on every upstairs light and banish the shadows. Peering over the banisters at the darkness downstairs, it releases the memory of another dream and of leaping the stairs to flee the house, but the cold floor tiles in the bathroom snap me wider awake and the toilet seat sends an extra shiver through me. It's what I need.

In Angie's room, I check inside the wardrobe like a scared child, pushing her remaining clothes to one side, and I kneel down to look under the bed too. I glance around her studio, behind the old sheet draped over her easel, but there's no one there. Of course there's not. I'm glad I looked, though, because sitting against one end of her tatty, paint-smeared cupboard is her plastic tub of inks, fabric dyes and cans of spray paint.

The sight sickens me. I want to cover them with another box, or hide them in a cupboard, until I realise two of the cans – black and fluoro pink – are exactly the same brand as the fluoro green one I used. It's not good. I've seen enough TV crime shows to know that Forensics has probably matched the graffiti paint with a particular brand and batch number already, and I can't afford to let the police find the same brand here. Why haven't I realised this before? I can't afford to let little details betray me.

Pulling them out, I jumble the remaining cans and pots so it doesn't look like any have been recently removed. I have to think of everything. I'll get rid of the black and the pink one first thing in the morning. If Angie asks – if she notices once she's got her new friend back here, or when she's packing up to move to some distant place – I'll tell her I used them when I was marking out a garden design on a client's old lawn. I'll offer to replace them if that's what she wants.

Being sensible and logical takes my mind off the stupid stuff and nudges me back towards being in control. Even so, that doesn't stop me from drawing a golf club from the umbrella stand when I'm downstairs and keeping a firm grip on it as I move through the rest of the house, turning on the lights and checking doors. No one really coughed, I tell myself. It would have been a tree limb creaking and snapping, or something similar. Grabbing an old plastic carrier bag from the kitchen drawer, I drop the two cans of spray paint in and leave it on the kitchen table, where it'll remind me in the morning about dumping it.

Angie's outside lights just about illuminate her whole

garden. There's been summer evenings when we've sat on the verandah or on a picnic blanket under one of her trees, chatting and drinking against a chorus of cicadas and a distant coodylark or two, with the garden lit up like a party and the forest standing in the shadows, and when we might have remained immersed in that warm halo of light all night long. We probably would've stayed there too if not for the mosquitoes and the fact that, back then, I'd have had to get home. As I flick on these lights now, I tell myself there's no reason they can't stay on all night for comfort and peace of mind, but when I pull the kitchen blind back to check whether any of Angie's trees have blown down, the first thing I see, apart from the coating of frost on the lawn, are the scuff marks across it: dark slashes across the glistening grey-white. Someone has been here. They have. The man with the cough. Dragging his feet.

Victor. Choking and crawling.

I drop the blind, tighten my grip on the golf club.

It can't be Victor. It's someone else. Some weirdo.

Maybe even now he's standing amongst the dark fringe of trees, pleased with himself at having caught me looking out. Or maybe he's crouched under this very window and has been following my movements across the kitchen through a gap between the window and the blind.

If I call the police they might send a patrol car, except I mustn't. It's not just because of the spray cans, but because the more I speak to them the more I'll be in their focus and the greater the chance I'll let something slip. I mustn't phone them again. That was a mistake.

The house is all lit up like a Christmas tree, except there's no festive warmth in this, and I'm shaking so much as I check the last couple of windows that my fingers are practically useless, and I wonder how I'll find the strength to swing the bloody golf club at someone (or some thing) if I have to. All the same, back upstairs, I manage to nudge and slide the chest of drawers against my bedroom door, so no bogey-man can get me if I fall asleep... unless he sets fire to the house.

The thought startles me. Usually I'd enjoy the irony.

If the house was on fire I'd have to jump out the window, onto the verandah roof. It'd be the only way out. Which makes me realise that someone could climb up and onto it and into my room that way too. I hadn't thought of that when barricading the door.

One part of me is shaking and another part is shivering, and I think I'll rattle apart if it doesn't stop soon. I turn off the bedroom lights and peer from behind the curtain to double-check the window is latched and that no one's on the verandah roof. Then I peer down into the garden, but can't make out any footprints from this angle, only some of the dragging marks I saw from the kitchen, as if someone was crawling across the lawn.

The cough was a while ago and there's been nothing since, so maybe they've gone. Maybe they ran off when the lights went on. Perhaps it was a stalker, a peeping-tom, someone who's read about the fire in the newspaper, someone who knows I live here by myself. Some creep or toss-pot loser.

I turn my bedside lamp back on, pull on a pair of socks, climb into bed in my dressing-gown and rest the golf club on top of the doona. I'd forgotten I'd switched the electric blanket on and the sheets are toasty, but I'm still shivering.

Should've made a hot drink and got a book to read from Angie's study, to help keep me awake, but really I'm tired and all I want is sleep. Rearranging my pillows so I can sit upright, I glance toward the curtains, wondering how many hours before it'll grow light, but I know I'll fall asleep at some point. I won't be able to stay awake through the night.

It's strange how we think darkness is less natural than light, as if light existed before darkness, but that's not the way it is: everything grows from darkness. Darkness is the backdrop to all we do and everything we are. Light is nothing but a temporary thinning of darkness.

I'm thinking about this and getting dozy and beginning to drift off, but when my head drops I wake with a jolt. From the ceiling, in one corner of the attic, comes a scurrying and scratching, followed by three or four soft taps. I freeze and strain to hear more. Part of me knows it's a mouse or a bush rat nestling down, but another part of me is sure that whoever's been creeping around outside has let themself into the house and is hiding up there; someone who's seen what I've done and who's waiting for me to fall asleep again before they pounce.

Again, I think of Victor. Victor could easily crawl out of my dreams and be hiding there.

Anything's possible in the middle of the night.

Listen. Listen.

I'll know for sure if I catch the faintest sound of them breathing or sighing or whispering my name. Although they're probably holding their breath too, straining to hear me drift back to sleep.

I'm struggling to stay awake now, but I won't sleep – I'll fight it – not until I'm sure. I won't let myself.

Then, from outside, in the garden, comes the cough again: a loud, rough cough. Very real.

Except I immediately recognise the husky coarseness of it now. It's a deer barking. Once, twice, it barks, followed by a silence which drags the forest into the room. A couple of minutes later, it barks again. A deep, short, sharp sound, that could easily be mistaken for a cough or someone shouting your name if you were half-asleep. The deer will also have been pawing at the ground, leaving scuff marks in the frost.

You really are a silly goose, Meg.

Flicking off my lamp to darken the room, I clamber out of bed once more and stand by the curtains. At the edge of the garden, a couple of metres beyond the halo of outside lights, are three young deer and, even as I look at them, the one in front stamps a hoof and barks again.

How ridiculous I've been. Pathetic.

I'm smarter than this, I scold myself. I have to be. And without switching my lamp back on, I return to bed, rearrange the pillows, pull up the doona and close my eyes.

The thin frost had thawed by the time I woke up, giving way to a mild, cloudy morning. When I stepped outside to put the bag with the two spray cans in the cab of my truck, the air smelt sweetly mildewy, of pine needles, leaves and rotting vegetation, but a fine drizzle of rain swept in as I returned to the house.

Over breakfast, I'd been agonising whether I should phone Stella or not, until I reminded myself that she was the one who'd hung up on me and that the best thing was to let her stew. But when someone rapped on the front door as I was cleaning away my dishes, my first thought was that it must be Stella and I was glad. She'd borrowed Pete Lailer's or Jasmine's car to drive out, apologise and to ask if she could move in with me.

Except it wasn't Stella, it was the police. Detective Earles and Officer Aitkens. She was in uniform, he was wearing a thick, padded jacket over the top of ordinary clothes. No Mick Droyler.

'I wonder if we might have a quick word?' he said. They were standing on the verandah, side-by-side, except he stood slightly in front. A bank of dark clouds were looming over the forest now, which was a sure sign heavier rain was on the way. 'You've met Officer Aitkens before, I take it?'

I did my best to smile and tried to be more friendly towards Earles. 'You best come in. It's about to get nasty out there.' As I closed the door behind them, and only for the sake of small talk, I added, 'Don't you guys get any days off?'

'No rest for the wicked,' he said, but I don't think he meant himself.

'Through here.' I led them into the lounge. 'It's warmer in here. Would you like a coffee or tea or something?'

'We're fine for the moment,' he said.

'Have a seat,' I said, but they remained standing. 'Have you heard anything? Do you have news? Is that why you're here?'

He said, 'We're following enquiries,' and took out his notebook.

It seemed strange she wasn't saying anything and I wondered if they were about to arrest me. He'd probably instructed her not to say anything and to observe; to be on hand in case Her Royal Craziness turned crazy. It was obvious he was the sort of person who enjoyed bossing other people around and I hated the way he said things in a monotone most of the time, void of emphasis and expression, as if everything he uttered was a fact and he couldn't be bothered making it sound interesting for plebs like me.

'Okay. Good. Thank you,' I said, and smiled again. I

didn't know why I said 'Thank you.' They'd flustered me, turning up out of the blue, and I told myself to relax, to concentrate on my breathing. Easier said than done.

Earles said, 'On the night of the fire, did you phone your father at all?'

'No,' I said, but too quickly and too definitely because I'd completely forgotten that I actually did. However, because of the way he'd phrased it, making it sound like a trick question, as if he already knew the answer, I was wondering what he was driving at and then I realised my mistake. 'No, wait, yes, I did. I forgot about that. I tried phoning him, but he didn't answer. Why?'

He glanced from me to his notebook and back again. 'What time was that?'

It seemed this was important and I couldn't work out why, as if I might not have anticipated a key move in the chess game, but there was only one response, only one way to move. 'I'm not exactly sure, but it was probably around midnight. Sometime around midnight.'

'At six minutes past twelve?'

'About then, yes. Why?'

Earles: 'Why did you call him?'

'Because I went to bed early, like I said before, but I woke up. I couldn't sleep for a short while and thought it'd be nice to talk to Dad, if he wasn't in a meeting or something. I thought it'd be the middle of the day for him because I thought he was still overseas, but he didn't answer, so I read for a while and then went back to sleep. Why?'

Earles: 'Why didn't you mention this before?'

'Because I'd forgotten all about it, and besides I didn't get through.'

Earles: 'So you didn't speak to him at all?'

'No.'

Earles: 'You didn't phone his hotel and ask for him?'

'No, of course not. How could I? I didn't know which hotel he was staying at.'

Earles: 'I see.'

'Why?' I asked again. 'How come you're checking my phone records?'

Earles: 'We're not. It's your father's phone log we're looking at.'

'Oh.' I didn't believe him.

He sort of smiled then, or attempted to smile, and glanced around the room, and his tone shifted, as if he could be all friendly now. 'Thanks, Meg. That's all for the moment.'

'That's all? You came all the way out here to ask that?'

'We have to be thorough. That's what you'd want, isn't it?'

'Yeah, I suppose so.'

He was playing with me. I'm sure he was. Perhaps that's what the police do if you're a suspect and they want to rattle you. It was too far to come to ask a couple of silly questions and to make such a big deal out of it, and it was the second time they'd done it. I looked at Aitkens to see if she was giving anything away, but she remained the picture of professional detachment.

'It's a lovely house,' he said, peering at the ornate, plaster centrepiece of the ceiling, before turning his attention to the fireplace. 'Victorian. Turn-of-the-century, isn't it?'

I had to be careful. I was regretting giving him a hard time before. It had set him against me.

'Angie says it's about a hundred-and-twenty-years old.' I was a bit breathless, so I covered it with a cough. 'Excuse me. Asthma,' I said.

'Hmm, that'd be right.' He stroked his hand across the

mantelpiece and then crouched down to look at the tiles around the hearth. 'All original,' he said.

I thought he was asking me.

'I don't know. I guess so.'

'It is,' he told me, twisting round and looking up. 'Now, if that coffee's still on offer, a white-with-one would be great.'

There was no choice but to play along.

I turned to Wendy Aitkens. 'How about you?'

'I'm fine,' she said, 'but I'll come through with you while you make it, if you like.'

'It's a lovely house,' he said again. 'I've always wanted a house like this. You don't mind if I take a quick squiz around, do you?'

'What for?'

'Because I'd like to. It interests me.'

So that was his game. Even though I was sure there was nothing he could find, now I'd moved the cans of spray paint, I didn't want him thinking he could trick me and do exactly what he pleased. I wasn't going to roll over for him.

'I don't know what you think you'll find,' I said, 'and I don't like strangers snooping through my stuff, but I've got nothing to hide, so go ahead.'

He gave his fake smile again. 'Thanks.'

'And if you think my dad's hiding here, you're wrong. He wouldn't have... he wouldn't have set fire to our house. Never. I know he wouldn't. He wouldn't have done that. He's not like that.'

I had to place Victor in the present tense and show how upset I was, but not overact, and I think I sounded fretful enough to be convincing. Nonetheless, I couldn't believe how quickly my eyes watered up and how I was almost crying by the time I'd finished. I think it was because

Earles upset me.

'No one's saying anything of the kind,' he said. 'Not at all.'

'Let's put the kettle on, shall we?' Wendy Aitkens suggested and ushered me out the room, as if it were her home and not mine. He walked out after us, but lingered in the hall to pretend he was looking at the architecture or something.

'Can he do that?' I said to her, even though he was in earshot. 'Is he allowed to nose around people's homes like this? Doesn't he need a warrant?'

'He did ask you, Meg. You can say no if you like.'

'But then it'd seem like I've got something, or someone, to hide, and I haven't. That's what he'd think.'

She reached for the kettle and passed it to me. 'Where do you keep your coffee, Meg?'

'I just don't like people snooping about, looking at my things.'

'Okay.'

I told myself to relax, but it wasn't easy with him nosing about, especially when I realised he might want to look in the garage or the cab of my truck again. He was probably just trying to rattle me and see if I'd do something stupid. Relax, I told myself.

It was hard enough keeping one ear on his footsteps as he walked from room to room upstairs while trying to have some sort of conversation with Officer Aitkens, who wanted to talk about Gustav and Persian cats, let alone having to make coffee too. Focus. Breathe. I'd give him his cup of coffee and watch him drink it. I had no choice. As long as I didn't go to pieces. That was the main thing. As long as he didn't want the keys to my truck. I'd tell him to get a warrant if he did.

When he joined us in the kitchen, clutching his mobile, he said, 'It's a lovely, big house. I'd never have thought it had so many rooms, not from outside. Your friend an artist, is she?'

'She teaches Music and Art.'

Earles: 'And you're house-sitting while she's away?'

I nodded.

Earles: 'Lucky. You could have got caught in the fire yourself.'

I nodded again. 'I know. That's crossed my mind a few times. Do you want a biscuit?'

'Thanks, but no. We can't stop for coffee after all. Sorry. I've just received a call.'

'About the fire? About Dad?'

He looked at me, but didn't answer.

It was a small price to pay.

I watched them drive away, but it didn't feel like they'd driven away. Even after I'd poured his coffee down the sink and washed the cup, they still seemed to fill the house. With Gustav following me, and sometimes running ahead, I went from room to room, making sure Earles hadn't moved anything or taken something, and I opened the lounge windows briefly to clear the air. Even after I'd tracked off into the forest to bury the paint cans, my head remained cram-jammed with his presence for an hour or two.

But I kept telling myself not to lose control. I kept telling myself I could survive this – one day at a time, move by move – and that helped.

By late afternoon, I hadn't heard from Stella and still couldn't figure what Earles thought he knew about me. Not knowing what other people might know or suspect is the hardest part. But it was the right thing to let him wander round the house; it was the right move. Maybe he'd leave me alone now.

According to several websites, about 30% of homicides don't get solved in the United States, but it's only 14% here, although there's a world of difference apparently between what gets included in those statistics. Still, they're not bad odds – 14 out of 100, or 1 in 7 – especially as most people would leave a trail of evidence behind them or get caught on CCTV or something, and especially as they don't know what happened to Victor yet. Victim or suspect? The more time that passes, the better. What with all the rubbish from the fire still strewn across the back garden and the water from the fire brigade's hoses saturating everything, they'll be nothing left for them to find. I might have had the means and the opportunity, but then so did lots of people, and there's no value in that without a motive. Stella would make a better suspect than me. Much better. But the A.A.R. is their best bet.

It's too horrible to be stuck indoors. I hate it. It's as if the day has given up, as if the world's itching to have night back again. It's weirdly quiet too and I can't hear a single bird, not even a raven or a pigeon; there's a couple of starlings on the lawn, but they don't make a sound. Angie's house has shrunk and, no matter what I start doing, I end up standing by a window, fogging the glass, wanting to be outside and a long way away from myself. I stare into the forest until it becomes a blur, and I know what I'm staring towards even if I can't see it.

After my dreams, I feel I should visit Victor and make sure he's okay, to make sure the forest animals aren't disturbing him, but I mustn't. Not yet. Not for a while. It wouldn't be safe. I have to act as if someone's watching me, following me, and as if they can hear every word I say. Having wasted so much of the day, though, I tell myself there's nothing to stop me from getting in my truck and driving someplace else. Not if I want to.

Pulling alongside the hedge of rambling wattle, I can't remember its botanical name for a moment and mustn't get out of my truck until I do. I have to remember because the small details hold me together.

Then I do: *Acacia perambulare*. It gives me confidence. Everything will be alright.

Night really is drawing in, even though it's only late-afternoon, and the little tunnel through the wattle is gloomy and dank in a way that makes it hard to imagine it'll ever be summer again. Except I know it will be; it can be.

There's a sharp, silver bright, sliver of moon rising out of the forest (as if that's where it sleeps during the day), and hovering above the river are the first wisps of more mist. The forest looms as a black and impenetrable vastness, while the darkening sky, for being cloudless again, seems infinitely high and overwhelmingly perfect.

I'm not going to haunt this place, but it was my home, so I'm allowed to return to look at it and gradually get used to it. That's all I'm doing.

There seems to be no one here, thank goodness, but all the same, as I walk round to the front, I place a hand against the glass and peer in through each blackened window to be sure. There are no cars in the driveway or parked on Rudely Road. Forensics have knocked-off or finished for good. There's plastic Crime Scene tape across the doors, as well as yellow tape with black writing: *Danger*

– *Keep Out!* A couple of windows have been boarded up and there's a dark, damning word sprayed across the front of the house.

I stand in front of the trampled rose bed and try staring it down.

It's a word. That's all.

'Sorry,' I whisper, to see how it makes me feel. 'I'm sorry,' I say a little louder, but it doesn't bring tears, only tiredness and self-consciousness at speaking aloud into an empty garden. I squat down to stare up at it. It's only a word and it's only a building – the old bones of a home – and everything else is inside my head. That's where the ghosts are. The past is dead and buried, and can only bother us if we keep digging it up and examining it.

A car heading into Three Creeks decelerates, as if turning onto the Wallan River Road, but turns into our driveway. The slowness of its approach gives me time to retreat to the side of the house. It's a small, red hatchback and not a car I recognise, and the windows are all reflected twilight and unfathomable shadow, but it stops well short of the garage and the engine is left running for almost a minute before it's turned off and the driver's door slowly opens.

Stella.

She climbs out and stands behind the open door. Her hands are covering her mouth and she's staring at the front of the building – at *that word*.

I keep back, watching from the corner of the house, and she doesn't see me. When she tries to cram her fingers into her mouth, I can tell she's crying, even though there's no sound. When she begins to wail, it's a long, high-pitched keen, like a tortured dog snapped in a fox trap, and I'm unsure whether I should edge further back and leave her alone or step out and comfort her.

'Stella,' I call. It may only be a few metres, but there's a gulf between us. She sees me and crumples, and I open my arms to her – she needs me – but she shakes her head, turns and vomits on the lawn.

My first thought is that she knows. She knows I did it. She saw me from her bedroom on the night of the fire, or heard me. It drains me. It blanks me out for a moment and I don't know what to do next... or how to go about doing it. But she can't have seen me. It's impossible. She'd have said something by now.

I place my hands on her shoulders while she's bent double and retching, and she doesn't shake me off. She takes the tissue I offer and wipes her eyes and her mouth.

'Stella.'

'It's horrible, it's evil,' she sobs. 'I never imagined...' and she stands, turns into the embrace I offer and continues crying.

I shake my head. *Evil* is completely the wrong word. I wish I could explain so she'd understand, but I don't think anyone, including Stella, could really understand.

'It'll be alright,' I say, although I feel more alone than ever. 'Everything'll be alright.'

'How can it be? How can it be?'

'It will be,' I assure her. 'In time.'

'No.' She begins crying again. She's simply sobbing at first, but then, as if hit by the realisation of something bigger and worse, she begins wailing with a new wretchedness – harder, louder – and she clings to me tighter. 'Meggy,' she wails, 'Oh I'm sorry. I'm sorry.'

She's sorry.

Relief floods through me and I almost smile.

I pull her to me in the way Angie hugged me once, as if

we need never let go of one another again, and it's a relief to know that everything definitely will be alright because she really is sorry and she's realised how much she needs me. My fears and doubts of the day begin to wane and I'm growing strong again. The lesson is obvious: I'm vulnerable when I'm too much on my own, but tougher and sharper when I've got Stella to look after and fight for. She needs me like she's always needed me, but she knows it now, and I hug her in the way our mother never did.

'Sorry? Why are you sorry?' I ask. I want to hear her say it. I want to hear her tell me she should never have gone with Pete Lailer and how revolted she is by the thought of him; she'll apologise for being mean to me and she'll be grateful I was looking out for her. She'll start to understand everything I've been through. She'll come back to Angie's and she'll stay with me until we're sure what's happening with this ruined house, and I'll look after her. We'll cook and eat together, slouch next to one another on the settee when we watch television in the evening and she'll sleep in the next room to me at night, and there'll be no more ghosts.

'Oh, Meg,' she sobs. 'I didn't mean it to happen. Really.' She's all tears and snot, more like an eight-year-old than an eighteen-year-old. 'Why me?'

I wait, but she doesn't continue.

'It wasn't just you. It was me too. Everything she put me through because of him. It was both of us, Stella.'

Shaking her head, she pulls away a little. 'No. No.'

Her eyes are red raw and I guess we've both cried a flood across these last few days. She takes a few quick breaths and will only look at me briefly. I wish I had another tissue, but maybe there's some in the car. It must be Jasmine's car.

'You weren't to know. Neither of us could have —'

'No!'

'What?'

'I'm pregnant,' she howls.

I let go of her. 'You can't be. No.'

'I am. Found out today. Everything's turned to crap. Everything. My life's... down the toilet.'

'No. You can't be.' She mustn't be. I try to remember how long she said she'd been seeing him, but it must have been longer than she admitted. She must have lied about that too. 'No. You said...' But I can't remember. 'You must have...'

'I didn't mean it. It wasn't supposed to... Oh, Meggy.'

This shouldn't be happening. Why me? It's one thing after another. I don't know what to say or do. After everything I've done for her. Even the graffiti, the roses, the fire – I did it as much for her as anything.

A colder belt of damp air wheedles its way into my clothes, but this latest news finishes me and I've lost the will to stamp my feet and shake it off. I sense that I'm staring at her, even while I'm not properly seeing her, and there's a part of me wants to slap her.

'Don't, Meg.' She's looking at me and she's stopped howling now, although her face is white and as wet as can be. 'Hold me, Meg. Don't look at me like that.'

Beyond the thick cypress hedge, which marks some of the front of the property, a tractor chugs along the Rudely Road, away from Three Creeks, and then all's quiet once more.

If only I could be the person sitting on the tractor, instead of me.

'Meg?'

Mechanically, I open my arms and she steps closer to me again, and I fold my arms around her.

'I'm sorry,' she says.

I nod and start stroking her hair. It may not be fully dark yet, but the silence of night is already lapping around us, creating stillness and long pauses, growing deeper and deeper. We're both exhausted. There's a numbness creeping through my toes.

'What should I do? What do you think I should do?'

She wants me to be the one to say it. To name what has to be done.

Despite the wash of silence and tiredness, there's no way I'm going to let myself drown in this place. Nor will I let her off the hook. Not that easily.

'Isn't that between you and... its father?' I say, but with one hand still stroking her hair. 'What does *he* want to do?'

She's like a frightened bird and the mention of him starts her trembling and crying again.

'It's over,' she blubbers. 'What you said... his mum... they argued.'

I stop the stroking. 'They argued? She didn't deny it?'

'No, they argued. I don't know. He was wild. He said I had to leave. I told him I was —'

'But she didn't deny it?'

'No — I don't know. I wasn't there. It's what you said —'

'What Mum told me,' I remind her.

'He said he was going to quit his job, leave town. That he was sick of the police. He said horrible things about you, Meg. We argued.'

'He's a weak, gutless arsehole,' I point out. Although, even as I'm saying this, I'm wondering what it means if his mum and him argued about it and she didn't deny it. What if, despite all Victor believed, or claimed to believe, Pete Lailer's mum didn't deny it because... because the only reason she'd moved to a place like Lapishot — to the back of nowhere – was to be near her son's father? The thought spins me around.

'Our...' Stella cries. 'Dad's...' She twists from me and begins to gag. She heaves a couple of times, but nothing comes up, and she groans and dabs at her mouth with the crumpled tissue.

'Our half-brother,' I mutter, finishing the sentence for her. 'Your baby's father.'

She spits a look at me, but dissolves into tears instead. 'Don't say it. Don't!' Turning her back, she folds her arms against the roof of the car and pushes her face down into her arms. Her shoulders rise and fall with each sob.

She can be so self-centred at times. She always has been. As if she's the only one. 'It's not just about you, you know,' I tell her. 'This is happening to me too.' I begin moving my toes back and forward in my boots, stamping my feet.

'I'm pregnant,' she howls again.

'Welcome to the real world, Stell. They had me committed, remember. She bust up my relationship, said things behind my back, that I was sick, had me locked up on the loony ward – anything rather than the truth. How do you think that makes me feel?'

She turns round again and rubs at her eyes. 'But you *were* sick,' she says. 'You had a breakdown.'

'Only because of what she did. Because of the unfairness. Don't you think you'd have spat the dummy if you were me?'

By the way she glances away, I can tell she doesn't believe me. She's going to humour me or pity me, but she's not going to believe me. She thinks she's different to me, she thinks she's better than me.

'You don't know the half of it,' I begin, but stop. I

mustn't harp on about Mum, in case I say too much and she tells the police. Instead, I turn it on her. 'What do you think she'd do to you if she knew you were expecting your brother's baby?'

Her eyes well up and she can't say anything. She glances towards the house, but only briefly. Her face is white but her eyelids are swollen and red; her hair is lank and lustreless. I can see the ghost in her.

'You mustn't tell the police a single thing more than you have to,' I say. 'Whatever you do, don't let them know you're pregnant by him.'

She sort of shakes her head, but is listless now, as if she can barely register what I'm saying. It's too cold to be standing here. Not cold enough for the river to freeze, but there'll definitely be another, heavier frost tonight.

'Why?' she asks, and seems smaller, more fragile.

I take her in my arms again and can feel her trembling. She stands there as I embrace her.

'They might think you set fire to the house,' I say, but gently. 'Or you and him together. They know these things usually start as family arguments. They look to the family first; they always do.'

'I didn't,' she mumbles, barely audible. 'I didn't.'

'I know you didn't. I'm sure you didn't. But they don't know that, do they? That's why you mustn't tell them about... that he got you pregnant. They'll think Mum and Dad found out, and that you argued.'

She tries to push away from me, but I hold her. I've always looked after Stella, especially when we were little.

'No.'

'They'll examine every possibility until they find out who did it, who had the motive and the opportunity, or until there are no more leads.'

'Animal Rights... ' she begins.

'They're never going to track them down,' I point out. 'Unless they can pin it on someone who's part of their group. Like Pete Lailer. But then –'

She starts shaking her head again. 'He's not. He said he wasn't.'

'Are you sure?'

'He wouldn't.'

'You mustn't have anything to do with him, Stell. You mustn't.'

'He's gone,' she moans. 'He's gone.'

'Good,' I say, but perhaps too quiet for her to hear. It's growing dark now. 'What are you going to do about... you know?'

She says nothing and I feel as if I'm reaching out into the silence again, except I'm managing it this time and swimming with it. Her breathing is fast and shallow, like tremors and ripples, and the warm moisture of her breath clings to my neck. She simply stands like a rag doll, arms dangling at her side, while I hold her. It's only when she sniffs, and I feel her lift and drop her shoulders in a more pronounced way, that I realise she's weeping, and I continue stroking her hair. She leans into me and puts her arms around me. It reminds me of holding Victor.

'Oh Meg, what can I do?'

She still wants me to be the one to say it, but I don't mind anymore.

I pat her on the back, once, twice, and draw in a long breath that's partly the tearful scent of her, my sister, and partly the iciness of night. 'You can't have it,' I say. 'There's no way you can have it. You'll have to get rid of it.'

'Oh, Meggy.'

'It'll be alright,' I say. 'Trust me. I'll look after you.'

She sobs once and clings to me tightly, and it reminds me of when we were little and how I'd tell her a story sometimes at night. Except it's real now.

'You can move in with me,' I tell her, 'and I'll help you through all this. We'll get everything sorted together. Angie won't mind, she'll understand. Okay?'

When she doesn't respond, I say again, 'Okay?'

She nods or squeezes me or something, but her head's nestled on my shoulder and it's almost as if she wants to go to sleep now, except every now and then she shakes or trembles.

'I'll make you an appointment with the doctor, if you like,' I tell her, 'and I'll come with you to the clinic if you want me to. Then, afterwards, together, we'll sort out what's going to happen to the house. We'll get solicitors and insurance agents to work through all that stuff. Okay?'

'Okay,' she mumbles against the collar of my jacket.

'The main thing is to get you through the last couple of months of school and exams. I can drive you to the bus stop and pick you up each day. That's not a problem. You don't need to stay with Jasmine. I want you to stay with me. If I have to, I'll drive you to school myself. In the evenings, you can do your homework and I'll cook tea, and then we'll sit down and watch television together – pig out on chocolate – or we'll play duets on the piano like we did when we were kids. I'll move into Angie's bedroom and you can have my room. At the weekend, we'll cook together, go for walks and we'll get past all this.'

I can almost see it. There'll be warm, summer days to look forward to, with brightness and butterflies again. The past will be forgotten and there'll be new beginnings.

She lifts her head and sniffs. 'You're not mad at me? You don't hate me?'

I hug her tighter and think of Angie with her new friend. 'Of course I don't. You're my little sister. I can't stay mad at you for long, can I? And I'm not just going to abandon you, am I?'

She relaxes and quietens. Snuggling against me, she definitely reminds me of a little bird, nestling to sleep, and it makes me wish I could nestle down to sleep too. Tonight, I think I will sleep.

'Really? You mean that? You're not just saying it?'

'No, I'm not just saying it. We've both been through a lot, but we'll get through everything else together.'

Out the corner of my eye, I see the yellow warning tape and the chequered blue and white Police tape, and wish the house had burnt to the ground, eating every last bone of the past with it – ashes to ashes, dust to dust and all that. I do. One day, the place will be bulldozed, though, and everything here will be forgotten. It's only a matter of time.

'It'll be fine,' I say, and start stroking her hair again. 'When the insurance is settled, we'll do whatever has to be done to the house and we'll sell it. You'll go to university and we'll buy something in the city and live together. Or, if you don't want to go, you can do something else. You don't have to go to uni. We'll move away from here and I'll look after you. You'll see. Everything'll be alright.'

She nestles against me and I rock her gently.

'Really? Do you think it will be?'

'There, there,' I coo, stroking her hair and rocking her.

I think of Dad, buried deep in the forest, beneath blankets of loam and leaves, in a remote beech glade marked by a monumental rock. It might be cold and bleak right now, but it's a perfect spot in many ways and idyllic in the summer – better than any cemetery – and I'd certainly prefer to sleep through eternity there if ever I had the choice.

We're warmer for being huddled together, Stella and I, even though the grass has lost its glossy sheen to the milky opaqueness of coming frost. The waning moon has risen higher and will soon be climbing over the broken roof of the house, and what we both need, more than anything else, is a good night's sleep, because things often seem better after a good night's sleep.

'It's been a hell of a week, but I'll look after you, Stell. Don't worry,' I coo. I stroke from the crown of her head down to the nape of her neck and I take another long, deep breath. 'Everything's going to be alright, one way or another. There, there.'

Also by Paul Burman

THE SNOWING AND GREENING OF THOMAS PASSMORE

Something strange is happening to Thomas Passmore. Waking from a warm Australian beach, he finds himself at Heathrow Airport on a winter's morning, but can't remember getting there. Haunted by his father's suicide, his mother's rejection and by increasingly vivid dreams of Kate Hainley, his first love, Thomas's increasingly bizarre journey takes him into a world where one man's struggle to live again is as timeless as the battle of the seasons.

A quirky and magical tale of loss, love and learning to live.

THE GREASE MONKEY'S TALE

Once upon a time, in a land too close for comfort lived a man on the run: Nic the mechanic, a man whose passion for fast cars and the beautiful Siobhan McConnell sets him on a series of journeys that turn his life upside down. When Siobhan first hurtles into his world, Nic senses his own story finally shifting from tragedy to romance... until he's framed for an armed robbery and Siobhan disappears. Enter Mary King, his would-be fairy godmother, who offers him the 'job-of-a-lifetime' in the remote township of Gimbly, where very little is what it appears to be and where Nic's search for the truth - beyond the deception and the lies - threatens to destroy everything he loves.